A VERY DUTIFUL DAUGHTER

Lady Denham sighed. Sensible, obedient Letty Glendenning was the perfect wife for her son: she would manage his house, and more important, manage him, put an end to Lord Roger Denham's scandalous bachelorhood. And Lady Denham was not mistaken: the young couple was passionately in love.

Letty's refusal was inexplicable. Something must have happened at Vauxhall, Lady Denham mused thoughtfully.

But what...?

Elizabeth Mansfield

Berkley Books by Elizabeth Mansfield

MY LORD MURDERER
THE PHANTOM LOVER
A VERY DUTIFUL DAUGHTER

A Very Dutiful Daughter

ELIZABETH MANSFIELD

A BERKLEY BOOK
published by
BERKLEY PUBLISHING CORPORATION

Published by arrangement with the author's agent

Berkley Publishing Corporation
200 Madison Avenue
New York, N.Y. 10016

SBN 425-04084-4

BERKLEY MEDALLION BOOKS are published by
Berkley Publishing Corporation
200 Madison Avenue
New York, N.Y. 10016

BERKLEY MEDALLION BOOK ® TM 757,375

Printed in the United States of America

Berkley Edition, APRIL, 1979

Chapter ONE

"I THINK MAMA is going to faint again," remarked Augusta from her position at the keyhole.

"Oh, Gussie, not again!" responded her older sister, Prudence, in tones of deep disgust. "Get away from the door and let me see."

"It's *my* turn," whined Clara, the youngest by several years. "I haven't had *one chance* to peek. You both have been positively piggish about that keyhole ever since Letty and Aunt Millicent came home and locked themselves up in there with Mama!"

The accusation, though totally ignored by the two older girls, was quite true. Gussie and Prue had taken alternate turns at the keyhole for the past half-hour, pushing aside the fourteen-year-old Clara heartlessly and ignoring her persistent questions as if she did not exist. Indeed, the entire morning had not been a good one for Clara. The day had begun with a message from their governess, Miss Dorrimore, to the effect that she intended to remain in bed to nurse her cold and that the girls were to spend the morning working on their French declensions. The older girls, ignoring these instructions, had spent most of the morning poring over the fashion plates in a treasured copy of *La Belle Assemblée*. Clara, not yet old enough to be concerned with modish gowns and the art of hairdressing, had threatened to report her sisters' transgressions to the indisposed Miss Dorrimore. Her sisters had responded with threats and jibes of such malignity that Clara had been reduced to tears. In the midst of this *contretemps*, they'd heard the sound of a carriage pulling up at their front door. They'd rushed to the window in time to see the door of their Aunt Millicent's impressively ancient equipage open to discharge their eldest sister, Letitia. Letty looked woebegone and red-eyed, and Gussie and Prue had exchanged looks of surprise. The surprise soon turned to consternation, for Letty had been followed out of the carriage by their Aunt Millicent whose customary cold, forbidding features were so distorted with suppressed anger as to make her ordinarily stern expression seem positively beneficent in comparison.

"Something's gone wrong," Prue had remarked in sepulchral tones. "She must have botched it somehow."

"Oh, no!" Gussie had moaned. "It can't be! Prue, didn't you tell me that Lord Denham was *certain* to make an offer?"

"Yes, it *was* certain. I overheard Aunt Millicent telling Mama all about it. Lady Denham assured her that her son Roger was ready to take a wife, and Letty was the girl they wanted."

"You *overheard* all that? Ha!" sneered the put-upon Clara. "*Eavesdropped*, more likely."

"And who's eavesdropping now, may I ask?" Gussie had asked quellingly. "This conversation is not meant for the ears of *children*, if you please. So take yourself off to your bedroom, or the nursery, or somewhere out-of-the-way."

"Listen to you, Miss Augusta High-and-mighty Glendenning! Just because you're sixteen, don't think you can queen it over me!" Clara had declared bravely, sticking out her chin in defiance.

"Stop squabbling," Prue had demanded with all the authority of her seventeen years in her voice. "Letty is in some sort of fix, and we ought to find a way to help her, not stand here brangling." With a toss of her red-gold curls, she'd turned quickly to the door and run to the landing. The two younger girls had followed hastily behind, and the three had peered over the banister to the floor below. They were barely in time to see Mama, the epitome of confused alarm, following Letty and Aunt Millicent into the small sitting room and shutting the door behind her.

Prue had lost no time in getting to the door and kneeling down with her eye at the keyhole. Gussie had cupped her hand to her ear and pressed it against the door. And thus it had been ever since, the two of them changing places periodically and pushing poor Clara aside whenever she attempted to come close to the door.

Gussie now surrendered her place at the keyhole to Prue, who reported promptly that Aunt Millicent was holding a bottle of vinaigrette to Mama's nose. "Can you hear anything?" Gussie asked impatiently.

"No," Prue muttered, "but they've not permitted Letty even to take off her bonnet and pelisse. She's just sitting there, staring at the floor. Aunt Millicent appears to be furious with her. But I don't see *why*! Is it *her* fault that Lord Denham didn't come up to scratch?"

Gussie looked down at her sister questioningly. "Do you think that's what happened? That Denham didn't offer after all?"

Prue, without taking her eye from the keyhole, shrugged. "What else could it be?"

Further speculation was interrupted by the opening of the front door. Their brother, Edward, strode in, his riding boots clattering loudly on the worn marble of the entryway as he hurried to the stairs. But he stopped short at the sight of the three girls grouped before the sitting-room door.

"What on earth are you doing?" he demanded suspiciously.

Two pairs of eyes looked at him guiltily. "Oh, Ned, it's Letty!" Gussie said breathlessly. "Aunt Millicent is furious with her, and Mama has fainted twice, and—"

"They're eavesdropping, that's what they're doing, Neddie," Clara declared self-righteously. "You ought to make them stop."

"That's just what I intend to do, infant," Ned said,

looking down at his youngest sister with distaste, "though you needn't think I'm doing it as a result of your tattling."

Prue had returned to the keyhole and now made her report. "Aunt Millicent is pacing again. And Letty is biting her lip. That means she's about to cry, the poor thing."

Ned pretended a disinterest he was far from feeling. "Get up, Prue, before someone catches you! Hang it, it ain't the thing for a girl your age to behave like a parlor-maid!" he scolded.

Prue rose calmly and brushed off her skirt. "And what do *you* know of parlor-maids? Was *that* why you were sent down from Oxford? For shame, Ned!"

Ned took a threatening step toward her. "Mind your tongue, goosecap! Get back to the schoolroom at once, and take your sisters with you, or you'll have to deal with me!"

Prue regarded him speculatively. He was only one year her senior, and barely an inch taller than she, but although he had not yet reached his full height, his shoulders were broad and the muscles in his arms fully developed. Previous experience had taught her that he was not easily bested in a fight. Besides, now that she was seventeen, it was no longer seemly to engage in a tussle with her brother. She shrugged and marched in brave retreat to the stairs. Gussie, meeting his glare, took Clara's hand and ran quickly after Prue. Ned waited until they had disappeared around the bend in the stairs. Then he listened for the closing of the schoolroom door, after which he promptly knelt down and peered into the keyhole to see for himself what was going on.

Inside the room the tension was palpable. Letty, seated in the far corner of the room, seemed immobile, her back straight, the hands in her lap hidden inside her fur-trimmed muff, her head lowered, her face shaded by the brim of her plumed bonnet, her eyes fixed on a worn patch of carpet at her feet. Only the sharpest of observers could have detected the movement of her fingers inside the muff as they clenched and unclenched in distress, and the frequent flicker of her eyelids as she battled valiantly to keep the tears from flowing over.

Her aunt paced the room with an angry stride, the stiff silk of her rather old-fashioned skirts whispering with matching anger every time she turned about. Letty began to count her aunt's paces... eight steps to the window, swish... eight steps back to the sofa, swish... eight steps to the window, swish...

A groan from the sofa caused Letty and Aunt Millicent to turn their heads. Lady Glendenning, stretched out full-length, sighed and raised her hand from her eyes. Her arm made a tremblingly nervous arc through the air and fell to her side where it dangled over the edge of the sofa in listless despair. "Whatever are we to do now, Millicent?" she asked in a quavering voice. "Whatever are we to do?"

"Ask your daughter!" Millicent said with asperity. "*She*'s the one who whistled a fortune down the wind!"

"Letty, my love," her mama asked tearfully, "*how* could you have done it? How could you have *refused* him?"

Letty, her lovely hazel eyes filling with tears, merely shook her head. Her aunt looked at her closely. Aunt Millicent, the formidable Lady Upsham, was no fool. No girl in possession of her senses could turn down a man like Lord Denham without a very good reason. "There *must* be someone else," she said for the third time. "You've fixed your heart on some ineligible wastrel, no doubt, and hope to make a match of it, in spite of your mother's wishes and your family's need, isn't that it?"

Letty looked up, blinking, as two tears rolled down her cheeks. "I've told you and told you. There's no one else. N-no one. I j-just c-could not..."

"You could not accept an offer from the most eligible bachelor in England? I fail to understand you, Letitia. It is not as if we were marrying you to an ogre. Or even to an old dodderer with nothing to recommend him but his purse. Denham is *more* than a wealthy peer. He is nothing if not charming and witty. His address is excellent, his mind superior to most of the young men of your flibberty-gibberty generation, and God knows he's as handsome a man as I've ever seen, even if his complexion is darker than I like, and his eyebrows somewhat heavy..."

"Was *that* it, Letty dear?" her mother asked in concern. "Did you take an aversion to his eyebrows?"

Letty had to smile, even if somewhat tremulously. "Oh, Mama, of course not!"

"His complexion, then?"

Letty's smile faded, and she returned her eyes to the patch in the carpet. "There's nothing at all amiss in Lord Denham's appearance," she said in a flat voice.

Lady Glendenning pulled herself up on one arm and peered closely at her daughter. She had never seen Letty in such distress. The poor girl looked positively hagged, although Lady Glendenning had to admit that even her excessive pallor failed to detract appreciably from the loveliness of Letty's face. Letty was blessed with thick auburn hair, high cheekbones, a clear complexion and a full, expressive mouth. And her eyes, even when red-rimmed and tearful, were large and lustrous and showed clearly the gentleness and intelligence that were her nature. Lady Glendenning had waited for two years, ever since Letty's come-out at eighteen under the auspices of her sister-in-law, Lady Millicent Upsham, for Letty to choose one of her rich suitors to marry. It was Letty who would save the family from sinking into a mire of debt. But Millicent had urged Lady Glendenning to curb her impatience. Millicent had a match in mind for Letty that would solve all their problems. Letty would marry the man most girls in London only *dreamed* of attaching. Millicent was saving Letty for Roger Denham, the Earl of Arneau.

Lady Glendenning sighed. Millicent's hopes for Letty had made her, Letty's own adoring mother, uneasy from the first. Lord Denham was past thirty and had never succumbed to matrimony. All Millicent's assurances that Roger Denham would come up to scratch failed to ease her mind. Lovely as her daughter was, Lady Glendenning knew that there were others more beautiful, more well-connected or more lively, and that Lord Denham had ignored them all. Letty, quiet and self-effacing, was not likely to catch quite so big a fish. Couldn't Millicent be content with a lesser prize?

But Millicent had been adamant. Her connection with the Dowager Lady Denham was very close, and she knew that she, Roger's mother, was quite taken with Letty. And, just as she had predicted, Lord Denham had taken an interest in Letty and had *offered*! Millicent and Lady Denham, between them, had done the trick. It was Letty herself who had ruined everything! What maggot had found its way into her devoted and very dutiful daughter's head to cause her to do such a terrible thing?

Lady Glendenning lay back on the pillows with a groan. "I don't understand you at all," she said tearfully. "If you don't hold his appearance in aversion, what *is* it that made you refuse him?"

Aunt Millicent snorted. "The answer is obvious. There's nothing about Lord Denham to revolt a girl. Why, there's not another girl in all of England who would refuse him. Your daughter has her eye on someone else. It's the only possible explanation."

Lady Glendenning shook her head. "No, Millicent. Letty wouldn't lie to us. She has always been the most devoted, the most obedient, the best behaved of all my children. She's never lied to me or given me the slightest trouble. She would not ruin her family by refusing a fortune—not for such a reason as that. You are not in love with some penniless fellow, are you, my darling?"

"No, Mama," Letty said quietly. "I swear I'm not. I'll marry anyone else you say. *Anyone.*" Her eyes filled with tears again. "But not Lord Denham."

"Then at least tell us *why*!" her aunt demanded impatiently.

She shook her head. "Please don't ask me to explain. I...can't explain it to you. I c-can't!" she answered in a choked voice.

"Don't you realize, you silly pea-goose, that there's not much chance of finding someone else now?" Millicent asked in disgust. "No one will believe that you turned Denham down. They will all say that he found *you* unsatisfactory and did not come up to scratch."

"Oh, my God!" wailed Lady Glendenning from the sofa. "I'd never thought of that..."

"Neither had your daughter, apparently," Millicent muttered angrily. "Perhaps if she had, she would not have been so quick to refuse him."

"It would have made no difference. I would have refused him in any case," Letty said in a flat, dead voice that her mother barely recognized.

"Stop badgering the girl, Millicent," Lady Glendenning said helplessly. "I can't bear to see her so unhappy."

"What about *your* unhappiness? And the rest of the family's?" Millicent demanded. "Why didn't she think of *that*?"

There was no answer. Lady Glendenning covered her eyes with trembling hands, and Letty stared in miserable silence at the carpet. Finally, Millicent sighed in defeat. "Well, go up to your room, Miss. I want to talk to your mother in private."

Letty rose quickly and hurried out, almost colliding with her brother who had not moved quickly enough from the door. "Ned!" she gasped.

"Quiet!" he hissed nervously, carefully shutting the door behind her. "Do you want Aunt Millicent to know I've been eavesdropping?"

"Then you heard—?"

"Most of it. Whatever made you do it, Letty? Do you really dislike him so much?"

"Oh, Neddie, don't *you* start on me, too!" Letty cried, and she burst into long-suppressed tears and fell against his shoulder.

Ned looked down at his sister's bonnet in perplexity. "There, now, don't cry," he said, patting her shoulder awkwardly. "You know I can't abide water-works. Besides, there's no need for tears *now*. It's all over and done with."

"D-done with?" Letty raised her head from his shoulder. "W-what do you m-mean?"

"You've turned him down, haven't you? It's done with. However much they may scold, they can't make you marry him now."

This brought out a fresh flood of tears. "You d-don't understand," she sobbed against his shoulder. "You d-don't unders-stand at all!"

"What is there to understand? Lord Denham asked you to marry him. You didn't want to marry him, so you refused him. Let Aunt Millicent carry on all she likes. It's too late for her to force you to marry him now, isn't it?"

"Yes," his sister nodded, still sobbing.

"Then I'm dashed if I can see what you're crying about. Stop it, will you? You're soaking my riding coat. Here." He lifted her head and handed her his handkerchief. "Dry those eyes, you silly puss. Everything is going to be fine."

Letty took a deep breath and tried to control her tears. Sniffing bravely into his handkerchief, she muttered, "Everything is going to be dreadful."

"Nonsense," her brother said decidedly. "You've only to weather a little scolding. They're bound to give up sooner or later. And when the noise is all over, you'll no longer have to marry a man you dislike."

"That's just it," Letty said, gulping back her tears and thrusting his wet handkerchief into his hand. "I *don't* dislike him. In fact, if you want to know the truth, there's no man in the world I'd *rather* marry than Roger Denham!" And she fled up the stairs, leaving her brother staring after her in open-mouthed bewilderment.

Chapter TWO

THE SIGHT OF his mother's blue-and-gold coach at his doorway caused Roger Denham, Fourth Earl of Arneau, to groan out load. Lord Denham had not had a good day. First, his morning call at the home of his mother's bosom-bow, Lady Millicent Upsham, to make an offer for her good-looking but rather mousy niece, had ended in disaster. Not that his heart was in any way touched. (He sometimes wondered if he would ever learn to feel the tender emotions so rapturously described by the poets.) But he had certainly suffered in his self-esteem. He had been given to understand by his mother that the chit was more than eager to receive his addresses, but when he had made his speech to her, (and it was in his most charmingly polished manner, too) she had looked up at him with eyes that he had to admit were remarkably lustrous and had stumblingly told him that she was very sorry for the inconvenience (as well she should be! He had wasted the entire morning!), but that she was unable to accept his very flattering offer. (If she had been in any way flattered, she certainly didn't show it.)

He had made a hasty retreat and had promptly repaired for solace to the residence of Mrs. Brownell. The captivating Kitty, a notorious widow whose opulent apartments and costly wardrobe he had been financing for some years now, was (as usual) completely compliant, but he found her practiced lovemaking neither stimulating to his depressed spirits nor soothing to the wound which had been dealt to his consequence.

The evening had been as flat and dull as the afternoon. His club had seemed to be devoid of good company, and his usual luck at the card table had quite deserted him. He'd left early, hoping that a good night's sleep would wipe away the memory of this irritating day. Thus, as he approached his residence, the sight of his mother's carriage fixed at his front door struck him as a particularly treacherous twist of fate. This ill-fate was intent on dogging his steps as closely at the end of the day as it had at the beginning.

With a sigh, he submitted to the inevitable and went in to face his mother. He found her seated in his study in his favorite wing chair, her eyes closed. But he knew she was not asleep. Her tapping foot, her frowning expression and the motion of her quizzing glass (which swung from a long chain which she dangled between her fingers) gave mute evidence that she was (1) wide awake and (2) quite angry. He smiled down at her affectionately. His mother sometimes enjoyed affecting an acerbic manner—her sharp tongue and aloof dignity brought her admiration and respect from her peers, her servants, and all who met her—but she couldn't hide from her son the deep warmth and affection she felt for him and which he returned in no small measure. He bent and kissed her cheek.

The Dowager Lady Denham opened her eyes, raised her quizzing glass and looked at her son coldly. "So, you're home. Quite early, too. I fully expected to have to wait for you at least another hour."

"Good evening, Mama. I suppose you will think me quite beetle-headed to be surprised to find you here."

"Beetle-headed, indeed, if you *truly* didn't expect me. Did you think that I would take no interest in the result of your interview with Miss Glendenning this morning?"

"I was persuaded that you'd have heard the result of that interview from other sources," Roger responded drily.

"And so I have. But I want to hear from *you* exactly what happened today."

"I've nothing to add that you've not already heard from your friend, Lady Upsham. I presented myself at her door promptly at the appointed hour. I made my speech to Miss Glendenning in my most charming style. She looked up at me with those remarkably speaking eyes of hers and told me bluntly that she was unable to accept me. I responded that I quite understood, hoped we might remain friends, made my bow and departed."

"And that's the whole of it?"

"I'm afraid so."

Lady Denham rose and began to pace with impatient strides. "The girl gave you no explanation for this astounding turn of events?" she asked incredulously.

Roger grinned at her affectionately. "How like a doting mother you sound."

She glared at him. "Doting? Balderdash! In what way am I doting?"

"In your ready assumption that any female's refusal of me is astounding," he answered promptly.

Lady Denham gave a ripple of laughter. "Obnoxious boy! Do you think I'm so besotted a mother as that? We are not speaking of *any* female. Only this one. I've met Letty Glendenning on more than one occasion, and I had the distinct impression that she was more than a little interested in you. And, in addition, her family has everything to gain by the match. The whole matter is quite puzzling."

"Not at all. The girl has simply taken me in dislike, or—"

"Taken you in dislike!" his mother cut in with asperity. "Rubbish! Why on earth should she?"

Roger's eyes twinkled. "I have no idea. Such a paragon as I am, it *does* seem incredible that a lady could bring herself to reject me."

Lady Denham did not deign to respond, but merely favored him with a glower and returned to her chair. Roger dropped onto an ottoman near the fire and settled himself comfortably. While he gazed into the flames, his mother studied him closely. Despite his denials, she was well aware of his desirability on the Marriage Mart. Besides the advantages of birth and wealth which he had in abundance, he had a generous share of those personal qualities which women admire and men envy. She was by no means one of those foolishly fond parents who cannot see their children's faults. She looked at him now, closely and dispassionately, as a stranger might. There in the firelight, his face looked quite appealing. His eyes were intelligent, humorous and kind, his mouth generous, his dark hair thick and curly. He had placed one booted foot on the fender of the fireplace and was resting his elbow on the knee of the other leg. Tall and masculine as he was, his body in repose seemed surprisingly graceful. What on earth was there about him that Letty had found to dislike?

"The girl's behavior is completely bewildering," she said, voicing her thoughts aloud, "unless she was playing a skittish game with you."

Roger made a dismissive gesture with his head. "Skittish? Not she."

"Why not? Many girls believe they ought to refuse a man the first time he offers."

"Not this girl. There was nothing coy in her refusal. She meant it."

"How can you be sure?"

Roger turned and faced his mother squarely. "Listen to me, Mama," he told her firmly, "and believe what I tell you. I'm thirty-one years old. I know the way of the world. I'm neither a coxcomb nor an innocent babe. I know when a young lady is flirting with me and when she is not, when she wants my attentions and when she doesn't. Miss Glendenning was not flirting. She was not skittish. She was not coy. She obviously doesn't want to become my wife. So I'm afraid you'll have to look elsewhere for a daughter-in-law. Sorry, but that's the end of it."

His mother stared at him in frustration. Damn the boy, would he *never* marry? Lady Denham winced to remember all the ploys she had used to stimulate Roger's interest in various eligible females. And she had not been alone in the attempt. She couldn't *count* all the designing mothers who had thrust their daughters in Roger's path. Not one of those girls had made the slightest mark on him. When he had at last agreed that the time had come for him to take a wife, he'd admitted to her that there was no girl at all for whom he had the slightest preference. He'd been quite willing to let his mother handle the selection of a suitable bride.

The result of that selection process had been Letty Glendenning. Lady Denham's closest friend, Millicent Upsham, had long spoken of her niece and had finally brought her to Arneau House for Lady Denham's inspection. Lady Denham had been delighted with the girl. Not only was she lovely and wellbred, but Lady Denham saw that under her outer softness, Letty had a character of moral strength. In addition, she had recognized, by Letty's carefully phrased questions and the unmistakable gleam in the girl's eyes when Roger's name was mentioned, that Letty was strongly attracted to him. If any girl could entice her son from the joys of bachelorhood, Lady Denham was sure Letty was the one. The plan had seemed so perfect, so simple, so foolproof. What could have gone wrong?

But she would let the matter drop for the nonce. There were too many unanswered questions to form a coherent plan of action. She stood up and wordlessly reached for the pelisse she had thrown over the back of her chair. Roger jumped to his feet and put it over her shoulders. Rubbing her cheek with the back of his hand, he smiled at her comfortingly and said softly, "Don't feel so put out, my dear. I'm sure you'll find another candidate for the post before very long."

"I haven't given up on *this* one yet," she answered curtly.

"Now, Mama—!" Roger began in annoyance.

"You must have said or done *something*!" his mother

said, ignoring his disapproval. "*Think*, you irritating jackanapes! Are you sure you said or did nothing which could have offended or upset her?"

"What *could* I have said? We barely exchanged a dozen sentences since we were introduced three weeks ago. And those exchanges were the merest commonplaces, I assure you."

"I see." She buttoned her pelisse and started for the door. "Well, ring for Trebbs, will you? There's no point in pursuing this subject any further tonight."

"There is no point in pursuing the subject at *any* time. Miss Glendenning has refused me, and the subject is closed. And I shall *not* ring for Trebbs. I shall see you out myself."

Lady Denham took his arm. "Don't think to deter me from my object by playing the gallant. You may accompany me to the door if you wish, but I will not refrain from pursuing the subject further. Millicent may have learned something from the girl herself. When I hear from her, we shall talk again. Please come to see me before the week is out."

"Mama—!" Roger exclaimed in disgust.

"No later than Saturday, if you please—or if you don't please!" his mother said firmly, and went out to her carriage without a further word.

The following morning the Glendenning household was as somberly quiet as if a death had occurred in the night. The servants moved about the house on tiptoe. Lady Glendenning, who had taken to her bed immediately after the departure of Aunt Millicent on the previous afternoon, had made no appearance at the breakfast table. The tray which had been brought to her door had been rejected with a moan. The rest of the family sat at the breakfast table eating listlessly. They spoke to each other only in subdued whispers. Miss Dorrimore, who had emerged from the sickroom well before her symptoms had disappeared, because she felt that her presence was needed in this emergency, stifled her sneezes in the voluminous folds of a very large handkerchief. Ned had dared to guffaw at something in a note a friend had sent round, but he was quickly silenced by the glares of disapproval his sisters shot at him.

Letty, getting up to help herself to a second cup of tea from the pot on the sideboard, looked up from her cup to find every eye upon her. Her sisters, her brother and everyone in the household had been following her every movement with solemn, lugubrious stares. Since she had been doing her very best to maintain a cheerful countenance, and to behave in a normal way, their stares were irritating in the extreme. She heaved a sigh of disgust and faced them squarely. "Will you all stop looking at me in that apprehensive way? You watch me quite as if I were dying of consumption of the lungs!" she burst out.

"It would serve you right if you were," pouted Clara under her breath.

"*What* did you say, you noddy little brat?" her brother growled. "Take that back at once!"

"I won't. Why did she have to make all this trouble for us?"

"Trouble?" asked Letty in surprise. "What do you mean, Clara?"

"You've refused Lord Denham, haven't you? Now we shall have no money, and we shall have to give up Hinson and the other servants and Miss Dorrimore, too. And we shan't be able to buy coal for the fire, or new dresses, and we shall all starve!"

Prue looked up from her plate in shocked disgust. "I'd like to slap your silly face!" she said. "Wherever did you hear such nonsense? Besides, who told you that Letty refused Lord Denham?"

"Everyone knows it, even Katie."

"Katie? Who's Katie?" Ned demanded.

"Katie in the kitchen. She helps Cook. She knows everything."

Miss Dorrimore rattled her cup with a nervous hand.

"Is this true, Miss Letty?" she asked with a trembling underlip. "Shall I have to go?"

"No, of course not," Letty assured her. "Really, Clara, you are getting too old for such silliness. Mama has an adequate income, if only we are frugal."

"Frugal? What's frugal?" Clara asked.

"Why don't you ask Katie-in-the-kitchen?" Ned put in with a satiric grimace. "She knows everything."

Miss Dorrimore, not to be outdone by a kitchen maid, immediately offered instruction. "From the Latin, *frugalis*, meaning economical and prudent in expenditure."

"Yes, Miss Dorrimore, but what does it *mean*?" Clara persisted.

"It means, love," Letty explained, "that we can't spend money on fripperies or ball gowns or parties or such things."

"Do you mean we won't be able to go to balls and parties?" Gussie asked, the import of Letty's action belatedly dawning upon her. "Oh, Letty, perhaps Clara is right. You shouldn't have done it."

"Gussie," Prue frowned, "that's a dreadful thing to say! Would you want your sister to sacrifice herself on the Altar of Matrimony just so that you can buy ball gowns and go to parties?"

"Prue's right," Ned said, nodding agreement. Then, turning to Gussie and Clara, he added vehemently, "Dashed if I ain't ashamed that you two are my sisters. You ought to know that Letty would do anything for us if she could. This was something she couldn't do, that's all."

"But I don't understand *why* she couldn't," Gussie argued. "Lord Denham is the best catch in the world. And now everyone will be saying that *he* didn't want Letty, and nobody else will offer for her. And then what will become of us?"

"Really, Gussie, I suppose I could have expected this from Clara, but I never thought to hear *you* talk like such a ninny," Prue said. "Letty is the prettiest, most sensible girl any man's likely to find. Do you suppose a man worth his salt would keep from offering for her just because of rumors that the toplofty Earl of Arneau didn't want her?"

"The Earl of Arneau is *not* toplofty," Clara informed them smugly. "Katie-in-the-kitchen says he's very pleasant and kind, besides being handsome and rich as King Midas."

"Katie-in-the-kitchen seems to be a veritable fount of information," Letty said drily.

"So it would seem." Ned laughed. "Perhaps, Miss Nodcock, you could ask your Katie-in-the-kitchen to recommend another lord for Letty to marry."

"I already did," Clara responded promptly, "but the only other lord she knows anything about is the Marquis of Atherton. Her cousin works in Lord Atherton's stables, you see. But Lord Atherton is not in the least eligible."

"No?" Prue asked with heavy sarcasm. "Why not?"

"Because he is fatter than the Prince and at least seventy-five years old."

Gussie and Prue giggled, but Ned, keeping his face in rigid control, held up a restraining hand. "That doesn't seem so bad. He might do for you sister, mightn't he, Clara? Especially if the marriage would mean gobs of money for the family to spend on balls and such."

"That's what I thought," Clara agreed with perfect seriousness, "but Katie said that he's not nearly rich enough to make up for his other defects."

The laughter could no longer be held back, and it burst forth from everyone at the table but Clara and Miss Dorrimore, Clara because she failed to see anything at all funny in what she'd said, and Miss Dorrimore because she felt that the whole conversation was far from proper and had listened to all of it with an expression on her face of profound disapproval.

"Good for Katie-in-the-kitchen," Prue gasped as soon

as she could catch her breath. "I think I'd prefer *her* to be my sister, Clara. She seems to have a great deal more sense than you do."

"Shall we put it to a vote?" Ned chortled. "All in favor of moving Clara down to the scullery and Katie up to Clara's room—"

"Now, that's enough, Neddie," Letty said calmly. "We've had a good laugh, Clara's frankness has given us a chance to clear the air, and you all have stopped looking at me in that odiously solemn way. So no harm has been done."

Gussie looked up at her sister guiltily. "I'm sorry for what I said, Letty. Neddie is right—you would have accepted him if you could. Mama always says that you are the best, the most obedient of us all. So If you couldn't do this, the most important thing she's ever asked you to do, you must have had a good reason."

Letty lowered her eyes to her cup. "I *think* I had," she said hesitantly.

Prue looked at her earnestly. "Aren't you sure, Letty? Maybe you should tell us why you rejected him. If we all understood—"

Letty shook her head. "I *can't*! Please don't ask me." She put down her cup and made for the door. "Miss Dorrimore, please excuse me. I'd like to go to my room."

"Of course, my dear," Miss Dorrimore said, sensing some romantic drama behind the tearful expression in Letty's eyes.

Gussie, too, seeing a look in her sister's face she had never seen before, was overcome with a wave of sympathy. She jumped up, ran to her sister and threw her arms about Letty's neck. "You're not upset with me, are you?" she asked in self-reproach. "I'm sorry I sounded so selfish. And Clara is sorry, too, aren't you, Clara?"

"I suppose so," the petulant Clara said reluctantly.

Letty forced a smile and looked down at her sister. "Of course I'm not upset with you, Gussie dear. Don't look so downcast. After all, Prue is the *real* beauty in the family.

She'll have her come-out next year, and before she is on the town a month, she will have found a lord even richer and handsomer than Denham. And she'll marry him, and we shall all live happily ever after."

Ned snorted. "*Prue*? You must be blind!"

Gussie agreed. "You're being silly, Letty. With her freckles and her lack of height, any man who's at all up to the mark would be unlikely even to *look* at her."

Prue drew herself up proudly. "Is that so? Well, I've been told by several gentlemen already that one need not be tall to be fashionably elegant, and that freckles are very *comme-il-faut*! So there!"

And while the merry discussion over Prue's charms—or lack of them—ensued, Letty quietly slipped from the room, ran to her bedroom and barricaded herself behind her locked door for the rest of the morning.

Chapter THREE

ALONE IN HER ROOM, Letty's outer cheerfulness dropped away. Poor Clara had been closer to the truth than Letty had wanted to admit. The future was indeed bleak for the family and for herself. Not only had she doomed herself to spinsterhood, but she had condemned the family to a life of near-poverty. She lay down on her bed and shut her eyes. Had she tossed away all their futures for a silly scruple?

She had met Roger Denham during the month of her come-out two years ago. From the moment she had been introduced to him at Almack's, she had adored him. He had seemed to her a model of masculine perfection—a top-of-the-trees Corinthian, Ned would have called him. His dark curls, his sardonic smile, his easy manner with his friends, his polished address with young ladies, the stories of his sporting exploits which were repeated in all the drawing rooms with such admiration, even his reputation for immunity to the lures of ladies of quality—all these things combined to make him a hero in her eyes.

As a result of the worshipful adoration with which she viewed him, her one and only dance with him had been a complete disaster. He had stood up with her for an interminable country dance during which she'd been completely tongue-tied and had kept her eyes fastened to the floor. Naturally, he did not again seek her companionship, and on those few occasions when they met again, she was favored with nothing more than a small bow. A puzzled expression would cross his face, as if he were trying to remember who she was.

This lack of interest on his part did nothing to diminish Letty's adoration. She would often daydream of attending a glittering ball, looking ravishing in green silk. He would see her and be irresistibly drawn to her. He would ask her to dance the evening's first waltz. She would grant his request, and they would float around the ballroom, the most beautiful couple in the room. Ignoring the eyes on them, they would exchange the most witty banter, each verbal riposte laughingly returned. He would become completely enchanted, and she, of all the lovely, brilliant women in London, would win his heart!

But her month in the midst of the London social scene soon came to an end. Aunt Millicent could not be expected to finance indefinitely the high costs of the social whirl which a young lady in her first year in society must necessarily undergo. Letty's time on the town had ended without a second chance to stand up with Lord Denham. She had returned to the quiet, withdrawn life in her mother's household without any further expectation of seeing the great Earl of Arneau again, except at a distance, at the opera or the theater. Nevertheless, her daydreams of him continued. Until that terrible night a few months later...

The memory of that night came flooding back to her. The night she had gone to Vauxhall Gardens. If only she'd obeyed her better instincts and stayed at home...

The weather had been fine, that autumn of 1805, and a group of Ned's cronies had decided to visit the Gardens. Several young ladies had been invited to join the expedition, and a Mrs. Lorimer, the mother of one of them, had been prevailed upon to accompany them as chaperone. When Ned invited Letty to make one of the party, she had been ecstatic. She'd never seen Vauxhall, but of course she'd heard a great deal about its wondrous charm. The Gardens were said to be spacious and picturesque, with delightful walks, magnificent hedges and greenery, and a wonderful assortment of pavilions, lodges, groves, grottoes, lawns, temples, cascades, porticoes and rotundas. It was crowded with gay company who strolled its walks, ate cold collations at its lodges, listened to the merry sounds of the musical bands and singers, and in general cavorted through its twelve acres with happy abandon.

One could not be sure of the quality of the people one might meet at Vauxhall, for anyone who could afford the one-shilling admission fee was welcome to roam its walks at will. Mixing freely with the *ton* were merchants, foreigners, farmers, servants, ruffians, robbers, pimps and prostitutes. The prospect was a bit frightening to a young girl of nineteen who had never gone on such an excursion before.

When Letty had applied to her mother for permission, half hoping that her mother would refuse to let her go, Lady Glendenning had acquiesced, feeling that the chaperonage of Mrs. Lorimer made the outing somewhat respectable. Besides, Ned had assured her that there was to be a masquerade that evening, so that, even if Letty were seen in such surroundings, she would not be recognized behind her mask.

By the time the evening had arrived, Letty had been quite eager for the excursion. She'd felt wildly adventurous as she covered herself with the green domino which Ned had provided for her. Ned himself had chosen to dress as a character from literature. He looked quite convincing as Prince Hamlet in his dark-colored doublet and full-sleeved shirt. He'd asked her to dress as the Lady Ophelia, but Letty was too shy to dress in costume and had decided that a simple domino would be exciting enough. She tied the shimmering, cloak-like garment at the neck, raised the hood over her well-brushed auburn hair, put on the matching mask and gazed at herself in the mirror. She appeared strange to herself, taller and more sophisticated and mysterious. She smiled at herself in sheer pleasure. The smile remained on her face as her brother escorted her by coach to Westminster where they joined the band of laughing companions with whom they were to spend the evening. The whole group boarded a wherry to take them across the Thames to the garden entrance.

The entrance to Vauxhall was at the foot of a dark alley, which made their first glimpse of the gardens overwhelming. The prospect that greeted them seemed even more resplendent in contrast to the dim alley they had just passed through. The innumerable colored lamps, the music, the laughter, the gay crowds—it was all as she had dreamed. People romped by dressed in all manner of colorful costumes. There were a goodly number of King Arthurs and Guineveres, Robin Hoods and Maid Marions, Arabian Sheikhs and dancing girls from their harems, Roman Legionnaires, Romeos and their Juliets. There were animals of all sorts—several kittens, a few lions, and one rather lumpy-looking unicorn. Some of the costumes were as shocking as they were ingenious. One lady wore a gown made entirely of silk leaves. It reached only to her knees and exposed (for all the world to see) a pair of very shapely but very bare legs. One gentleman, who seemed to represent the sun, had gilded himself from top to toe, not only his shoes, trousers and coat, but the skin of his face and hands as well.

Letty and her party proceeded down the Grand Walk to the Grove, the central quadrangle which held a large pavilion from which issued forth some lively music. A great number of indecorous dancers whirled about the grove, and it was not long before Ned and his companions were tempted to join. Two by two they paired off to participate in the festivities. Even Mrs. Lorimer succumbed to the blandishments of a young buck and allowed herself to be led into the throng. Only Letty resisted the various requests for her participation. One young man, who had been at her side since they'd boarded the wherry and whose name she could not remember, pleaded with her to dance with him. She shook her head, telling him that she preferred to stand here on the sidelines and watch. The young man remained dutifully at her side for several minutes, but suddenly spied a friend across the quadrangle. Promising a quick return, he set out through the crowd and was soon lost from view.

Letty, realizing that she was quite alone and unprotected, experienced a complete change of mood. People who a moment ago had seemed happy and innocent suddenly appeared menacing and sinister. The eyes of strangers seemed to be watching her with mocking leers. A raucous burst of laughter from somewhere behind her made her jump. Her eyes searched the crowd of dancers for a glimpse of Ned, but she couldn't locate him. What if he never found her in this sea of people? What could she do? How would she find her way home?

Suddenly she felt a hand on her shoulder, and she was wrenched around to face a tall, dark gentleman in a silver domino who was frowning down at her. "So here you are, my dear," he said in a tone of icy contempt. "I had not thought to find you alone."

"Sir, I think you m-mistake me—" Letty said timidly, trying to back away from him.

"Let us not play any more games," the stranger said curtly, and, grasping her hand in an iron grip, he turned and pulled her behind him as he strode rapidly away from the Grove. She was dragged down a walk darkened by the interlacing trees which lined it. He walked so quickly that she had to run to keep up and had hardly breath enough to repeat her cry that he'd made a dreadful mistake. The walk was not as crowded with people as the wider, brighter thoroughfares had been, but occasionally a passerby appeared. Letty's feeble cries for help were either ignored or she was stared at with suspicion, amusement or distaste.

At last they arrived at a little alcove, surrounded by Greek pillars, in which she glimpsed a table set for two and covered with cold meats, cheeses, cakes and wine. Here she was unceremoniously thrust into a chair. The stranger loomed up before her and looked down at her threateningly. "I've told you, Madam, that I don't relish these lovers' games you so enjoy. These attempts to arouse my jealousy are worse than pointless—they degrade us. I've had no liking for such behavior in the past and see no prospect of changing my mind in the future. If you wish to continue under my protection—"

"Sir," cried Letty in dismay, "please say no more! You've made a terrible mistake and—"

The gentleman's expression of disgust could be discerned even through his mask. "Do you think to disarm me by this *newest* charade? I've no stomach for games, I tell you, even this nonsense you're attempting now."

Letty, breathless and frightened, could scarcely hold back her tears. "Sir, I b-beg you to l-listen to me—" she pleaded, her voice choked with fear.

"If I were in a better mood," the gentleman said, the anger in his voice receding, "I might find this playacting of yours a bit amusing. I had no idea that you were so good at it." With these words he took a seat opposite her, threw back the hood of his domino and removed his mask, tossing it carelessly on the table. "There, now, let's forego this wrangling and try to salvage what is left of the evening. Shall I pour you a glass of madeira?"

Letty stared at her abductor speechlessly. She had recognized him as soon as he'd removed his mask. It was Roger Denham! She could scarcely believe her eyes. For months she had daydreamed of meeting him again, and here he was. And in surroundings that could have been delightfully private and romantic. But there was nothing romantic about being abducted by a man who was behaving like a veritable lunatic. As she stared at him in horror, she was filled only with the desire to run away from the place as fast as her legs could carry her.

With shaking knees she rose from her chair and stood before him. "Sir, I cannot tell you my name or remove my mask—it would embarrass us both. But please believe that I am not the lady you think me. I beg you to excuse me and permit me to return to my friends—"

He looked up at her, a reluctantly admiring smile appearing at the corners of his mouth. "You've disguised your voice very well, my love, I'll say that for your performance," he remarked. "Come here. We'll try something you *can't* disguise." And with that, he reached out, pulled her on his lap, put a strong arm about her shoulders and, before her cry of "My lord—!" had left her lips, his mouth was pressed to hers.

Letty couldn't even struggle, so tight was the grip in which she was held. Powerless to move, she submitted to the most intimate embrace she had ever experienced. She felt her blood burning in her cheeks and pounding in her ears, while she shivered from head to toe. Lord Denham's head came up sharply. "My God!" he gasped. "*You're* not—! You're trembling! What have I done? Who . . . who are you?" And he reached for her mask.

Shaken and breathless, Letty knew only that she must not let him learn her identity. "No, please!" she gasped and tried to fend off his hand.

At that moment there was a cry behind them. "So, my lord," came the shrill voice of a woman standing like a fury at the entrance of the alcove, "*this* is what happens the moment my back is turned!"

Denham hastily set Letty on her feet and jumped up. He stared at the lady who stood before them with her arms akimbo and her mouth stretched into a caustic smile. "Kitty . . .?" he asked in confusion.

At last Letty understood, for the lady wore a shiny green domino, the twin of her own, its hood covering a mass of auburn curls quite similar to her own hair in style and color. And the lady's height and girth, too, were remarkably like hers. There, however, the resemblance ended. From what she could see of the lady's face under the mask which obscured her eyes and nose, Letty was not a bit flattered by Lord Denham's mistake. The lady was years older than Letty, and, in Letty's opinion, not at all pretty. Her lips were too thin, and there were hard lines around her mouth.

Denham looked from one to the other in amazement. Turning to Letty, he said quietly and shamefacedly, "Madam, forgive me. I don't know what to say to you. I *have* made a dreadful mistake—"

"Well, how long do you intend to ignore me?" the lady demanded. "Introduce me to that slut you've been fondling."

Denham whirled around and grasped the lady by the shoulders. "Damn it, Kitty, take a damper! Can't you see I mistook the girl for *you*?"

Letty, her breast heaving with a host of tumultuous and conflicting emotions, desired only to be gone from this place. Taking advantage of the momentary diversion of Lord Denham's attention, she ran between the two closest pillars into the shrubbery behind them. She heard Lord Denham swear and start to follow. The lady tried to restrain him, but he told her curtly that he had to find the girl, to apologize and restore her to her friends. Letty did not wait to hear more. The lady had detained Lord Denham just long enough to permit her to escape. Silently she darted across the lawn in the direction of the Grove and did not stop running until she had come out on the brightly lit quadrangle.

Almost immediately, she saw her brother, who was searching about for her with an air of desperation. Near hysterics, she pleaded with him to take her home. It took only one look at her strained face to convince him, and without questioning her further, he sought out Mrs. Lorimer, explained that his sister had the headache, and the two departed.

Once safely on the way home in a hired hack, Ned had turned to Letty and demanded to know what had occurred. Letty would say only that a gentleman had mistaken her for another and had handled her rudely. Ned hotheadedly had demanded that they return to the Gardens, seek out the miscreant and demand satisfaction, but Letty would have none of it. "Only take me home, Neddie," she had pleaded, "and let me forget the entire incident. The sooner forgotten, the better."

Ned obligingly had forgotten it within a week. But Letty could not forget. Her hero, she'd discovered, had feet of clay. A shrew of a woman—someone named Kitty, with auburn hair and a shrill voice—was "under his protection." Letty was not such an innocent that she was unaware of the meaning of the phrase; Kitty was his mistress. Kitty was a woman whom he kissed with passionate intensity. Yes, she now knew how men kissed their mistresses. It was disgraceful, shocking, appalling! And if Roger Denham were ever to come near her again, *she would want him to kiss her again in that very same way.* It was *that* awareness that shocked her most of all.

She had not stopped dreaming of him, but her dreams had changed. She no longer saw them waltzing together in a brilliantly lit ballroom watched by hundreds of envious eyes. Now, she pictured them alone in a tree-shaded grove, imagining herself lying in his arms in an intimate, blood-tingling embrace. Just thinking of it made her blush with shame and cover her face with trembling hands. What had that dreadful man done to her?

What an ironic twist of fortune it had been to have him approach her again—this time as a suitor for her hand! If she did not feel so much like crying, she would laugh at the way her fate had mocked her. Roger's mother had no doubt convinced him that the time had come to take a wife, and she, Letty, had been chosen as a likely candidate. It had been done through the machinations of her Aunt Millicent, she had no doubt. She could almost hear her aunt and Lady Denham discussing the advantages of the match—"Oh, yes, Letitia Glendenning is a perfect choice. So properly reared, so unexceptional, so unexciting and undemanding." To them she was Lady Glendenning's complaisant, dutiful daughter. *Ha*!

Roger had evidently been a dutiful son, for he had let his mother arrange everything. Letty, completely in the dark, had been invited—was it only three weeks ago?—to spend some time visiting her aunt at Lady Upsham's elegant town house in Jermyn Street. She had been stricken speechless when Aunt Millicent had informed her that she was soon to receive a call from none other than the elusive Earl of Arneau, who had expressed his intentions of offering for her. When she could find her tongue to express her objections, her aunt had summarily dismissed them as "nothing but missish nonsense." Roger had paid a polite morning call, had driven her about the park in his curricle several times, had escorted her aunt, his mother and her to a play at Drury Lane and had proposed.

As a dutiful daughter, she knew what was expected of her. She was to make the best match she could, marry the man no matter what she felt about him, accept whatever connubial demands he would make upon her, bear his children, run his home and ask no questions about his activities and liaisons away from home. She was sure she could accept those conditions—with any man in the world but Roger Denham.

No one could deny that Roger was as good a catch as it was possible for a young lady in her position to capture. She owed it to her family to accept him. And she had tried. When his intentions had at first been made clear, she had allowed herself to hope that he had changed—that he had given up his paramour and intended to turn over a new leaf. But it had not been hard to ascertain, from the many acquaintances who were only too delighted to pass on such juicy tidbits of gossip, that Mrs. Kitty Brownell was known to have rejected several recent overtures—one from a duke!—declaring that she was quite content with her "present arrangements" with her Earl.

Could Letty marry Lord Denham, accept his bored but polite presence at her dinner table, his bored but polite kisses on her cheek, his bored but polite excuses when he absented himself from home? Could she play the game without flinching when she knew she would find herself filled with jealousy, realizing that he was finding love in the not-very-polite but not-at-all-boring arms of Mrs. Kitty Brownell? Lady Glendenning's dutiful daughter thought long and hard, through many sleepless nights and agonizing days, and she had come to the inescapable realization that she could not. She could not sentence herself to a lifetime of the sort of pain she was feeling now. She could *not*.

She turned over and buried her head in her pillow. "Mama, please forgive me," she whispered tearfully. "Your daughter can't be dutiful this time. Let me be wayward, just this once!"

Chapter FOUR

LETTY WAS NOT permitted the luxury of private tears for very long. An urgent knock at her bedroom door cut short her gloomy musings and brought her reluctantly to her feet. A quick glance at her mirror showed her that her eyes were too red-rimmed and her nose too swollen to permit speedy repair, so she shrugged helplessly and went to the door. Prue bounced in excitedly. "Aunt Millicent is back," she announced and perched on the bed. "They want us both in Mama's room right away."

"Both of us?" Letty asked in surprise. "Whatever for?"

"I can't imagine. Unless they want Lord Denham to offer for *me*!" Prue suggested with a giggle.

"That would be very obliging of Lord Denham, wouldn't it?" Letty muttered sarcastically, turning back to the mirror to see if she could in some way disguise the ruin of her face.

Prue tucked her legs up under her contentedly. "*I* wouldn't mind accepting an offer from Denham. It might be fun to be mistress of an enormous country house and queen it over hordes of servants, to come to London every month for balls and theaters, to buy lots of exquisite bonnets and—" Catching her sister's eye in the mirror, she gasped, "Letty, for heaven's sake! Have you been here *crying* all morning?"

"Yes, I have, if you must know. And how am I to face Aunt Millicent looking like this?"

Prue regarded her sister in sympathy. "What's the matter, Letty? Can't you tell me?"

"It's nothing, Prue, really. I'm just being missish. Be a dear and pay me no mind."

"Well, if you're sure... But we mustn't stay here talking, in any case. Aunt Millicent is waiting."

Letty sighed. "I thought I'd heard everything she had to say already. What else has she thought of, I wonder."

"And how does it involve *me*? Well," Prue said, getting to her feet, "we may as well go and find out."

"Can I go looking like this? Am I presentable?" Letty asked.

"You look terrible, but there's no time to do anything about it now," Prue answered encouragingly. And the two girls left the room.

Mama was sitting up among a dozen pillows, her face pale and her eyes underlined with purple shadows. Millicent was sitting at her side on a spindly-legged chair, still wearing her hat and pelisse. "There you are at last," she said sourly as the girls entered.

"Good afternoon, Aunt Millicent," Prue said with a quick curtsy.

"Good day, Aunt," Letty echoed. Then turning to her mother, she smiled and went to sit beside her on the bed. "You look quite done in, dearest," she said, taking her mother's hand in hers. "I've made you ill with my disobedience, haven't I?"

"What did you expect, goosecap?" her aunt asked in irritation.

Lady Glendenning patted her daughter's hand soothingly. "Never mind, sweetheart," she said. "I shall be up and about tomorrow, I promise."

"May I take your hat and pelisse, Aunt?" Prue asked primly.

"No, you may not," was the curt reply. "I don't intend to remain above a few minutes."

"Your aunt has a rather pleasant surprise for you both," Lady Glendenning put in cheerfully. "I think you'll both be delighted with the news."

The two girls turned to their aunt questioningly.

Millicent looked from one to the other, frowned and spoke. "I've come to offer you a temporary solution to the predicament which you, Letitia, have made for yourself. Your name is already the subject of gossip and conjecture in the salons of London. Your mother and I have decided that it will be to your advantage to remove you from London for a few months, until the talk has died down. Since I always spend the late summer months in Bath, I propose to take you and Prudence with me for a while."

"To Bath?" Letty asked bewilderedly.

"With *me*?" Prue added with delight. "Oh, my!"

Millicent grunted. "At least *Prudence* shows some gratitude."

Letty forced a smile. "I'm grateful too, Aunt. Most grateful. I'd be delighted to accept, if Mama thinks she can spare me."

"Of course I can spare you. It will be the very thing for both of you," Lady Glendenning assured her.

"Oh, Mama," beamed the overjoyed Prue. "Bath! Only think of it! I've never traveled anywhere in my life." And she ran and hugged her aunt in enthusiasm.

"Enough!" muttered Aunt Millicent sourly, pushing her niece away. "I intend to be on my way by noon tomorrow, so don't waste time in effusive demonstrations. Go and pack your things."

"Yes, of course, Aunt Millicent," Prue said, trying to contain her excitement.

"Will you excuse us, Mama?" Letty asked.

"Yes, dears, go along. I feel so much better that I shall get up and come to help you select some suitable clothes in a little while."

When the girls had closed the door behind them, Lady Glendenning looked at her sister-in-law with misgiving. "Are you sure it's wise not to tell her that Denham will be there?"

"Yes. Lady Denham and I agreed it would be best. She is convinced that the reason Letty refused him is that their acquaintance was too short. She feels—and I am quite inclined to agree—that Roger was too precipitous. Half-a-dozen meetings in three weeks—they scarcely had time to become acquainted. A month or two in Bath, with very few other young people about to distract them, should do the trick. Of course, Lady Denham has not yet broached Roger on the subject..."

"Suppose he refuses to go?"

"He may balk, but he won't refuse. The attachment between him and his mother is quite strong."

"As yours is to my girls," Lady Glendenning said, smiling affectionately at her sister-in-law, "though you pretend to be indifferent. I hope you know how grateful I am to you for all you've done for my children."

"Whom else have I to care for?" Millicent said gruffly, standing up and adjusting her bonnet. "They are my brother's children, after all." She stood up and held out her hand to her sister-in-law. "I don't despair. With luck, we shall have them married before the year is out."

Lady Glendenning's smile clouded over. "I hope we're doing the right thing. All I want is my children's happiness."

Millicent dismissed her qualms with a wave of her hand and went to the door. "I don't know what maggot has got into Letty's head," she said firmly, "but don't let it get into yours. If those two do not make a perfect couple, I know nothing of human nature."

Lady Glendenning, mysteriously cured of the ailment which had sent her to bed, appeared in Letty's doorway an hour later, fully clothed and looking surprisingly healthy and cheerful. There on Letty's bed lay a huge mound of garments of all colors and descriptions. Prue was sorting the clothing into piles, watched by an abstracted Letty and the two younger girls who were observing the activity with envious faces. "I see you've made a good start," Lady Glendenning said optimistically and entered to lend assistance.

"Here," Prue said to Gussie, "fold these petticoats. You

may as well make yourself useful if you're going to sit here with us."

"I won't," said Gussie with a pout. "You're the one going, so *you* do the folding."

"Gussie, you jealous cat," Prue said accusingly, "you sound just like Clara."

"I'm not a jealous cat," Clara said sullenly, but she was ignored, as usual.

Lady Glendenning patted Gussie's head. "Don't be envious, Augusta. Your time will come one day, you'll see."

"I don't see that there's anything to be envious of," Letty added with a small sigh. "Bath is no longer a very exciting place to visit, unless one is elderly or infirm."

"Why, Letty!" her mother said in mild reproach. "How can you say so, when your aunt has provided you with the constant companionship of your sister to sustain you, and has undoubtedly planned any number of amusements and outings for you both to enjoy?"

"I'm sorry, Mama," Letty said, lowering her eyes. "I don't mean to sound ungrateful. It's just that I'm tired of being grateful to Aunt Millicent for things I don't want. If she hadn't . . ." But here she stopped herself, bit her lip, turned and went to the window where she stood staring out at the summer blooms with unseeing eyes.

"Hadn't *what*, Letty dear?" her mother asked in concern.

"If she hadn't pushed Lord Denham to offer," Letty said from the window, "I wouldn't be in this fix, and we wouldn't have to go to Bath at all."

Prue looked up from the red Norwich crepe gown she was folding carefully and frowned at Letty in annoyance. "Well, I, for one, am glad she did. There's nothing lost by it—you are not being forced to marry him against your will, are you?—and *I* have gained this chance to travel. I don't care what you say about Bath—I shall love it. I've never been beyond ten miles of this house and, as far as I'm concerned, this trip will be a great adventure."

Letty, on whom the strain of the last few weeks was beginning to tell, wheeled about and snapped back at Prue curtly, "An adventure? You'll see what a great adventure it will be! We shall be beholden to Aunt Millicent for every bite of food, every night's lodging, every penny of pin-money. Wait until you try to thank her, and all you get in return is a cold grunt. Wait until you try to dress for dinner and her sour-faced abigail, Miss Tristle, comes in to dress your hair, grumbling that she's neglecting her generous mistress who insists on indulging spoiled young ladies at her own expense. And if you tell her you will not need her, she will sniff and say, 'Lady Upsham insists!'"

Prue stared at her sister, shocked. It was not at all like Letty to burst out in complaints. Letty had always been so gentle, softspoken and accepting. "Oh, Letty," she asked contritely, "is it really going to be as bad as that?"

Ashamed at having made an outburst, Letty shrugged and turned back to the window. Lady Glendenning sighed. "I know it's difficult for you to have to accept so much from her," she said. "Would it make things easier to bear if I told you that your Aunt Millicent *loves* doing things for you? With no children of her own, she delights in being a surrogate parent to you all."

"Does she?" Gussie asked in disbelief. "She always seems so . . . gruff."

Letty turned around. "Does she *truly*, Mama?"

"Yes, she does. Truly. Her gruffness only covers up a tender heart. All the Glendennings are like that. Even your father spoke in that grunting way whenever his emotions were involved." She sighed in melancholy recollection. "Dear man, he so hated to be thought sentimental."

Letty, thoroughly contrite, ran to her mother and knelt down before her. "Oh, Mama," she said tearfully, "I'm an ungrateful wretch."

Lady Glendenning smiled down at the auburn head in her lap and gently smoothed her daughter's tousled curls.

"How can you be a wretch, you silly goose, when you are the very *best* daughter a mother could want?"

"Well, I *say*!" Prudence declared in mock offense. "What are *we*, your other daughters, to think of that, pray?"

Lady Glendenning laughed. "You are *all* my best daughters, as well you know. But, Letty, I've been thinking about what you said, and in a way, you're right. One doesn't like to feel beholden to a benefactor for *everything*. Perhaps we can find a way to provide you with your own abigail."

"Our own abigail?" Prue gasped with delight.

Letty looked up at her mother hopefully. "Can we afford it? It would be heavenly not to have to face Miss Tristle every evening."

"We might spare one of the maids . . ." Lady Glendenning said dubiously. The house was large and already understaffed, but she couldn't bear to see Letty so unhappy.

The neglected Clara let out a cry of dismay. "No, that's not fair! With Prue and Letty gone, that would leave too much housework for Gussie and me."

The justice of the complaint was apparent to everybody. They all fell silent. Prue looked at Clara speculatively. Soon her eyes lit up, as a delicious idea dawned. "I have it!" she said with a giggle. "Let's take Katie-in-the-kitchen!"

"Katie-in-the-kitchen?" Letty laughed. "What an idea! Prue, you're a genius!"

Lady Glendenning looked at her daughters in confusion. "Who *is* this Katie? Are you speaking of Cook's little cousin—the scrawny little thing who helps out in the kitchen?"

Clara nodded. "She's the one."

"But . . . what makes you think she'd make a satisfactory abigail?"

"I'm sure she'll be fine. Clara says that she's very knowing," Prue said, winking at Clara like a conspirator.

"I never said anything of the sort," Clara said sullenly. "And if you take her with you, who will help Cook?"

"Cook won't mind," Prue said airily. "She'll have two fewer mouths to feed, when we go."

Clara pouted again and flounced to the door in disgust. "I might have known I'd get the worst of it," she muttered. "Now there'll be no one in this whole household who'll tell me *anything*!"

Katie-in-the-kitchen was sent for. She was indeed a scrawny girl, undersized for her sixteen years, but with a pair of shrewd eyes that looked out from her peaked little face and seemed to tell the world that here was a person not easily daunted. She was never at a loss for words. Even the surprising news that she was being invited to accompany Miss Letty and Miss Prue to Bath did not discomfit her. She cocked her head and looked from one to the other suspiciously. "Are you tryin' to tip me a rise?" she asked.

"Not at all," Prue assured her, the expression having been made familiar to her by Ned's frequent use of it. "Why would we want to fool you?"

"'Cause I ain't never been a abigail afore. And I don't look so nice or talk so nice neither."

"We shall give you a lovely blue bombazine dress and a brand new white cap, and you shall make a very fine appearance," Lady Glendenning said soothingly.

"And as for not having been an abigail," Letty added with a smile, "Clara tells us that you know everything, so you should have no trouble."

Katie didn't blink. "I ain't sayin' as how I know'd *everything*, but I don't miss much. I suppose I could pick up the way of it quick enough. Don't know that I'd be much good at dressin' 'air, though."

"That's all right," Letty said. "We're quite accustomed to dressing our own hair."

"Well? Are you willing to come along with us?" Prue demanded eagerly.

Katie smiled broadly. "Willin'? If you 'ad to work in a

kitchen, you'd a know'd the answer to that. I'll say I'm willin'! When do we start?"

They started the following morning. An impressive number of trunks and boxes were tied to the top of the Upsham coach, and three young ladies were helped aboard: first, Prue hopped up, her red-gold hair bouncing and her spirits soaring in joyous anticipation; next, Letty stepped up, subdued, brave and determined to show a cheerful facade to the world and to make herself forget what might have been; and last, the diminutive Katie, dressed in the finest gown she'd ever worn, her head erect as a queen's, permitted herself to be helped aboard as if she'd been to the manor born. Right on schedule, as a nearby steeple bell chimed noon, the coach lumbered off down the street bearing its occupants to adventures which would turn out to be quite different from their various expectations.

It was not until three days later that Roger Denham paid the promised call on his mother. She lost no time in informing him that she wanted his escort to Bath. He readily agreed to provide it, but when he realized that she expected him to remain with her for several weeks, he firmly declined. Bath, he told her, was a dowdy, outdated, stodgy locality where neither good sport nor good company could be found, and he had no intention of rusticating there when he had everything he needed for contentment and amusement right here at home.

His mother then launched into a full explanation of her reasons for asking him to remain at Bath for so long a time. She wanted him to see Letty again. She told him bluntly that his pursuit of Letty had been inadequate—if not downright insulting to the girl. He had accused his mother of believing that his charms were such that no girl could refuse him, but was *he* not guilty of the same sort of conceit if he expected a girl to fall into his arms after a mere three-week acquaintance? "Did you ever have a sincere conversation with the girl?" she asked. "Have you ever spent more than two hours at a time in her company?"

Roger had to admit that he had not.

"Then what was the poor child to think of your proposal? Only that you wanted a suitable wife and didn't care much who she was."

"Well, that's really the truth of the situation, is it not?" Roger reminded her reasonably.

His mother looked at him disapprovingly. "It needn't be, if you'd only try to know her better," she suggested.

"If you have any expectations of my falling in love like a schoolboy, you're out in your reckoning, Mama," he told her flatly.

She sighed in discouragement. "I suppose I cannot expect too much," she said, "but you needn't have let the girl know how completely indifferent you are."

"At least my approach was honest. You wouldn't want me to mislead her into expecting more of me than I can offer her. If she's looking for a love match, she is right to refuse me."

"She has a right to expect some interest and affection from a suitor, even if some elements of romance are lacking. Marriage requires intimacy, in any circumstances."

Roger had to admit she was right. He had not gone out of his way to attach Miss Glendenning or to convince her that he had every intention of being a gentle, thoughtful, generous husband. He was certainly aware that the prospect of marriage could be frightening for an innocent young woman, and the prospect of marriage to a stranger might well seem terrifying. He had been thoughtless and unfeeling.

Once his mother had won this point, she was able to convince him to reconsider. Bath was very small, by London standards, and people mingled with each other constantly. He would find many opportunities to see Miss Glendenning, to draw her into conversation, to develop an understanding, to teach her to trust him, and to permit them both to feel comfortable with each other. Surely, she argued, he owed this chance to the girl and to himself.

Reluctantly, he agreed to remain in Bath for a fortnight. If, as he suspected, Miss Glendenning was quite indifferent to him, he would then return to London and the subject would be dropped. If, on the other hand, his renewed suit showed promise, he would abide by his mother's judgment and remain until the time was ripe for him to make his offer again. He chaffed a bit at the terms, but he had to admit they were sensible.

Roger left his mother's house with a feeling of resentment against all women. How they managed to cut up a man's peace! Until the subject of marriage had come up, he had been quite content. What was wrong with a bachelor's existence? He had everything a man could want—his home was comfortable, he had an army of servants to minister to his every need, a host of friends to provide amusing conversation and companionship, a mistress who was available when he desired her, and the freedom to spend his time exactly as he chose. A wife would only complicate his days and disturb his routine. What could a wife provide that he did not already have? His mother had given him the answer to that question—an heir. A man must do his part for posterity. Unfortunately, for him that meant spending a fortnight or more of numbing boredom at Bath. Oh, well, if it couldn't be helped, he told himself, he might as well accept it with good grace. With a shrug, he hurried off to his club to make as merry an evening as possible of his last night in London.

Chapter FIVE

THE GLENDENNINGS' ARRIVAL at Bath coincided with the arrival of a week of chilling rain, a circumstance which not only dampened considerably the town itself but the high spirits of its newest inhabitants as well. As a result, Prue, who could not be restrained from venturing out to do a bit of exploring of her new surroundings, shortly came down with a head cold and was confined to her room until, her aunt told her firmly, all her symptoms had disappeared.

When three days of gloomy downpour had passed without the least sign of clearing, Aunt Millicent decided to pay a visit to the Pump Room in spite of the weather. Prue, she felt, was not well enough to join her in this expedition, but there was no reason why Letty might not be cheered by the outing, and she had no doubt that a drink of Bath's mineral water, ill-tasting though it was, would be beneficial to her. Strictly admonishing Letty to don a pair of thick-soled galoshoes, Millicent opened a large umbrella and the two ladies ventured forth under its protection. With the umbrella above and the galoshoes below, they walked the short distance from their lodgings on the North Parade to the Pump Room without too serious a soaking.

The Pump Room was surprisingly full of people who had been tempted out of their houses by a need for social intercourse stronger than their instincts to stay warm and dry at home. Letty looked around the imposing room with interest. Opposite the entrance was the focal point of the room—the pump itself, set before a window so large it provided light for the entire room. In a recess of the wall at some distance from her on the left she could see the famous equation clock which had been presented to Bath by its maker, Thomas Tompion, almost a hundred years earlier. In a matching recess in the wall to her right sat a small group of musicians playing a selection of country airs. The music, combined with the cheerful sound of voices echoing in the high reaches of the ceiling, made a very pleasant din which did much to lift her spirits.

Millicent, after pressing Letty to drink a glass of the much-praised mineral water, took her arm and began to parade around the room searching among the other strollers for a familiar face. Letty had barely time enough to note that the occupants of the room were preponderantly of middle-age or older when a feminine voice was heard behind them calling, "Lady Upsham! Lady Upsham!"

They turned to find a large-bosomed, gray-haired matron approaching them with a look of eager recognition. Trailing reluctantly behind her was a short, spectacled, thin-faced though handsome youth looking decidedly embarrassed. Aunt Millicent's face broke into an unaccustomed smile. "Why, Mrs. Peake! How good to see you here!"

The two women touched cheeks, and Mrs. Peake turned to introduce the young man. "I don't believe you've met my son, Brandon, Lady Upsham," she said, pulling the young man forward.

"How do you do, Mr. Peake? I thought you were at Oxford," Lady Upsham observed. Brandon Peake opened his mouth to respond, but Millicent, not really interested, went on. "And I don't think you know my niece, Letitia Glendenning. My brother's eldest daughter, you know."

Before the two young people could bow, the ladies had linked arms and proceeded to circle the room. Brandon Peake and Letty fell in behind them, Brandon surveying

Letty shyly from behind his spectacles. Letty, searching for something to say, noticed that the young man carried a book with his finger marking his place. "I'm afraid we've interrupted your reading," she remarked.

"Oh, no," he said earnestly. "Not at all. I had hoped to find... That is, by your leave... I mean, I'm delighted to discover someone like you to talk to."

"Like *me*?" Letty asked.

"Well, yes... I mean... By your leave, someone more in my... That is to say..."

Letty smiled. "I know what you mean. Someone under the age of fifty."

Brandon colored and smiled gratefully. "Yes, by your leave, that's *just* what I mean. We've been here for over a fortnight and you're the first person of my age I've met."

"How terrible," Letty said with real sympathy. "Do you not have a brother or sister to keep you company?"

"No, I have none. Have you?"

"Yes, indeed. I have three sisters and a brother. Although only one sister is here with me."

"You have a sister here in Bath?" he asked interestedly.

"Yes, my sister Prudence. She has a slight indisposition and had to stay indoors today, but I'm sure she'll be out as soon as the weather turns."

"Well, well," Brandon smiled, "there will be three of us. That *will* be a merry change, if I may say so." Then, realizing that he was perhaps taking too much for granted, he looked at Letty shamefacedly and added a stumbling, "By your leave, of course..."

Letty suppressed a laugh and asked him what he'd been reading. The young man explained that he'd been studying the classics at Oxford, but that he'd contracted a severe inflammation of the lungs and had been sent home to recover.

"I'm surprised, in that case," Letty said, "that your mother permits you to come out on a day like this."

"Oh, I'm quite recovered now," Brandon assured her. "Healthy as the proverbial horse, actually. I'm only marking time until I can get back to school next month."

"I see. So your reading is by way of preparation?"

"Yes. I've fallen a bit behind, you see, and I'm trying to catch up. Today, I've been going over Thucydides again."

"Really? Reading history in Greek doesn't sound like much fun for someone just recovering from a long illness," Letty said with both admiration and commiseration.

"Oh, by your leave, I beg to disagree," the young man said earnestly. "I love history, and the story of the Peloponnesian War is particularly fascinating."

"My!" Letty said with a smile, "I suppose it must be."

The admiring look was all the encouragement the pale young man needed. He launched into a detailed explanation of those parts of Thucydides which he found particularly exciting and only stopped when Letty saw that her aunt and Mrs. Peake were saying their adieus. Brandon took her hand, thanked her for listening, hoped he had not been a crashing bore, told her that she was "very easy to talk to, for a female," and hoped, by her leave, to see her again on the morrow.

Letty, walking home with her aunt through the continuing rain, felt quite content. Brandon Peake was small of stature, shy, gauche and somewhat pedantic—certainly not the sort of man about whom she could weave romantic dreams—but he was well educated, sweet-natured and interesting to listen to. He had helped her while away the morning so pleasantly that she had thought of Roger Denham scarcely more than half-a-dozen times. Perhaps her aunt was right—perhaps here she would recover from the depression which had enveloped her for so long.

The following morning, Letty and Lady Upsham returned to the Pump Room. Brandon Peake immediately appeared to take Letty for a stroll around the room, while his mother and Lady Upsham sipped the waters and enjoyed a cozy chat on one of the rout benches which were placed in every convenient nook. No sooner had Brandon launched into his topic for the morning, which was to illustrate the greater objectivity and re-creative powers of Thucydides over Herodotus—a point which Letty had no intention of disputing—when he was interrupted by the appearance of the Master of Ceremonies who begged leave to introduce Sir Ralph Gilliam to Miss Glendenning. Sir Ralph was a lad of twenty, with two large front teeth and an occasional stammer. He expressed his delight at having discovered "some k-kindred souls" at what had previously seemed an unconscionably dull resort, and he followed them around the room, staring at Letty in adoration and interrupting Brandon's lecture at the most crucial points to say how delighted he was to have made Miss Glendenning's acquaintance.

"I thought you said there were no other young people here," Letty remarked to Brandon when Sir Ralph had at last taken his departure.

"By your leave, that was certainly my impression," Brandon said, puzzled. "I wonder if there are any others lurking about."

There were indeed others, as the next morning was to prove. The threesome was further increased by the addition of two more gentlemen—one was Osbert Caswell, a London youth who affected the *dégagé* in his hair-style and casual dress, and the other a Mr. William Woodward, the stocky, sturdy and serious son and heir of a Lincolnshire country squire—and a young lady named Gladys Summer-Smythe, whose large and somewhat vacuous blue eyes shone with joy as she declared her surprise at discovering so many young gentlemen sojourning in Bath. Letty, Brandon and Sir Ralph gathered with the three newcomers near the alcove which housed the clock and spent the morning exchanging foolish pleasantries. Only Brandon remained silent, glowering at the others helplessly. Letty, noticing his displeasure, took his arm and drew him aside to whisper, "I thought you would be delighted to have so many young persons with whom to consort."

"Not any more," he said bluntly. "By your leave, Miss Glendenning, they are all too foolish to converse with on any worthwhile subject. I can only say, as did Dionysius the Elder, that 'unless speech be better than silence, one should be silent.' And where," he added somewhat jealously, "were they before *you* arrived? You seem to be the flame, if I have your leave to say so, which has attracted this group of moths."

Letty laughed and turned to Sir Ralph, who was so overjoyed by this bit of attention that he confided to her that his friends all called him "Rabbit," and he hoped she would do the same. Brandon, completely disgusted, announced at this point that he had promised to restore Miss Glendenning to her aunt and, ignoring the vociferous objections of the other gentlemen, bore her away.

But Letty's reign as the Queen of Bath was to be short-lived. At the end of the week, as soon as the sun made its appearance, Prue emerged from her "sickroom" and announced her intention of joining her aunt and her sister on their daily expedition to the Pump Room. After lengthy argument, she succeeded in convincing Aunt Millicent that she was indeed free of any significant symptoms (for anyone could see that the slight sniffle which still troubled her was the merest trifle and might well disappear after she'd drunk a few glasses of Bath's salubrious water), and she ran gleefully to her room to begin the arduous task of picking the perfect dress in which to make her first appearance in Bath society.

Katie, who had been taking care of her during her illness, was consulted at every step of the dressing process, and it was Katie who decided that the pink dimity was too schoolgirlish, the blue linen more suited for early spring and the red Norwich crepe too unflattering to her coloring. At last, bedecked in a new morning dress of green jaconet, tied tightly under the bosom with silver ribbons, peasant-style, and wearing a fetching bonnet of beige straw with the tiniest poke and a mass of green feathers, she won Katie's approving smile and set off with her sister and her aunt to set Bath afire.

Her entrance into the Pump Room caused all heads to turn, a situation which made Letty blush with embarrassment but which did not at all disturb Prue, who reveled in the attention. "It's better to be looked at than to be ignored," she whispered to her sister flippantly.

Mrs. Peake expressed the view of the majority of the onlookers when she remarked to Lady Upsham that her younger niece was a striking-looking young woman, "although perhaps not quite as lovely as the elder, who, being taller, slimmer and more subdued in coloring, has a beauty which is more haunting because it is more subtle."

The subtlety was lost on most of the young men, however, and the ease with which they dropped their hearts into Prue's hand boded ill for the development of her character. From the moment that Letty introduced her sister into their circle, Prue became the focus of their attentions. Unlike Letty, who had treated them all with equal and polite indifference, Prue smiled flirtatiously at each one of them, laughed at their quips, teased them out of their shyness and played one against the other with a skill that belied the fact that she was just out of the schoolroom and had never met a young man in her life before, if one didn't count the dolts her brother had brought home from time to time.

Brandon Peake, however, remained aloof. Prue had smiled and flirted with him at this first meeting as she had with the others, but Brandon had not responded. He remained at Letty's side, watching the little scene Prue was enacting. After a while, he drew Letty away from the others, led her to a bench and endeavored to entertain her by expounding on Plato's view of the immortality of the soul as set forth in the *Phaedo*. But while he spoke, his eyes flitted to Prue every few moments. Something about her behavior disturbed him, yet he couldn't help watching her. "By your leave, Miss Glendenning," he said to Letty after a while, "I hope you won't mind my remarking that I find your sister's behavior a little forward."

"Forward, Mr. Peake? I don't know what you mean."

"I mean . . . by your leave of course . . . that perhaps it will not be considered seemly—Bath being a rather respectable place, you know—for a young lady to flirt so obviously with three gentlemen at once."

Letty jumped up and frowned down at Brandon angrily. He had never seen her in such a mood before. "Oh . . . I . . . beg your pardon. Perhaps I should not have spoken . . ." he began.

"No, you should not have," Letty said coldly.

Brandon got to his feet awkwardly, realizing that his words had been ill-chosen. Letty, ignoring his embarrassment, drew herself up to her full height, which was a full three inches greater than his, and said curtly, "If Bath society finds anything objectionable in a young lady who is doing nothing more reprehensible than laughing with her acquaintances, then it is made up of more dowdy a group of gudgeons than I had supposed!"

"I . . . I did not mean to offend you, Miss Glendenning," Brandon said miserably. "I only meant . . . After all, even the great Sophocles said—in the *Ajax*, you may remember—that women should be seen and not heard."

"Well, I *don't* remember, not having read it. And it is an extremely silly statement, even if it *was* Sophocles who said it, and the Greek women were very wise to ignore it, which they certainly did, if I know anything about Greek history."

Brandon lowered his head. "I most humbly beg your pardon, Miss Glendenning. I should not have presumed . . . That is, it was not my place . . ."

Letty, observing his discomfiture, softened. "Very well, Mr. Peake. Let us speak of it no further. Now, please sit down again and continue with your description of Tartarus. I find it most interesting."

Brandon, sighing with relief, resumed his lecture. Her ready forgiveness and her sincere attention to a subject so close to his heart did much to restore the pleasant comfort of their relationship. By the time they parted, they had agreed to call each other by their given names. It was only when he had to take his leave of her sister, Prue, that his awkwardness reasserted itself. He colored, stumbled over his words, and he took Prue's proffered hand so gingerly that one would have thought she carried the plague. When Prue glanced at Letty with questioning eyes, Letty could scarcely refrain from giggling.

"What on earth was wrong with Mr. Peake?" Prue demanded as soon as Brandon had left, and they stood waiting for Aunt Millicent to accompany them home.

"I'm afraid, Prue," Letty said with a laugh, "that Brandon finds you a bit overwhelming. I think he finds you *fast*."

"Fast!" Prue repeated, coloring angrily. "Of all the nasty—! What a stuffed goose! If you ask me, I find *him* a slow-top! He and his incessant 'by-your leaves' are the outside of enough!"

"Well, you needn't fire up at *me*. I'm not responsible for what he says and does."

"You spent the entire morning in his pocket! What you see in him I can't imagine. He may be somewhat handsome, if one ignores his horrid spectacles, but he is inches shorter than you, and such a bore besides—"

"That's not fair. *You* may find him a bore, but I do not. I admit that he may be somewhat stuffy, but his conversation is so scholarly that I can't help but learn a great deal from him."

"Honestly, Letty, what can you possibly learn from him that's interesting?" Prue demanded sceptically.

"Many things. For instance, did you know that the saying 'Children should be seen and not heard' originally referred to *women*? Sophocles wrote it, in the *Ajax*."

Prue glared at her sister. "*Women* should be seen and not heard? Hmmmph! I can well imagine in what context *that* was quoted! It was directed at me, I have no doubt. Thank you so much, Letitia, for your scholarly lesson-of-the-day. But if tomorrow's discourse is like today's, I hope you will spare me the recital of it!" And she flounced off to find her aunt.

With the Bath season already well under way, the Assembly Rooms were the scene of nightly activities of great variety and interest; yet circumstances had conspired to prevent Lady Upsham and her charges from attending a single play, concert or ball since their arrival. Therefore, Lady Upsham's announcement that they were to attend the evening's concert in the Upper Rooms so delighted her two nieces that their little tiff of the morning was forgotten. The afternoon was happily spent in a shopping expedition to Milsom Street where Aunt Millicent, in an unaccustomed burst of good spirits, insisted on buying a new pair of gloves for Letty and a Florentine shawl for Prue. "It will be a special evening," she said, as if in apology for her unwonted generosity, "for it is your first formal appearance in Bath society. And nothing makes an evening feel more special than wearing something new."

Her generosity was more than rewarded, not only by the sincere gratitude of her nieces, but by the looks of admiration the girls received on their entrance into the Upper Rooms that evening. Both girls had chosen to wear blue. Prue wore a graceful lustring with small puffed sleeves and a three-inch flounce at the bottom, and had thrown the new shawl lightly over her shoulders. Letty wore a Tiffany silk overdress which was buttoned beneath the bust with a pearl clasp and revealed a glimpse of its white satin underdress when she walked. A large number of people had gathered to hear the concert, and the din of their voices was perceptibly lowered when Letty and Prue entered the room and stood hesitantly in the doorway. Heads turned and people stared. Had they been alone, Prue would have been strikingly attractive with her red-gold hair, diminutive figure and laughing eyes, and Letty, lovely with her auburn curls, willowy grace and serene expression. But together in the doorway, the girls made a breathtaking picture. Aunt Millicent, aware of the admiring attention her nieces had attracted, was content.

Letty and Prue were too fascinated by their surroundings to notice the stir caused by their entrance. The elegant room, with its impressively high ceilings, gracefully shaped windows and magnificent chandeliers, was as lovely as any that could be found in London. Letty, absorbed in admiration of a particularly fine lustre, was suddenly jolted by Prue, who whispered urgently, "Hurry, Letty! Aunt Millicent has found seats and is beckoning to us." And she hurried down the aisle, not aware that her shawl had slipped from her shoulders to the floor. Letty stooped to pick it up. At the same moment, a gentleman who had been sitting on the aisle jumped up from his seat and bent to pick it up for her. Kneeling, their hands touched, and Letty glanced up to find herself looking directly into the smiling eyes of Roger Denham.

Chapter SIX

"ALLOW ME, MISS GLENDENNING," Lord Denham said, helping her up.

"M-my lord!" Letty gasped. "I didn't know... That is, I didn't expect to s-see you here."

"But I expected to see *you* here," he said, smiling at her with polished aplomb, "and I hoped I should find an opportunity to renew our acquaintance."

His self-assurance only succeeded in shaking her own. "Thank you... I mean, I don't think... That is..." and her voice petered out in hopeless dismay. She had no idea of what to say. She was so startled by his unexpected appearance that her mind didn't seem to be functioning. What had brought him to Bath of all places? This was scarcely the sort of place to attract a Corinthian whose activities had always been at the very center of the fashionable circles. But there was no time now for puzzling over riddles. She must say something—anything!—and make her escape. "I believe," she murmured, "that my aunt is... er... waiting for me. Please excuse me, sir."

She glanced up at him to find him regarding her with a most disconcerting look of amusement in his eyes. "Of course, my dear," he said, "but can you not spare a moment to greet my mother? She's sitting right there, directly behind you, and is eager, I'm sure, to say hello to you."

"Your mother?" Letty wheeled around.

Lady Denham was smiling up at her warmly. "How do

you do, Letitia, dear?" she asked, holding out her hand. "How very lovely you are looking this evening."

Letty took the proferred hand and made a nervous curtsy. "Good evening, Lady Denham," she said awkwardly, and relapsed into blushing silence. She knew she should make some response to Lady Denham's compliment, but something seemed to have happened to her wits. A few phrases flashed through her mind—"I didn't see you sitting there," or "How delightful to see you here in Bath," or, "You, too, are looking very well this evening"—all of which she rejected for the inanities they were. But before her silence had become noticeable, a movement at the front of the room drew their eyes. The musicians were making their entrance.

"Oh, dear," murmured Lady Denham, "we shall have to postpone our conversation. But never mind. You are with your aunt, are you not? Tell her that Roger and I shall look for you both at the intermission."

Letty bobbed another awkward curtsy, smiled weakly and started quickly down the aisle. Suddenly, realizing that she had not said good-bye to Roger Denham, she turned and glanced back over her shoulder. He was standing where she had left him, looking after her. Meeting his eyes, which seemed to her to have a rather unholy gleam of mischief in them, she gave him the briefest of nods and turned quickly to rejoin her aunt. So precipitous was she in turning away from his amused regard that she blundered into a gentleman who was proceeding up the aisle in the opposite direction. Ready to sink into the ground in mortification, she made a blushing and incoherent apology to the stranger who smilingly assured her that it was all his fault.

To add to her chagrin, she had a feeling that Roger had witnessed the entire scene. Unable to keep herself from confirming her fear, she glanced back up the aisle and saw, to her horror, that not only had he been watching but that he was coming toward her again. What can he want *now*? she wondered as she watched his approach fearfully.

But when he came up to her, he merely grinned and said, "I'm afraid I neglected to return this to you." And he held out Prue's forgotten shawl.

"Th-thank you," she murmured miserably and, taking the shawl, fled down the aisle.

Her cheeks burning with embarrassment, she slid into the seat beside Prue just as the first notes of Handel's *Water Music* sounded. Prue, not the least bit interested in the music, leaned toward Letty. "What kept you?" she asked in a loud whisper.

"This!" Letty hissed, and tossed the trouble-making shawl on Prue's lap.

Lady Upsham, on the other side of Prue, frowned and leaned forward. "Is there anything the matter, Letty?" she asked.

"No, no. Nothing," Letty whispered back. "But Lady Denham is here and said to tell you she will join us during the intermission."

Aunt Millicent nodded without any apparent surprise at the news and sat back to enjoy the music. Prue, sensing some drama behind the little announcement, looked at Letty questioningly. But Letty shook her head and put a finger to her lips. Then she turned to face the orchestra and tried to concentrate on the lovely strains that had won for their composer the affection and support of a previously angry king.

But Letty couldn't concentrate on the music. Her cheeks still burned in embarrassment at the memory of her mortifying performance, her heart still beat rapidly at the remembered gleam in Denham's eyes, and her head still reeled with unanswered questions. That look in his eyes, as if he were enjoying a joke at her expense, was only to be expected when one thought of her behavior. She had acted like a veritable ninnyhammer. Never before, even when she had danced with him at Almack's so long ago, had she felt so gawky and maladroit. Even more bothersome to her peace of mind was her inability to sift out the confusion of her own emotions about facing him again at intermission. She was well aware that her emotions were a chaos of contradictions. Mixed with her misery was a strong feeling of anticipation. Mixed with her fear was a tingle of excitement. Mixed with her pain was a very distinct element of joy. None of these feelings was appropriate to the situation. None was a sensible reaction to a chance encounter with a man who was little more than a stranger to her. Inexplicable as Denham's appearance at Bath might be, Letty was sure it had nothing whatever to do with her.

Handel's music had never seemed so interminable. She could not wait for it to end. Yet she dreaded the moment the last chord would be sounded. She needed every moment to compose her mind and still the racing of her pulse. For this, the *Water Music* proved to be an ally, for by the time the music had ended and the applause had faded, she had regained some semblance of composure and was able to face the approach of Lady Denham and her son with at least the *appearance* of equanimity.

Lady Upsham and Lady Denham greeted each other effusively, and Lord Denham was made known to Prue, who, when learning the identity of the splendid-looking nobleman who smiled down at her, did all but gape at him open-mouthed. When he turned away to exchange some remarks with Lady Upsham, Prue drew Letty aside and whispered excitedly, "I never took you for a fool, Letty, but fool you must be! How could you have refused him? He's *devastating*!"

"Hush, you idiot! Do you want him to hear you?" Letty answered in irritation. "And if you find him so devastating, why don't you ask him to offer for *you*?"

Prue was given no opportunity to respond, for Denham was approaching. With his practiced smile, he asked to escort Letty to the Octagon Room, where a table of refreshments had been laid out. Letty was about to make a polite refusal when she caught her aunt's eye on her. There was no mistaking the order in that glance. Letty was to accept. She threw her aunt a look of desperate appeal, but the answering glance held a command of such ferocity that Letty knew she had better agree.

Diffidently, she took Denham's proffered arm and walked with him out of the room. Roger, who had missed nothing of the little byplay between Letty and her aunt, gave her hand a sympathetic squeeze. "I know you're quite reluctant to accept my company, Miss Glendenning," he said with disarming candor. "I can't say I blame you. I perfectly understand that our situation is somewhat awkward."

"Very awkward, my lord," Letty admitted.

"But it needn't be. Even though you won't *marry* me, you may still *talk* to me, you know. Accepting my company to the refreshment table won't commit you to accepting my offer of marriage."

He was smiling down at her with his roguish look. It made her feel foolish and naive, and she lowered her eyes and said nothing.

Denham tried again. "If I promise to say nothing of marriage, I'm sure you will find me quite easy to talk to," he assured her with his unnerving self-confidence.

Letty felt a wave of resentment. He was talking to her as if she were a wilful child—as if her awkwardness came from her own lack of spirit rather than a dreadful situation which was completely of *his* making! With an intake of breath, she made a decision to match his candor with a bit of her own. "*Will* I find you easy to talk to?" she asked in a tone that was decidedly challenging. "I have not hitherto found you so."

Lord Denham looked at her in astonishment. This was not the sort of answer he'd expected. "What did you say?" he asked doubtfully. "Have you found my conversation . . . er . . . troublesome in some way?"

Letty, realizing that the answer to his question might lead her in a direction that was much too dangerous to approach, tried to draw back. "I . . . We . . . I see that we've arrived at the Octagon Room. Do you suppose they serve ratafia?" she asked innocently.

Roger cocked an eyebrow and surveyed her suspiciously. "You are trying to put me off the scent, Miss Glendenning, and I'm much too good a hunter for that. But, to answer *your* question before we return to *mine*, yes, I'm sure I can procure a glass of ratafia for you, if you're sure you want the dreadful stuff."

"I think I should like some, if you please," she answered mendaciously, well aware that ratafia was the most insipid drink imaginable.

Roger led her into the room, brought her to an unoccupied bench, bowed and went to the refreshment table. But the short interruption did not suffice to make him forget the subject under discussion. He quickly returned, handed her the drink and seated himself beside her. She peeped up at him to find him staring at her with interest—more interest, she thought, than he had shown when he'd asked her to marry him. Meeting her eye, he repeated his question abruptly. "In what way has my conversation been troublesome to you, Miss Glendenning?"

Letty lowered her eyes. "I've been too frank, I fear."

"Not at all," he assured her. "Frankness is a quality I very much admire."

Letty looked at him earnestly. "I've no wish for you to reproach yourself about... about anything in regard to me. Indeed, you've been... almost always... quite proper and kind. I should not have said what I did just now."

"*Almost* always?" Lord Denham persisted. "That means that, at some time, I was *not* proper and kind. Can you tell me when I was not?"

"Oh, dear, I *have* gone too far. Please, Lord Denham, may we change the subject?"

"Of course, if you wish. I don't want to make *this* conversation troublesome." His disarming smile made a sudden reappearance. "But I shan't let the matter rest for long. You've stirred up my curiosity, my girl, and it must, sooner or later, be satisfied."

Letty couldn't resist an impulse to tease. "You see?" she

accused, with an impish smile. "You've done it again."

"What have I done?"

"Said something troublesome."

"What?" he asked in puzzled amusement. "Now?"

"Yes, you have."

"I can't think what it could have been," he said, watching her intently. The girl was almost enchanting, and he was surprised that he had not noticed it before. He smiled at her challengingly. "Either I'm a complete clodpole, or you are oversensitive."

"I don't choose to call you a clodpole, sir, but you *did* call me 'my girl,' which you must admit is a troublesome epithet for a young lady who . . . who . . ."

Roger laughed appreciatively. "A young lady who refused to be my wife. You are quite right. I *am* a clodpole."

With that disturbing gleam back in his eyes, he kept them fixed on Letty's face while he removed the glass gently from her hand (having noted that she had not drunk a drop), held it out to a passing waiter without even glancing round, and took both her hands in his. "Were my other troublesome remarks of the same nature," he asked her softly, "or were they even worse?"

Letty's smile wavered, her eyes dropped and she tried in vain to remove her hands from his clasp. "I thought we were going to change the subject," she said, her heart beginning to race.

"Tell me," he demanded with a smiling urgency.

She looked up at him with a show of defiance in her eyes. "Much worse," she said bluntly.

His smile faded, and he stared at her in dismay. "You're quite serious, aren't you? I *have* offended you in some way."

"You are being troublesome again, my lord. And I think you'd better release my hands. I'm afraid that we're becoming the object of a few curious stares."

Roger looked round to find her accusation to be quite true. With real reluctance, he released her and helped her to her feet. "Very well, Miss Glendenning, you win this round," he said as he took her arm. "We shall go back, though I'll admit to you that my pleasure in the music is quite at an end. But I intend to get to the bottom of this, and in the very near future, so take warning."

"You make too much of my nonsensical remarks, my lord," she said in the colorless tone she had used when he'd met her in the past, and nothing he said could induce her to say another word.

Roger was rather silent on the walk back to their lodgings, so Lady Denham took the bull by the horns and broached the subject in a direct assault. "I trust you made some headway with Miss Glendenning this evening," she said candidly.

Roger, who had been in a brown study, started. "What did you say, Mama? Headway?" he asked abstractedly. "Oh, you mean to ask if I encouraged her to look upon my suit more favorably. No, my dear, I've made no headway at all."

Lady Denham sniffed disgustedly. "Nonsense, you *must* have. Why, you spent over half-an-hour with her. Everyone remarked upon it."

"Did they?" Roger asked drily. "How very delightful. Shall all our encounters be clocked and watched like that—as if we were a pair of racehorses?"

"Roger, I hope I need not remind you that I'm your mother and will brook no disrespect. You needn't get on your high ropes with me. And you can't disappear with a refined young lady for over half-an-hour without having it remarked upon."

"I have often disappeared with a young lady—and for much longer than half-an-hour—without any ill consequences," he insisted.

"In London, perhaps, in that fast set with whom you choose to hobnob. But here in Bath, with the daughter of Lionel Glendenning, no, my dear boy, no."

Roger snorted. "Fast? *My* set? Really, Mama, you

can't mean it. Denny Wivilscombe and Stosh St. John and Marmaduke Shackleford *fast*?" He laughed loudly.

Lady Denham was not amused but regarded her son with sceptical disdain. "If you think to put me off my question by this obvious irrelevancy, you're off the mark," she told him curtly.

"I thought I'd answered your question," Roger said with false innocence, "but, to repeat, I saw no sign—in our over-half-an-hour *assignation*—that Miss Glendenning was any nearer to accepting me than she'd been when I asked her before."

"But *something* must have transpired between you. You've been completely abstracted since you restored her to her aunt."

"Have I been?" Roger asked. "If I have, it's because I've discovered some surprising facets in the girl. I'll admit to you, Mama, that she is not at all mousy, as I'd first supposed. She's hidden herself behind a rather thick wall of reserve, but when she reveals what lies behind it, she is quite—"

His mother looked at him keenly. "Quite what?" she prodded.

He grinned down at her boyishly. "Quite enchanting," he admitted.

"Well!" sighed his mother in satisfaction. "That is a remarkable discovery to have made in a half-hour *tête-à-tête*."

Roger laughed. "I know. You needn't say it. You told me so."

"So I did. Over and over. I'm delighted, though, that you've discovered it for yourself. It's not the sort of thing one wants to take another's word for—even one's own mother's word."

"I've made another discovery, too, that proves I have a very shrewd mother," Roger said, his smile fading.

"As if that needed proof," she retorted quickly. But, seeing his changed expression, her own smile disappeared. "Oh, dear, what now?" she asked anxiously.

"I'm afraid you were right about my having offended her. She hinted as much to me."

"I knew it! What had you done, you scoundrel?"

"I don't know. She won't speak of it."

"Won't speak of it? Why, Roger, it sounds as if you've done something rather dreadful to the girl!" she said, aghast.

"It does, doesn't it," Roger muttered, rubbing his chin ruefully.

"She gave you no clue at all?"

"No, none. She was completely immovable in her refusal to reveal the circumstances to me."

They had, by this time, arrived at the house, and their conversation was interrupted while the butler took their wraps. Roger requested a brandy to be brought to the study, but Lady Denham chose to go directly to bed. With a hand on the banister, she turned to her son. "Roger, it's incredible to me that you could so offend a young lady and not realize it. Think! Try to remember everything of your courtship. What could you have said or done to her?"

Roger sighed. "I've tried, Mama, truly. I've gone over it and over it in my mind. I tell you, our conversation was made up of the most trivial of commonplaces. I paid her compliments which she answered in monosyllables. I made little pleasantries, to which she smiled wanly. I can think of nothing—nothing!—at all out of the way."

"But the girl is neither stupid nor mad. She cannot have *imagined* a slight!"

"I agree completely. I must have done *something*. But what? The only thing I can think of is my offer itself. You said I was by far too precipitous."

Lady Denham rejected the idea. "An offer of marriage is not *offensive*, even if it *is* precipitous. Unwelcome, perhaps, but not offensive."

Roger could only shrug helplessly. Lady Denham shook her head, sighed and went up the stairs. Roger retreated to the study, where he sank into a comfortable chair and sipped his brandy thoughtfully. But brandy offered no answer either, and in due time he gave up the puzzle and went wearily to bed.

Letty, too, found herself being subjected to close questioning by her family when they returned home that evening. First, Aunt Millicent asked her what she and Lord Denham had talked about for upwards of half-an-hour. Getting little satisfaction from Letty's evasive answers, she gave up and retired. Then Katie came in to help her into her nightclothes and asked a number of questions which clearly indicated that the perspicacious abilgail had already learned—from what source heaven only knew—that Lord Denham had been present at the concert and had spent some time with Letty. Letty refused to answer. She dismissed the girl, telling her to see to Prue and leave her alone. But just as she was brushing her hair, the last chore before she would blow out the candles and retire for the night, her door opened and Prue, dressed only in a muslin nightdress, tiptoed in. "Oh, you're still awake," she observed cheerfully. "Good. I want to talk to you."

"Not tonight, Prue, please. I'm worn to the bone. Go to bed."

Prue ignored these remarks with such complete indifference that her sister could not be sure she had heard them. She perched on the bed cheerfully and tucked her legs up under her comfortably. "I think you must be mad," she said. "He's everything Aunt Millicent said he was—handsome and charming and kind. And he likes you. Really. I could tell by the way he looks at you."

"Prue, go to bed," her sister pleaded wearily.

"Did he do something dreadful to you?" Prue persisted. "Did he fondle your breast or some such thing?"

"Fondle my breast!" gasped Letty incredulously. "Good God, Prue, wherever did you get such an idea?"

"Well, promise not to tell anyone, but I read all about such things in a most shocking book called *Pamela*.

Neddie's friend, Tom Vanleigh—do you remember him? The one with the spots—well, he gave it to me. All eight volumes. And I've had a terrible time hiding them, especially from Gussie, I can tell you! Well, anyway, in the story, poor Pamela is pursued by a Mr. B. who loves her but doesn't want to offer wedlock. So she refuses his advances, but he keeps attempting to seduce her, and he always comes up behind her at the most unexpected times and puts his hand—"

"Prue, that's enough!" cried Letty, horrified. "Such a story is too shocking to *read*, much less to repeat, and—"

"It's a *wonderful* story to read," Prue said defiantly. "I loved every word of it!"

"For shame! If you were a lady, instead of a brazen little hoyden, you would not admit to being the least bit interested in such a tale! And to suggest that a gentleman like Lord Denham would even *think* of behaving in such a monstrously rude fash—" But a sudden recollection of an embrace, in which she had been held so closely that a hand on her breast would have seemed tame by comparison, brought her up short. She fell silent and colored to her ears.

Prue did not fail to note her sister's embarrassment. Her eyes opened wide and, in an awed whisper, she gasped, "Oh, Letty! *Did* he—?"

"No, he did *not*!" Letty almost shouted. "And I'd be obliged if you'd remove yourself and your vulgar suggestions from this room at once!"

"Very well," Prue said, tossing her head proudly and getting up from the bed. "I'll go. But I'm not too far off the mark, I'm sure of that. *Something* made you color up like that." She went to the door and paused. Looking back at her sister, she said in a knowing tone, "I wouldn't let myself be too angry with Denham if I were you. He *did* ask you to marry him which is more than Mr. B. did for poor Pamela—until the end of the story, that is."

"Prudence Glendenning—!" her sister muttered warningly.

"I'm going, I'm going," Prue assured her. "But if you continue to behave like a prudish old cat, you'll *never* get married." And by darting quickly out the door, she managed to escape being struck by the hairbrush which her infuriated sister had thrown in her direction.

Chapter SEVEN

THE ALTERCATION BETWEEN the sisters could not be classified as more serious than a squabble, and since squabbles between sisters are quite frequent in occurrence and petty in nature, the irritations they generate are not likely to be lasting. So it is not surprising that the following morning, Prue and Letty greeted each other with smiles of perfect amicability. The clear, bright day had lightened Letty's spirits and, with Prue wisely refraining from any reference to the subject of the night before, they entered the breakfast room hand-in-hand, greeting their aunt with high-spirited warmth.

All three were agreed that this lovely day was to be spent outdoors, and soon they were happily engaged in making plans for a morning stroll through the famous Sydney Gardens. This was interrupted, however, by the announcement that a morning caller—none other than Lord Denham himself— waited below. Lady Upsham instructed her butler to show him up immediately. As soon as the butler left the room, Letty mumbled an excuse and made for the door, but Aunt Millicent ordered her to resume her seat and to refrain from such skittish behavior. "It's time you learned to behave like a lady, my dear," Millicent said implacably. "You should count yourself fortunate that Lord Denham bears you no ill will and is willing to seek your company."

"But why should he *want* my company?" Letty asked in desperation. "What purpose could there be—?"

But her question was not to be answered, for Lord

Denham entered at that moment. With a charming smile for each of the ladies, he wished them good morning and delivered a message from his mother, inviting Lady Upsham to take luncheon with her. As for himself, he would be delighted to have the companionship of the Misses Glendenning for a ride in his curricle.

Letty opened her mouth to refuse, but Lady Upsham broke in before Letty could utter a sound. "How thoughtful of you, Lord Denham," she said effusively. "It is quite the perfect day for a drive. And although I'm afraid I cannot spare Prue this morning—I require her assistance on an errand of some urgency—I'm sure Letitia will be happy to accompany you." With that, she turned to Letty with a look that brooked no opposition and said with a meaningful smile, "*Won't* you, Letty dear?"

Letty met her Aunt's eye with a rebellious flicker in her own, but realizing that an unpleasant scene would undoubtedly follow if she disobeyed the unspoken command, she submitted. Dropping her eyes to the floor, she nodded and said meekly, "Yes, of course, if Lord Denham can wait until I change into something more appropriate."

"I'll wait as long as necessary, of course," Denham said promptly, "although I think you look charming just as you are."

Letty glanced up at him distrustfully but met a look of such sincere sympathy that she was quite disarmed. Nevertheless, it was with a great deal of trepidation that, a few minutes later, having put on a fetching bonnet of natural straw and a camlet shawl, she permitted herself to be handed up into his lordship's curricle.

Prue and Aunt Millicent watched their departure from an upstairs window. "There," Aunt Millicent said with a relieved sigh when the curricle had disappeared from view, "that's done."

"What do you mean, Aunt?" Prue demanded forthrightly. "Are you making a game of poor Letty?"

Millicent frowned at her niece quellingly. "Never mind, Miss. Your manners are sadly in need of mending. For one thing, I don't like your tone when you address your elders. For another, I don't like your asking questions about matters that are not your concern."

Prue, never one to quail before an attack, remained undaunted. "I beg your pardon, but if you're going to tell whiskers involving me, then perhaps I'd best be in on the plot."

"Whiskers!" her Aunt exclaimed furiously. "Prudence, do you accuse me of telling a *lie*?"

"Well, didn't you?" Prue asked reasonably. "You don't *truly* need me for any errand, do you? You only said that so Denham would have Letty to himself."

Millicent Upsham fixed Prue with a level stare and, drawing herself up to her full height, declared with dignity, "I do *not* tell whiskers, young lady. And I *do* need you for an errand. I need your help to . . . to . . ." She hesitated, waiting for some inspiration to assist her.

Prue grinned mischievously. "To do what, Aunt?"

"To help me choose a gown to wear for my luncheon with Lady Denham," Millicent responded, without so much as a flicker of her eyelashes to indicate that she knew Prue would not be taken in by such a ridiculous answer.

"Oh, Aunt Millicent, really! As if Miss Tristle would permit *me* to—"

"Never mind Miss Tristle. I say I need you, and I do. And I don't intend to stand about bandying words with a jingle-brained snip of a girl who has more tongue than manners." She marched firmly to the doorway. "Now come along. We have a great deal to do this morning." She left the room without a further word.

Prue made a grimace at her aunt's retreating back which managed to combine annoyed impatience with saucy amusement. "Huh!" she snorted under her breath. "Jingle-brained snip, am I? Well, not so jingle-brained that I don't know a whisker when I hear one." And making one last, disrespectful face, she followed her aunt out of the room.

Prue had not minded in the least being excluded from

the drive in Lord Denham's curricle. Since Letty had not seen fit to confide in her sister about the true nature of her feelings for Lord Denham, Prue could not conceive how her presence on the drive would have been any help to Letty. The thought had crossed Prue's mind that perhaps she should try to attach Lord Denham herself and thereby rescue Letty from her predicament, but she soon realized that the scheme was too far-fetched. Lord Denham had taken no special notice of her and, as much as she admired his looks and demeanor, Prue had no personal interest in him. She was only seventeen and had never before gone into society. She looked on Denham as a member of an older generation. Although Prue wished her sister well, she was quite willing to allow Letty to deal with her own problems.

What Prue really wanted was the opportunity to develop her skill at coquetry on young men closer to her own age. Therefore, when Aunt Millicent suggested that she spend the morning in the company of her young friends at the Pump Room, she was quite content.

Aunt Millicent accompanied Prue to the Pump Room where she left her in the company of Miss Gladys Summer-Smythe while she went on to pay her call on Lady Denham. Prue, completely unchaperoned for the first time in her life, felt positively lightheaded with freedom.

Unfortunately, however, Miss Summer-Smythe, whose first few weeks in Bath had been depressingly uneventful and lonely, welcomed Prue's arrival with the enthusiasm of a lost puppy for the arrival of its master. She immediately drew Prue to a rout bench near the clock and eagerly attempted to establish an intimacy between them by confiding to Prue all manner of girlish secrets, in particular her newborn but overwhelming passion for one of the young men in their 'circle.' Prue, her eyes roaming the room in search of a rescuer to interrupt this *tête-à-tête*, answered in polite monosyllables, but these were evidently encouraging enough to Miss Summer-Smythe to make her reveal the identity of the object of her secret passion: Sir Ralph Gilliam.

"Rabbit?" Prue asked, staring at the girl incredulously.

"Yes," Miss Summer-Smythe admitted, lowering her eyes in maidenly bashfulness. "Don't you think he's . . . elegant?"

"Elegant?" Prue repeated, trying not to giggle. Sir Ralph was the most *in*elegant man Prue could imagine. It was not only his rabbity appearance which was inappropriate for elegance, but his entire demeanor. He wore his shirtpoints so high that he could barely turn his head, and he was so conscious of the fit of his clothes that he constantly tugged at his waistcoat or smoothed out his breeches. The stiffness of his carriage, combined with his incessant tugging and pulling, made him appear ludicrously uncomfortable. "I'm not sure I would have chosen *that* word to describe him," Prue ventured.

"Oh, yes, it's the very word," Miss Summer-Smythe insisted. "His manners, his address, his . . . waistcoats . . . Why, did you not see him last evening at the concert? He was wearing a waistcoat of puce satin with wide yellow stripes. I'm sure it must have been the most outstanding waistcoat in the room." She glanced up at Prue and, lowering her voice to a dramatic whisper, revealed (for Prue's ears only, of course) the most exciting tidbit she could offer. "I told him so! Truly. When he approached me at the intermission, I actually told him so! I know it was terribly daring of me, but I said it. 'Sir Ralph,' I said, 'yours is by far the most outstanding waistcoat in the room.' You don't think it was too forward of me, do you? Telling him that?"

Prue, accustomed to the outspoken style of a large family, could only stare at Miss Summer-Smythe in amazement. At length she managed to nod and say, "It certainly *was* an outstanding waistcoat. I . . . er . . . noticed it myself," and endeavored to change the subject. Again searching the room for a rescuer, her eyes met those of Brandon Peake, who had just entered. He came to them immediately. "Good morning, Miss Summer-Smythe, Miss Glendenning. By your leave, Miss Glendenning, may I ask where your sister is today? I don't see her anywhere about."

"She is otherwise occupied this morning, Mr. Peake. *Our* company will have to suffice, I'm afraid," Prue said, smiling at him teasingly, "unless you'd rather go off into a corner and read that book you've brought with you."

Before Brandon could answer, the other three gentlemen arrived and greeted them noisily. As soon as the greetings had been exchanged, Miss Summer-Smythe blinked up at Sir Ralph and, interspersing her words with a series of self-conscious giggles, told him that his waistcoat was again outstanding. Since Sir Ralph had buttoned his coat, covering over all but the very edges of his waistcoat (which, since he knew it would not show, was a rather innocuous one of pale blue loretto), he stared at her dumbfounded. Prue, to cover what she felt must be an awkward moment for poor Miss Summer-Smythe, immediately directed her most enticing smile at the three gentlemen and demanded to know what had kept them all away until this advanced hour. The three, delighted that they had been missed, eagerly surrounded Prue and jostled with each other for her attention. Brandon had no liking for superficialities of this kind. He caught Prue's eye and, with a brief by-your-leave, took himself off. Prue was the only one who took note of his abrupt departure, her eyes following him until he took a seat across the room and opened his book.

Osbert Caswell, the tallest of the young men and the one most casual in his dress, leaned toward Prue, pulled at the ends of the handkerchief he'd tied around his throat and announced proudly, "I've written a poem about you, Miss Glendenning."

Prue, aware that Brandon's withdrawal had irritated her unduly, tried to recapture her former good spirits. "Have you indeed?" she asked with eager insincerity.

"Yes. I sat up half the night composing it. It's

somewhat in the manner of Ben Johnson's 'Celia.'"

A giggle and nudge from Miss Summer-Smythe reminded Prue of that neglected young lady's presence. In an unaccountable wave of generosity, Prue attempted to share with her the attentions of the young men. Slipping an arm around her, Prue drew Miss Summer-Smythe into the circle and said to her laughingly, "I'm not terribly fond of 'Celia,' are you, Miss Summer-Smythe?"

"I don't think I've ever met her," Miss Summer-Smythe answered blandly.

There was a stunned silence for a moment. Then Prue quickly attempted to cover the gaffe by requesting Mr. Caswell to read his lyric aloud. This Mr. Caswell refused to do. "It's for your ears alone, lovely lady," he insisted and would not be moved.

"I wonder where Mr. Peake has gone?" Miss Summer-Smythe asked suddenly.

Sir Ralph glanced around and spotted Brandon seated some distance behind them. "There he is. Shall I get him for you?"

"No, no," Prue said quickly. "He's deep in his heavy reading, as usual. We mustn't disturb him, must we, Miss Summer-Smythe?"

Miss Summer-Smythe looked around toward Brandon. "I don't think it's heavy reading," she declared seriously. "It's only a very *little* book."

For Prue, this was the last straw. While the gentlemen struggled to keep from laughing, Prue lowered her eyes demurely and said nothing. But her sympathetic feelings for Miss Summer-Smythe evaporated as suddenly as they'd come. The silly chit could manage for herself from now on. Prue washed her hands of her.

Sir Ralph restored the equilibrium of the group by referring again to Osbert's poem and demanding a reading. When Prue added her voice to the rest, Osbert weakened and took from his pocket his opus magnus, a poem of two eight-line stanzas which would have taken no more than two minutes to read had not every line been greeted with hoots, catcalls and derision. Every 'rosy lip,' every 'glance divine,' every 'coppery curl' was met with a loud laugh from the listeners. Every 'whilst' and 'beguil'st,' every 'lover pained' and 'kiss abstained' was ridiculed merrily. Before very long, even the poet himself had joined in the hilarity, for he was quick to learn what many writers had learned before him—that if one cannot move one's readers to tears, moving them to laughter is the next best thing. So successful was the comic rendering that his listeners demanded three readings before they were satisfied.

Prue, her sides aching from her laughter, looked up to find that Brandon had returned and was regarding her balefully. "Aha!" she clarioned, "You've returned! No doubt you've finished your book and, having nothing better to do, decided to rejoin us."

The others, their discrimination having been weakened by laughter, reacted as if Prue had said something of enormous wit. They roared. Brandon merely frowned and asked Prue if he might, by her leave, have a word with her in private. Prue raised her eyebrows in surprise, excused herself and walked away on Brandon's arm. "Well, sir," she asked when they were out of earshot, "what is it you wish to say to me?"

"I hope that you'll not take this amiss... That is, I realize that it is not my affair, but... by your leave..."

"I've given you my leave by accompanying you, sir. Please speak up," Prue said with a shade of impatience.

"With your own reputation as my only concern, Miss Glendenning, I merely wished to point out that you've been the object of some... er... disapproval from the... er..."

Prue frowned at him in dawning annoyance. "I think I begin to feel the direction of the wind," she said stiffly. "Are you about to offer me a scolding, Mr. Peake?"

"No, no, of course not. I would scarcely call it... No, indeed. Merely a cautionary word of advice from someone who—"

"Someone who is almost a stranger to me, isn't that right, Mr. Peake?"

"Perhaps. But, you see, my friendship with your sister is my justification for presuming to speak to you on a matter which I would otherwise not venture to broach."

"Indeed? Do you think my sister would countenance such presumption?" Prue asked angrily.

Brandon began to feel misgivings. "I suppose not," he admitted, "b-but I only wished to point out to you that your... by your leave... your beauty, if I may be blunt, is such that you attract many eyes, and therefore it behooves you to show even more restraint than is necessary for other young women—"

"I'm glad you find me beautiful, sir, but I fail to see—"

"I didn't say *I* find you beautiful, exactly. I mean, I do, of course... that is... I mean that *others* do, and therefore your rather unseemly conduct this morning seems all the more indecorous because people tend to keep their eyes on you..."

"I see," Prue said with dangerous restraint, her eyes giving off a steely glint. "Other people—but not you, of course—find me beautiful, and therefore I may not enjoy myself with my friends, is that what you're saying?"

"I'm afraid I'm not expressing myself at all well, Miss Glendenning," Brandon said, beginning to feel acutely uncomfortable in his chosen role as protective uncle. "I only meant to remind you of the wisdom of Aesop when he said, 'Outward show is a poor substitute for inner worth.'"

"I was wondering when you would come forth with a quotation. That was the one thing this conversation lacked," Prue said nastily.

"I'm sorry if my tendency to rely on quotations offends you," he responded lamely.

"Your tendency to rely on quotations is the least of it!" Prue burst out. "Your temerity in speaking to me at *all* on this matter offends me! Your calling my behavior unseemly offends me! Your avuncular manner offends me! And even your calling me beautiful offends me!"

Brandon, unaccustomed to the emotional outbursts of women, was completely taken aback. "I . . . I'm . . . sorry," he stammered, backing away from the angry flash of her eyes. "I m-meant no harm . . ."

"Meant no harm? Meant no harm? You call me a vulgar hussy and then say you meant no harm?"

"V-Vulgar hus—? I never said . . . ! Miss Glendenning, please believe me! I never meant to imply—"

"How else am I to interpret what you said?"

"I merely indicated that your rather noisy frivolity was a bit unseemly, that's—"

"Unseemly! That, Mr. Peake, is not much better than *vulgar!*" Prue snapped and turned her back on him.

Brandon came up behind her and said placatingly, "Please forgive me, Miss Glendenning. I meant it for the best. As Sophocles said in his great *Antigone*, 'None love the messenger who brings bad news.'"

Prue wheeled around and found herself face to face with her accuser. Staring at him stonily, her mind made irrelevant note of the fact that, slight in stature as he was, he stood at least an inch taller than she. Summoning all the control she could muster, she said spitefully, "But you see, Mr. Peake, I don't consider you to be the messenger. As far as I'm concerned, you are the bad news!"

Poor Brandon was stunned. "By your leave, Miss Glen—" he began.

"By *your* leave, Mr. Peake, I don't wish to hear any more. I intend to return to my friends and comport myself exactly as I wish. And I'll thank you to take no further notice of my behavior. In fact, I'd be delighted if you took your by-your-leaves and your classical quotations and never spoke to me again!"

She turned on her heel and ran quickly back to her friends, leaving Brandon bemused, remorseful and miserable. To make matters worse, he looked around to find himself the object of several curious stares. There was nothing for him to do but take his leave. Prue, on the other hand, resumed her laughter and flirtations with more energy than before, until she realized that Brandon was no longer in the room. Then some of her spiritedness seemed to desert her, and although she continued to smile indiscriminately on her three swains, she noticed that somewhere at the back of her throat she felt very close to tears.

In the meantime, Lord Denham was doing his best to find a way to penetrate his companion's thick wall of reserve. He had set a course for Limpley Stoke, promising Letty that she would have much picturesque scenery to enjoy, for the road ran along the Avon's banks for several miles. For the first hour he engaged in the kind of polite and amiable exchanges which had marked their conversation during his brief "courtship," but as the distance from Bath increased and the traffic on the road became lighter, he gave the horses their heads and turned his attention to the girl beside him. "It is quite lowering to realize, Miss Glendenning," he said disarmingly, "that I owe your company today to the coercion of your aunt."

Her eyes flew to his face and, finding him smiling down at her kindly, she colored slightly. "I . . . I . . . would not call it coercion, exactly. My aunt, despite a rather forbidding exterior, is really very kind."

"I didn't mean to imply that she would *beat* you, my dear," Lord Denham said drily. "I only meant that, without her urging, you would not have come."

"You are embarrassingly direct, my lord."

"I'm sorry if I make you uncomfortable, but I know no other way to learn to understand you. Why did you not wish to ride with me today?"

"I should think the answer to that would be evident," Letty said, matching his directness with her own. "People in our . . . situation do not usually seek out each other's company, do they?"

"By 'our situation' you are no doubt referring to the fact that I am your rejected suitor. I can perfectly understand your reluctance to accept me as a husband, Miss Glendenning, but does it necessarily follow that I am unacceptable as a friend as well?"

She looked up at him candidly. "As a friend, my lord? Is that your purpose in seeking me out? To develop a friendship between us?"

"Yes, *one* of my purposes. Why not?"

"I know that friendships between men and women do exist, but I can't believe they can come about after such a beginning as ours," Letty said sceptically.

"I don't think there are any immutable rules governing the conditions in which friendships can develop," he pointed out reasonably.

"Perhaps not, but in our case, there are . . . certain blocks . . ."

"Such as?" he asked intently.

She lowered her eyes. "Such as a feeling of discomfort . . . about the past."

"But I assured you last night that we need think no more about the past. I promise to avoid the subject of marriage completely—at least until or unless you give me leave to reopen it. Doesn't that dispense with the embarrassment of the past?"

Letty, intensely aware of a greater embarrassment by far than his rather uninspired proposal, did not answer.

"Doesn't it?" he insisted, looking at her closely.

She knew that a negative answer would prompt closer inquiries, and a positive one would be tantamount to giving him permission to pursue their relationship. Either course of action would give her pain. How like him to place her in this untenable position!

Before she could decide what to say, he abruptly steered the horses to the side of the road and brought them to a halt. He threw down the reins and turned to her, grasping her shoulder and turning her so that she had no choice but to face him squarely. "Letty, let's be honest with each other," he said earnestly. "I know I thrust upon you an unwanted proposal of marriage, and that I've said or done something that offended you. But please believe that I wish nothing more than to make amends."

Letty raised her eyes and looked at him levelly. "That is not honest. It's your *mother's* wish, not yours."

Roger dropped his hold on her and stared in astonishment. He had not expected quite so much honesty as that. "My mother's wish?" he asked awkwardly.

"Your mother's and my aunt's," she said calmly.

Roger smiled ruefully and rubbed his chin. "That's a leveler," he admitted. "You have me there."

"Then there isn't any more to be said, is there? I think you'd best turn the horses around and take me home."

"No, not quite yet, young lady," Roger said, undaunted. "There is still a great deal to be said. I admit that, at first, my interest in you was inspired by my mother. But since last night my interest has needed no outside prodding. In fact, I've been wishing that both your aunt and my mother would, in future, stay out of our affairs. I hope you believe me."

"It makes no difference whether I do or not," Letty told him bluntly. "A friendship between us is impossible in any case."

Roger shook his head. "If we were to be completely honest, my girl, we'd admit that even the things we've just been saying are nothing but subterfuge and nonsense. There can be only *one* real barrier to a friendship between us."

"Oh?" Letty couldn't resist asking. "And what's that?"

He took her chin in his hand and tilted up her face. "That you hold me in dislike," he said simply, his eyes fixed on her. "Only tell me *that*, and I shall disturb you no further."

Letty, forced to meet his dark, questioning regard, felt herself freeze. Tell him you dislike him, she told herself. It was much the simplest solution to this tangle. One simple little sentence—I cannot like you, sir—and he would be gone from her life. But her throat was constricted, and she could scarcely breathe. She couldn't even lower her eyes to escape his penetrating look. No words came.

The look in his eyes changed. Without taking his eyes from her face or releasing her chin, he slipped his free arm around her and gently drew her to him. "Does your silence mean that you *don't* dislike me?" he asked softly, his eyes glinting with a smiling warmth. "That you feel *some* little liking?"

Her heart was racing. He was too close, his look too intimate. She had to put an end to this—now! But still she couldn't speak.

"Say something, girl," he urged, smiling. "Just say that you feel enough liking to pursue a friendship. Just a *little* would be enough."

He had had no intention of kissing her. She was so young and looked so frightened, he knew that she would require the most gentle, sensitive handling. But at that moment her bonnet slipped back, and her face, which had been partially shadowed, was suddenly fully exposed. He was struck forcibly by its surprising sweetness and something that was not sweet—something unfathomable and mysteriously challenging—lurking in her eyes behind the fear, and he forgot himself. Almost without realizing it, he bent his head to hers.

Sensing his intention, she found her voice. "No!" she gasped, trying to push herself away from him. "No—!"

But it was a gentle kiss, soft and undemanding, and she realized that she could pull away easily if she wished. She felt dizzy, however, and everything seemed to be spinning around, requiring that she shut her eyes and cling to him for support. After a while, he let her go, but it took a moment more before she felt steady enough to open her eyes. When she did, she found him looking down at her with just the merest hint of a smile in his eyes and at the corners of his mouth. He leaned over to her, replaced her bonnet firmly on her head, then stooped and picked up the reins. She stared at him wordlessly as he calmly turned the horses around. Then he turned to her. "I think we may safely say," he said, his hint-of-a-smile broadening into an infuriatingly exultant grin, "that you like me enough."

Chapter EIGHT

LETTY KNEW SHE was not in her best looks when she entered the Pump Room with her aunt and her sister the following morning. The blue shadows beneath her eyes and the excessive pallor of her face could be directly attributed to the fact that she had spent another sleepless night. Even Aunt Millicent had noticed the ravages the night had wreaked in her appearance and had suggested that she return to bed. But Letty would not hear of it. She had an urgent need to visit the Pump Room this morning—a need which neither her aunt nor her sister could suspect. With luck, this morning's activities would bring a solution to her problem.

For Letty's sleepless night had not been in vain. With the early morning light an idea had dawned—an idea of such audacity, deceit and cunning that she was dismayed that she had thought of it. It was an idea completely unworthy of Mama's sweet, obedient, well-behaved, dutiful daughter, and she laughed aloud in pure pleasure as she imagined putting it into action. It was shockingly dishonest and unladylike, but it was the very thing to put that unprincipled libertine, Roger Denham, in his place.

Letty knew that she should reject the idea out-of-hand. There was no doubt at all that it was highly improper and unworthy. But it was the only way she could think of to keep Roger at arm's length, and she knew that he must be kept away from her at all costs. She had spent the last few sleepless hours reliving the events of that morning, enduring the humiliation of realizing that she had behaved in the most spineless, weak-kneed, addlepated manner imaginable. Lord Denham had certainly carried the day. Not only had she not repulsed his brazen advances—she had met his embraces with only the flimsiest, the most feeble pretense at resistance. She had lain in his arms as bedazzled as a schoolgirl, unable to utter a word. She had been an easy conquest, an almost-willing victim of his practiced charm. But this idea—if she could put it to work—would be her armor against him in the future.

She looked around the Pump Room gingerly, hoping for a glimpse of Brandon Peake, the person who would be most instrumental in putting her plan into action. But he was not there. At that moment, she was startled to hear Prue whisper in her ear, "Thank goodness he isn't here!"

"Who?" Letty asked, confused.

"Mr. Peake," Prue said, making a face. "I hope he's broken a leg or something."

"Prue!" Letty exclaimed, shocked. She had an uneasy feeling that Prue had been reading her mind. "Why?"

"Why! Because he's an odious, spying, priggish fool, that's why!" Prue declared venomously.

"Has he done something to offend you, Prue?" Letty asked in surprise. "He seems to be a most docile, agreeable young man."

"Agreeable? Not to me," Prue said. "I hope I never see him again. I'll tell you about it later."

Fortunately for Prue, Letty was too preoccupied with her own thoughts to notice that, for the rest of the morning, Prue's eyes flicked to the doorway every few minutes, unconsciously watching for the appearance of the young man she hoped never to see again. Letty, too, watched the door for the very same young man, but Brandon Peake did not appear.

Brandon, chagrined and embarrassed by the scene with Prue the day before, had decided to avoid the Pump Room. Instead, he went for a stroll in the Parade Gardens. He paced its lanes until he had traversed every corner of the park, but his spirits remained downcast. Finally, weary and depressed, he sat down under a shady tree, pulled a book from his pocket and tried to lose himself in his reading. So quickly did the book absorb him that he didn't hear the clatter of approaching hooves until a horse and rider flew by him, liberally spraying him with a shower of pebbles and mud. With a sharp oath, he got to his feet, berating the careless horseman loudly and brushing himself off.

The horseman, however, had pulled up, dismounted and, leading his horse behind him, was walking quickly back in Brandon's direction. "I say, I'm terribly sorry," the rider said as soon as he came within earshot. "I didn't see you sitting there until I was almost upon you."

Brandon, not one to hold resentment long, was perfectly willing to forgive him. "Oh, it was nothing. No real harm done," he assured the rider, who had now come up to him.

"But your breeches are badly stained!" the rider said. "I am most truly sorry. If you'd care to step round to my rooms—they're only a short distance from here—my valet will see to them immediately."

"Thank you, but that won't be at all necessary. It's the merest trifle, sir, I assure you," Brandon told him. "Oh," he added, recognizing the rider, "you're Lord Denham."

"Why, yes," Roger said, putting out his hand with a ready smile, "but I don't think I—"

"I'm Brandon Peake. We haven't met, but I saw you the other evening at the concert. You were speaking to Miss Glendenning. Lady Upsham told me who you were."

The two men shook hands warmly. "Are you well acquainted with Miss Glendenning, Mr. Peake?" Roger asked.

"With Miss Letitia Glendenning, quite well. She has been kind enough to show an interest in my studies."

"Really? You are most fortunate," Roger remarked casually.

"Yes," Brandon agreed. "Not many young ladies are

interested in the classics. Her sister, Prue, for instance, thinks my studies are the greatest bore."

"Oh? Does she?"

Brandon sighed. "I'm afraid so. She told me in so many words that my classical quotations were... were..."

"Were what, Mr. Peake?" Roger prodded, watching Brandon with amused curiosity.

"She said they were... *offensive*," Brandon admitted with a blush.

"Offensive! I'm sure you must have misunderstood—"

"No, I don't think so. Miss Prudence Glendenning doesn't mince words."

"It seems not," Roger said, trying to hide a smile. "I don't know her very well, but she seems a very lively girl. Sometimes lively young women are wont to say things they don't mean."

"Oh, well, I don't suppose it matters, one way or the other," Brandon said glumly.

"No, I suppose not, especially since the *other* sister is so encouraging," Roger ventured.

"Yes, the elder Miss Glendenning is quite interested. I've been thinking of reading some of *this* to her. Catullus, you know. I would like to hear her reactions to some of these lyrics—the more proper ones, of course."

"Are you reading Catullus?" Roger asked enthusiastically, reaching for the book and leafing through the pages. "I was quite fond of him, too, when I was your age."

"Oh, do you know the classics, Lord Denham?" Brandon asked in surprise. "I didn't think..."

Roger grinned at him. "Didn't think a man of my stamp would ever open a book, is that it?"

Brandon nodded guiltily. "I meant no disrespect, sir. It's only—by your leave—you Corinthians, especially those of note like yourself, are not usually known for your scholarly abilities."

"I don't claim to be a scholar, not by any means, but I did engage in serious study of the classics in my school days—with great enjoyment, I might add—and even now may be found in my library from time to time for purposes other than sitting by the fire with a glass of port."

"I do apologize, my lord," Brandon said in a chastened voice.

"Don't be a cawker. How would you be expected to know my interests?" Roger pointed out reasonably. "But to return to the subject of Catullus, what made you choose him to read to Miss Glendenning?"

"No special reason, exactly," Brandon said quickly. "It's only that it occurred to me today that he is the only Roman who knew anything about real love."

"You mean because he fell into it *per caputque pedesque?*" Roger asked with a small smile.

"Well, yes, for one thing. After all, 'head over heels' is the only way real love comes about, don't you think? Not casual and practiced, like Horace or Ovid," Brandon asked earnestly.

"I suppose, at your age, it is usual to think so," Roger answered thoughtfully. "Does it strike you that Miss Glendenning is especially interested in love poetry?"

Brandon seemed nonplussed by the question. "I thought *all* young ladies were interested in love poetry. Aren't they? Are you suggesting that you think she might not care for Catullus? I mean to read only the most proper and heartfelt of the poems, of course."

"No, I didn't mean to suggest anything at all," Roger assured him. "I'm sure she will enjoy the poems enormously. But I mustn't keep my horse standing any longer. Why don't you drop in to see me later on? I have a new translation of Horace that might interest you."

Brandon stammered an acceptance with obvious pleasure. He watched as Lord Denham mounted his horse, waved briskly and rode off. Brandon then walked back to his lodgings feeling more cheerful than he'd felt all day. How lucky he was to have found someone with whom he could talk!

To Brandon's surprise, his mother greeted him at the

door, obviously in a flurry. She seemed quite overset by the fact that Brandon had received a note from Miss Glendenning. She handed it to him with a hand that shook with agitation. "What does Miss Glendenning want with *you*, my dear?" she inquired urgently.

Brandon stared at the note, feeling a little agitated himself. "I'm sure I couldn't say, Mama," he answered, unwilling to open it in front of her. "Did the messenger say which Miss Glendenning had sent it?"

"*Which* Miss Glendenning? Why, I never thought to ask. Are you on terms of such intimacy with *both* of them?"

"Intimacy?" Brandon said, looking at his mother with annoyance. "Of course not. Not with either of them. What sort of question is *that*?"

"Well, I'm sure that when *I* was a girl, I would never have been so forward as to send a note to a young man with whom I was barely acquainted," Mrs. Peake said with a scornful sniff.

"Never mind, Mama. I'm sure that it's nothing of importance. If you'll excuse me, I'll go to my room," Brandon said impatiently.

"Very well, I'm sure it's none of my business if young ladies choose to write to you. I only hope you realize that a connection with the Glendennings is not what I'd hoped for you. I have it on very good authority that poor Lady Glendenning has been left without a feather to fly with."

Brandon groaned under his breath and made a hasty escape. As soon as he'd closed his door, he opened the missive and read it eagerly. It was a briefly worded but urgent request that he pay a call at their house on the North Parade that afternoon at three. It was signed L.G.

Promptly at the appointed hour, Brandon reached for the door knocker at Lady Upsham's house on the North Parade. Before he could knock, however, the door was opened by Letty herself. "I've been watching for you," she said in a whisper. "Come in quickly. I don't want anyone to know you're here." Taking his hand, she led him to a small sitting room near the stairs and closed the door behind them. "There. We shall be safe now. Aunt Millicent and Prue have gone out, so we shan't be disturbed."

"By your leave, Letty, if you've asked me here to scold me about what I said to your sister yesterday," Brandon said quickly, "you needn't have gone to all this trouble. I've scolded myself enough already."

Letty looked at him in bewilderment. "What? I don't know what you're talking about. Did you say something dreadful to my sister?"

"Didn't she tell you?"

"No, not a word. Although, now you mention it, she did say something this morning about hoping you'd break a leg."

Brandon reddened. "Break a—?"

Letty laughed. "You mustn't take offense. That's just Prue's way. She doesn't really mean it, you know."

"Oh, she meant it," Brandon insisted glumly. "She's furious with me for criticizing her behavior in the Pump Room yesterday."

"Is that all? Well, I shouldn't give the matter a second thought, if I were you. She probably deserved it, anyway. Please, Brandon, I must speak to you about a matter of much greater importance."

"But Letty, she didn't deserve it. I mean, I had no right at all to comment on your sister's conduct."

"Brandon, you make a mountain of a molehill. Prue's temper can be volatile, I know, but she cools quickly. She's probably forgotten the whole incident by this time."

"Forgotten it? I can't believe—"

"But I'm sure of it. Don't let it worry you any more. Come, sit down here. I have something to ask you of the utmost urgency." And she gently pulled him down on the sofa beside her.

Brandon, putting aside the subject of Prue with the greatest reluctance, looked at Letty dubiously. Something about the intensity of her manner made him distinctly uneasy. "Urgency?" he asked timidly.

"Yes. To me it is a matter of . . . of . . . my entire future. Brandon, will you do me the greatest favor?"

All Brandon's instincts set up loud warnings, but he hadn't the courage to be rude. "Well, if I can . . . of course. What is it you want of me?" he asked diffidently.

"I want you to be my . . . my betrothed . . . for just a little while."

"I don't understand, Letty. Your—?"

"My betrothed. My husband-to-be," she said distinctly, twisting her fingers in her lap nervously.

Brandon blinked at her in alarm. "Me? But . . . You don't . . . You can't mean that you—? I mean, by your leave, we are not so well acquainted that . . . I mean, do you think you know me well enough to . . . ?"

Letty smiled wanly. "Oh, Brandon, I don't mean it to be a *real* engagement! How can you think so? I could scarcely be the one to make such a proposal if I seriously wanted to marry you."

Brandon nodded thoughtfully. "Oh, I see what you mean. The gentleman is supposed to do the asking, I suppose. But if you *don't* want to marry me, then what *are* you asking?"

"Only that you *pretend* that we are promised. It would be very simple, really. We would pretend to have a secret understanding—secret because our families object to the match. We need tell no one at all about it, except—"

"Except?"

"Except . . . one person. In other words, we would go on exactly as before. Nothing at all would be changed, except that . . . if this person should ask you . . . you would say that I am indeed your betrothed, that we have had an understanding for several weeks, and that we hope to make the news public as soon as we win our families' approval."

"Letty, I hope you will forgive me for being quite dense, but I don't understand any of this."

Letty sighed. "I'm not explaining it at all well, I'm

afraid. It's a rather complicated story. You see, before I came to Bath, a . . . gentleman of my acquaintance asked me to marry him. He had the support of my family but I . . . I cannot like the match. I could not accept him, as I told him. But he's come to Bath and has given me . . . er . . . signs that he doesn't believe my refusal is final."

"You mean that he persists in bothering you after you've refused him?" Brandon asked, shaking his head in outrage. "He sounds like the greatest of coxcombs! I don't blame you at all for refusing such a fellow."

"No, you mustn't be misled. He is not a coxcomb. He is a very . . . personable gentleman. That's what makes the matter so difficult. No one can understand why I don't think he'd make a suitable husband."

"But *I* understand," Brandon insisted loyally. "Any man who would thrust his attentions on a woman who doesn't want him must not be the right sort at all!"

"As to that, Brandon, I must be fair. My manner with him has not been. . . . Oh, how can I explain? . . . has not been as . . . er . . . discouraging as it should have been. I really cannot completely blame Lord Denham for—"

"Lord Denham!" Brandon gasped in astonishment. "*He* cannot be the one you mean!"

Letty raised an eyebrow. "No? And why not, pray?"

"But Letty, I've met him. Why, he's the kindest, most considerate, the *finest* man I've ever met!"

Letty frowned at him in annoyance. "What has that to say to anything?"

Brandon was completely at a loss. "But . . . but . . . I can't believe any young lady would . . . That is, are you *sure* you don't wish to marry him?"

"There! You see?" Letty burst out. "Even *you* won't accept my right to refuse him!"

"Well, I wouldn't say *that*, exactly. It's only that I don't understand—"

"But why *should* you understand? Why should *anyone* have to understand? *I* understand, and that should be enough!" she cried in desperation. Then, realizing that she was losing control of herself, she clenched her hands and blinked back the tears that she feared were about to make an appearance. "Oh, Brandon," she whispered helplessly, "if I'm forced to marry him, I think I'll die!"

Brandon looked at her miserably. "But, Letty, I still don't see what I can do..."

Letty looked up eagerly. "But you *can*, Brandon, don't you see? If he believes that I'm truly in love with someone else, he will surely go away and not trouble me again."

"Oh, I see. Yes, I suppose he will."

Brandon hesitated. He liked Lord Denham. He had intended to pay him a call that very afternoon. But how could he face him if he knew that sooner or later he would have to lie to him? Besides, what if the lie should be spread about, and his mother should hear of it? How could he explain? "By your leave, Letty," he asked worriedly, "have you given any thought to what would happen if word got out that you and I were betrothed? You might *have* to marry me! And I very much fear, my dear, that such an occurrence might turn out to be, as the great Sophocles said, 'a remedy too strong for the disease.'"

Letty laughed. "Oh, Brandon, as if I would do such a thing to you! No, have no fear on that score. If word should leak out—which I very much doubt—I would simply cry off. I assure you that I have no wish to be married—to *anybody*."

"I don't know," Brandon said, still reluctant, "it seems a very shaky plan to me."

"On the contrary," Letty insisted, "I'm sure it will work. If Lord Denham decides to give up his suit—which he might at any time, you know—we shall never have to use the plan at all. But if he persists, I'll simply tell him that my heart is otherwise engaged, and I'll name a man in whose company I've often been seen—*you*—and he'll be bound to believe me. If he goes to you, you'll support my story, leaving him no choice but to accept it. Then he'll go away, and we can forget all about it."

Brandon was silent for a moment. Finally he spoke up. "I cannot like it, Letty. Dishonesty makes me very uneasy."

"I know," Letty said, shamefacedly. "If I were not driven to desperate measures, I should never suggest such a thing. But what else am I to do?"

"Are you sure you cannot find it in your heart to like Lord Denham? I spoke to him just this morning and learned, to my surprise, that he is a classics scholar, in addition to his other accomplishments."

"If I wanted to marry a classics scholar," Letty said with asperity, "I would sooner marry *you*!"

Brandon, who had no answer to that, hung his head.

"Oh, Brandon, forgive me," Letty said contritely. "I'm so upset that I don't know what I'm saying. It's such a strain. Everyone thinks Lord Denham is such a paragon, it makes me want to scream in vexation."

"There's nothing to forgive," Brandon assured her, patting her hand comfortingly. "But should you not sleep on it tonight? Euripides tells us that second thoughts are ever wisest.'"

"I have slept on it, Brandon. My mind is quite made up. But if you wish to think it over, I must certainly allow you to do so. I just wish to point out to you that you once told me that Socrates said, 'Heaven ne'er helps the man who will not act.'"

Brandon could not help smiling at her proudly. "That's true! How clever of you to remember that. I would be a poor sort of man to refuse a favor to my most apt pupil."

"Then you'll do it?" Letty squealed in delight. "Oh, Brandon," she sighed in relief and threw her arms around his neck, "I don't know how to thank you!"

Brandon, blushing with pleasure at the feeling of self-satisfaction derived from the knowledge that he'd made a noble—indeed a knightly—sacrifice for a lady fair, permitted himself to be led to the door. His goodbyes were said with a sincerely happy smile. His pleasure lasted until he reached the corner of the North Parade. There his sense of uneasiness assailed him again. Good God, what if his mother learned of this? What of his budding friendship with Denham? And what of Prue? What would *she* feel if she believed him to be in love with her sister? He didn't understand why the thought of Prue depressed his spirits, but he returned home filled with misgivings. Into what other difficulties, he wondered, would this devil's pact with Letty lead him?

Chapter NINE

THE WEATHER CONTINUED FINE, luring the high-spirited youths of Bath to seek activities out of doors. Letty and Prue, often in the company of Brandon, the Rabbit, Osbert and the others, strolled the circuses, crescents and squares of Bath until the city was as familiar to them as to the natives. They explored the parks which liberally surrounded the town center, and they made special expeditions to the Sydney Gardens, where they blundered through the well-known labyrinth, laughing and shrieking until they had found their way out again. They even climbed up the high streets to a point above Lansdown Crescent where, high over the lower city, they could make out through the trees the graceful curves of the city streets below.

On these bucolic rambles, Roger Denham rarely joined them, preferring to ride his horse through the countryside. But even he was soon tempted to explore more distant vistas, and when the young squire-to-be, the sober Mr. Woodward, undertook to organize an expedition to see the famous cathedral at Wells, some twenty-one miles to the south, Roger was prevailed upon to make one of the party. The group, which included (besides Woodward and Roger) both the Glendenning sisters, Miss Summer-Smythe, Sir Ralph and Osbert Caswell, was soon augmented when Lady Upsham and Lady Denham agreed to act as chaperones and Mrs. Peake declared her intense interest in making the trip with them. Lady Denham volunteered the use of her barouche which, if one of the gentlemen rode with the driver, could seat five. This, with the addition of Roger's curricle and Mr. Woodward's phaeton, would be sufficient for transportation, and an early hour on the following Wednesday was decided upon for the start of the journey.

On the appointed morning, Katie-erstwhile-of-the-kitchen arose before the sun, picked up the two dresses she had chosen for her mistresses to wear—they had long since given such decisions into her forceful and capable hands—and made for the little room off the kitchen where an ironing board was permanently set for use. To her chagrin (but not her surprise, since it had happened frequently before) Miss Tristle was there before her, busily pressing the ruffles on her mistress' voluminous traveling dress. "I might've know'd," Katie grumbled. "Don't you never sleep?"

Miss Tristle stared coldly at the diminutive wench whom she regarded as a vulgar, encroaching upstart, completely unfit for intimate service to ladies of quality and certainly not equal to herself in the household hierarchy. "You should have done your ironing last night," she said loftily, placing the flatiron she had been holding on a metal stand which had been heated by a bed of hot coals and picking up its twin which had been warming on the stand.

"So could you," Katie came back disrespectfully. Miss Tristle was the only irritant in Katie's new, clean, pleasant existence. The woman had resented Katie's appearance in the household from the first, although Cook had told Katie how Miss Tristle had complained for days before they'd left London that she didn't like taking care of Lady Upsham's two nieces as well as her ladyship. But the moment the toplofty dresser had learned that the Misses Glendenning were arriving with an abigail of their own, her nose had been quite out of joint.

"I do not deign to bandy words with such as you," Miss Tristle said coldly, pursing her lips primly and speaking down her rather elongated nose to Katie. "I'm in no mood for squabbles, seeing as I'm not in the best of health this morning."

Katie pursed her lips and crossed her eyes in a satiric imitation of Miss Tristle's expression. "I do not deign to squabble wi' you neither," she said impertinently. "Howsomever, I 'ave two gowns 'ere what must be pressed, an' what am I s'posed to do about 'em, eh?"

Miss Tristle was about to retort when a sharp pain in a tooth which had been giving her severe discomfort for the past several hours caused her to drop the iron upon the dress and press both her hands against her cheek. Katie, with her usual presence of mind, snatched up the iron before it could do any damage and placed it on the stand. Then, looking at Miss Tristle with sympathetic interest, she asked, "Took wi' a toothache, are you?"

Miss Tristle only groaned.

"I know a good remedy for toothache," Katie suggested.

Miss Tristle sniffed disparagingly and picked up the cloth needed to grasp the iron's hot handle, the spasm of pain having passed. "I have my own remedy, thank you," she said slightingly, lifting the iron again.

"It don't seem to be doin' you no good, from what I can see," Katie remarked bluntly. "What is it you're usin'?"

Miss Tristle was forced to stop her work and clutch her face again. When the pain subsided, she turned to Katie with less assurance. "I learned the recipe from my mother," she said. "It is concocted of a mixture of honey, juniper root and rock alum. But I must admit," she added with a moan, "that it doesn't seem to be working a bit well."

"I ain't surprised. Honey is the most dimwittedest thing to put on a bad tooth. It's the sweetness, y'know, what makes the tooth feel worser."

"Is it indeed?" Miss Tristle asked contemptuously. "And how did you become so expert, may I ask?"

"I know a thing or two," Katie answered cryptically. "Do you want to 'ear my remedy or don't you?"

"If it's to lay roasted turnip parings behind the ear, I've already tried that, and it didn't help either," Miss Tristle told her, the discouragement and suffering in her voice softening the unfriendliness of her words.

"I ain't never 'eard such gammon as that!" Katie declared. "No, mine is a simple 'erb wash. I'll make it for you after we've got our ladies off, if you've a mind to try it."

A simple herb wash had a soothing sound. Miss Tristle nodded almost gratefully. She hastily completed her work on Lady Upsham's dress and turned the irons over to Katie with unmistakable eagerness, even offering to help by smoothing ruffles and folding ribbons. But Katie, her object won, generously urged Miss Tristle to snatch a few minutes rest before her mistress should wake and demand her services. Miss Tristle, feeling an unexpected spark of affection for the hitherto despised kitchen girl, smiled as warmly as her sour disposition and her aching tooth permitted, clutched her cheek and left Katie to her work.

The results of Katie's labors with the irons were much admired, first by Letty and Prue and then by their aunt. Lady Upsham smiled with satisfaction to see how fresh and lovely Letty looked in her dress of white cambric with its rows of red flowers embroidered at the hem and the red satin sash tied in a fetching bow at the back. And Prue, too, was a credit to her, looking charming in her yellow-and-white striped dimity with its perky ruffle at the neck. She was so pleased with her nieces that she uncharacteristically complimented them both on their appearance. Katie, who hovered near the door to see them off, grinned with pleasure when Letty waved a happy goodbye and Prue gave her a congratulatory wink. Then she hurried off to the kitchen to brew her herbal concoction for the suffering Miss Tristle.

The meeting place for the members of the expedition was the square at the back of Bath Abbey. Before the hour of eight had struck, a number of the adventurers had assembled, bearing baskets, parasols, lap robes and shawls in abundance, for early September weather was unpredictable. No sooner did Letty and Prue make their appearance than everyone began a subtle but purposeful maneuvering for advantageous seating in the carriages. Lady Upsham immediately claimed a place beside Lady Denham in the barouche. Letty, determined not to ride with Roger, attempted to follow her aunt, but Millicent promptly declared that she had promised the two remaining seats to Mrs. Peake and Brandon. To Millicent's chagrin, however, Prue, with a mischievous twinkle (and blithely ignoring the pleas from all the gentlemen for her companionship), asked Roger if she might join him in his curricle. Whether her motive was to tease her swains or to help her sister she was not sure. What Roger felt, no one could tell. He merely threw Letty a quizzical look and smilingly helped Prue to climb into the curricle.

Mrs. Peake took her place in the barouche, but before Brandon could follow her, Roger approached him and offered to let him take the ribbons of the curricle. "What?" Brandon asked in pleased surprise. "Do you mean it? Would you really let me handle your grays?"

"Why not? They are quite well trained, you know," Roger said.

"But . . . but they're the most beautiful set of matched grays I've ever seen," Brandon said in awe. "If they were mine, I don't think I could bear to let anyone else touch them."

"I hope you're not trying to tell me that you're cow-handed with the ribbons," Roger said.

"Oh, no!" Brandon assured him hastily. "At Oxford, I'm considered to be rather a creditable driver. I'd take very special care, if—by your leave—you are truly in earnest about letting me take the reins."

Roger assured him of his sincerity with a warm smile and helped him into the curricle. Brandon's face glowed with pleasure, not only at the prospect of driving the beautiful grays but of showing off his prowess before none other than Prudence Glendenning herself.

Lady Denham, meanwhile, enticed Sir Ralph to ride alongside her coachman with the promise that the coachman would give him the reins from time to time. With excitement equal to Brandon's, Sir Ralph jumped up on the box in happy anticipation. Gladys Summer-Smythe, who had been following Sir Ralph around the square with doglike devotion, eagerly took the one vacant seat in the barouche, having decided that being near her "rabbit" was worth enduring the company of the three chaperones. That left Roger, Osbert and Letty to take their seats in William Woodward's phaeton. Osbert helped Letty into the phaeton and followed after her. Roger took his place on her other side, Mr. Woodward climbed onto the driver's seat, and the entire cavalcade set off on the twenty-one mile trip to Wells.

Letty glanced surreptitiously at Roger settling himself comfortably beside her and was almost certain that his eyes held a mischievous gleam of triumph. But nothing in his manner or conversation was the least bit out-of-the-way. He complimented Mr. Woodward on the balance of his carriage, admired Osbert's yellow pantaloons which he assured him were all the crack in London, and nodded in polite agreement when Osbert said in his flowery way that Letty was as pretty as the roses on her dress. Much of the conversation during the first hour of travel was made by Mr. Woodward who, because he had instigated the expedition, felt it incumbent upon him to point out the various places of interest along the way and to find something attractive about every vista they looked upon.

For a while, Osbert kept his eyes on the curricle just ahead of them, wishing it was he and not Brandon who sat beside Prue in that elegant, graceful curricle. But before long Brandon let the horses have their heads, and the curricle passed the barouche, which had led the way, and pulled out of sight. Having nothing better to do, Osbert found himself glancing more and more often at the subdued young lady seated beside him. The sun cast glinting highlights on Letty's hair, which was pulled back from her face and bound up in a knot at the back of her head, but Osbert noticed that little tendrils of sunlit curls had escaped their bonds and framed her face with entrancing charm. He noticed, too, the natural and delicate high color of her cheeks, the slender curve of her neck and the whiteness of the skin he could glimpse beneath her décolletage. Prue was quite forgotten as he gazed at Letty in dawning adoration. Suddenly he remembered a new poem he had composed the night before which now rested in his coat pocket. It had been written to Prue, but if he remembered it rightly, it was general enough to apply to *any* lovely young lady. With a broad smile, he turned to Letty. "I say, Miss Glendenning, would you care to hear a poem I've penned just for you?"

Letty started. "For me?" she asked in surprise.

"Yes, indeed. I'm a great admirer of yours, you know."

At this, William Woodward turned around in disgust. "I thought it was Miss Prudence you was nutty on," he remarked forthrightly.

Osbert glared at William furiously. "Why don't you tend to your driving?" he muttered savagely.

Letty, suppressing a smile, looked down at her hands. But Roger was too amused to let the matter pass. "You are not being kind to our poet, Mr. Woodward," he said. "A true bard must be given the freedom to take inspiration from any number of sources. He needn't be inspired by only one female."

"Exactly so," Osbert agreed with alacrity.

Mr. Woodward shrugged. "If you want to encourage his nonsensical rhyming, it's nothing to me," he said placidly and turned back to his horses.

"I, for one, am quite agog to hear your verses, Caswell," Roger said encouragingly. "With Miss Glendenning's permission, of course."

"*By my leave*, Lord Denham?" Letty couldn't resist

saying, hoping the teasing reference to Brandon's excessive formality would not be lost on Roger. They exchanged a smiling glance.

"By your leave, ma'am," he responded readily, with a nod of the head that signified *touché.*

"Of course you may read your poem, Mr. Caswell," Letty said, resuming her demure demeanor.

Osbert unfolded his paper and, enunciating carefully, gave his poem its first reading:

"When in this Chariot of Love
We twain together ride,
I cannot voice my Ecstacy
When you are at my side.

"Your copper Curls, your Skin so fair,
Your Smile that I adoreth—
I long to make them all My Own,
But dare not to imploreth.

"From azure eyes one flashing Glance,
From ruby lips one Smile,
Then I, in fear, am stripped of words
Or Talent to Beguile.

"So here in silent Misery
I gaze and yearn in vain,
And pray you'll turn those azure Orbs
To look on me again.

"Well, that's it. It don't do you justice, ma'am, of course, but I hope you liked it."

"Do her *justice*!" exclaimed William, turning around again. "It ain't got anything to *do* with her! Does she have copper curls? I ask you, does she?"

Roger's lips twitched. "It's . . . er . . . poetic license, Woodward. A poet may use poetic license in these matters."

"And how about 'azure orbs'?" Woodward demanded. "Are they poetic license, too?"

Roger was sure he heard a gurgle from Letty's throat. It took all his will-power to control the laughter welling up inside him. "Yes, indeed," he answered manfully.

"And how about 'imploreth'?" Woodward persisted, preferring the teasing they had given to Osbert at his last poetic reading to this politeness. "Are you trying to tell me you liked 'dare not to *imploreth*'?"

Roger choked. "It was . . . certainly ingenious," he managed.

"Thank you, Lord Denham," Osbert said, pleased. "Though I'll admit the last stanza is a little weak. I had a bit of trouble with that one."

"May I see it?" Roger offered. "Perhaps I can make a suggestion or two."

Osbert passed the paper to him, and Roger read the stanza carefully. Letty, her eyes brimming with suppressed amusement, looked over his shoulder. "Well, my lord, how do you propose to improve it?" she challenged.

"How about this?" he said promptly,

> "So here in silent misery
> I gaze and yearn in sorrow,
> And pray some *other* azure eyes
> Will smile on me tomorrow."

At this, Woodward gave a loud guffaw from his place on the box, slapping his knee in appreciation. This was too much for Letty, who burst into uncontrollable laughter. Roger tried for a moment to keep his expression serious but soon had to follow suit. Osbert, accustomed to hearing his verses greeted with merriment, good-naturedly joined in. The ice thus broken, the conversation in the phaeton became much less constrained, and by the time the halfway point had been reached, somewhere south of Midsomer Norton, the four were engaging in the comfortable raillery of old friends.

This was not the case in the curricle, where Prue had maintained her attitude of frigid indifference for almost two hours. Brandon had tried, at first, to maintain a stream of innocuous comments on the weather and the scenery, but her lack of response soon wearied him. He relapsed into silence and gave his attention to the magnificent horses. It was not long before he could drive the vehicle with skillful competence. He had left the other carriages far behind, and he bowled along the road at a pace lively enough to impress any young lady, but Prue showed no reaction. At length, he slowed the horses to a comfortable trot and settled back in his seat glumly. The ride which had seemed at the outset to be so promising was turning out in actuality to be a complete fiasco. Brandon turned to Prue in desperation. "Please, Miss Glendenning, won't you listen to me? I have apologized and apologized for my rudeness the other day. Can't you possibly forgive me—at least to the extent of speaking to me during this curst ride? We can't possibly travel all the way to Wells without saying a word to each other!"

"Yes, we can," Prue said coldly. "We'll be there in another hour."

"Nevertheless—by your leave—an hour can be interminable in these circumstances," Brandon pointed out.

"By your leave, I'm well aware of that," she answered drily.

"I seem to say 'by your leave' a bit too often, I suppose," Brandon said miserably.

"You say it every time you open your mouth," she told him in digust.

"I'm sorry..."

Prue shrugged. "It doesn't matter to me," she said bluntly. "But while we're on the subject of your silly repetitions, I also find that you are always saying you're *sorry* about one thing or another."

"Really?" Brandon asked thoughtfully. "I'm sor— I mean, I didn't realize. Well, as the great Homer once said, 'A noble mind disdains not to repent.'"

Prue merely looked at him with her eyebrows raised.

Brandon colored. "Oh, I see. You are thinking that I'm too full of quotations also. I'm sor—"

A giggle escaped Prue. "It seems that, if we eliminate your by-your-leaves, your apologies and your quotations, you have nothing at all to say for yourself."

Brandon turned away. "If you choose to mock me, go ahead," he said, the epitome of injured dignity.

"If you ask me, a bit of mocking may be good for you," Prue said waspishly.

Brandon, nettled, turned to her. "If you ask *me*, a bit of—" But he cut himself off.

"What?" Prue asked curiously. "Go ahead and finish what you started to say."

Brandon shook his head and stared straight ahead, his mouth compressed in a straight line.

"Say it," she urged. "You were going to say that a bit of *something* would be good for me. Tell me what it is. Although I don't see why I bother to ask. I wouldn't take advice or counsel from a . . . a . . . stuffed prig."

"A stuffed—!" Brandon gasped. Pushed beyond endurance, he wheeled himself around and grasped her by the shoulders. "I'll tell you what would be good for you—*this*!" And he shook her so violently that her teeth rattled. After a moment, aghast at his loss of control, he stopped. His hands still grasping her shoulders, he stared at her in shamefaced remorse. "I'm . . . I'm . . . *sorry* . . ." he stammered breathlessly.

Prue stared back at him, her heart beating violently against her ribs. Adept as she was at coquetry and flirtation, she was really quite inexperienced in the feelings which come from intimate encounters between men and women. She knew that her feelings for Brandon were strangely ambivalent. He was often in her thoughts, and she knew that, of all the young men who circled about her, he was the one whose approval she most desired. Ironically, however, he had made his *dis*approval of her quite plain. First, he had criticized her to her sister, then to her face, and now this. She had a strong urge to burst into tears and collapse against his shoulder, but her pride and a fierce resentment which seemed to well up inside her kept her from succumbing to an urge which was nothing more than mawkish sentimentality. Instead, she shook his hands from her shoulders. "Sorry!" she cried out in fury. "Sorry! Here's what I think of your sorries!" She put her two hands flat against his chest and pushed him with such strength that he tumbled out of the carriage.

Frightened at the result of her impetuous act, Prue looked down at the road to see if he'd been hurt, but the horses, ignoring the drama being played behind them, continued to trot on. "Brandon! Are you hurt?" Prue called back in alarm.

Brandon sat up in the road and shook his head in confusion. Then, with a dawning realization of what was happening, he looked up and shouted frantically, "Prue, *wait*! Stop the horses!"

But she, now relieved of any guilt, since he was apparently unhurt, laughed wickedly. "I will not!" she called back. "You can jolly well *walk* to Wells!" With that, she picked up the reins, gave Brandon an insolent wave of her hand and drove off round a bend in the road.

In desperation, Brandon jumped to his feet, only to topple over on one knee. His ankle was sprained. "Prue, *Prue*," he shouted in anguish, "you must stop! The *horses*... I promised Lord Denham! Prue, come back!"

Once round the bend, Prue felt a twinge of fear. She had never driven a vehicle by herself before. Gingerly, she pulled the reins. Lord Denham's well-trained horses placidly slowed to a halt. She breathed a sigh of relief and decided to remain where she was. Brandon would come along soon. She would apologize, and all would be well.

It was a full quarter of an hour before the much-abused Brandon hobbled into view. The sight of him caused Prue to gasp. He was covered with dust, his face was streaked with perspiration and grime, and he winced in agony at every step. Prue leapt from the carriage and ran to him. "Oh, Brandon," she said in a voice of sincere self-reproach, "you *are* hurt. I'm a beast! I'll never forgive myself! Here, let me help you."

Brandon glared at the infuriating minx who stood so remorsefully before him, offering her arm. Even his sense of relief when he saw that she and the horses were safe was not strong enough to ease the wrath she had inspired in him. "Don't touch me," he snapped at her. Limping to the curricle, he painfully lifted himself into his seat.

Prue climbed up and seated herself beside him. She glanced covertly at his face, but one glimpse of his tense, frozen expression and the look in his eyes as he stared implacably at the road before him told her that any words of hers would fall on deaf ears. With a silent, rather pitiful sigh, she settled back to endure the rest of the ride. She knew in her bones that it would be passed in a silence more insupportable than before.

Chapter TEN

DESPITE THE TEMPORARY SETBACK, Brandon's vehicle was the first to arrive at the King's Head Inn at Wells. Within half-an-hour the other carriages pulled into the courtyard. The gaiety of the four who spilled from Mr. Woodward's phaeton was so infectious that the whole group made a merry entrance into the inn and joined Prue and Brandon who were sitting glumly at opposite sides of a tiny but cheerful dining room. Prue greeted them with an affected eagerness, but she was soon laughing with perfect and heartless sincerity over the fulsome compliments being paid to her by Sir Ralph. Brandon, who was determined not to spoil the outing for the others by bringing attention to his injured ankle, gave strained smiles to everyone, gritted his teeth and said nothing. And since Prue had no idea of the severity of his pain, she, too, said nothing about his accident. Thus no one else noticed that anything was at all amiss.

They sat down to a noisy luncheon, during which great quantities of country ham, cold mutton, coddled eggs, hot biscuits, currant pudding and home-brew were consumed, after which they drifted out to take the short walk to the cathedral. Brandon, telling them that he would follow shortly, watched until they were out of sight and then hobbled to the innkeeper and asked for a room in which he could lie down for a while. The innkeeper helped him up to a small bedroom and offered to pull off his boots, but when they attempted to remove the boot from the injured foot, it caused such a spasm of pain that

Brandon decided to leave it alone. The innkeeper shrugged and, not knowing what else to do for him, left him alone. Poor Brandon lay back against the pillows and surrendered to self-pity.

The rest of the party arrived at the cathedral and promptly separated into small groups, since some wanted to go first to the Chapel, some to the Chapter House and some straight to the famous Wells clock. Thus the fact that Brandon failed to arrive was not noticed.

When Letty became separated from her group, her absence was not noticed either. Fascinated by the sculpture that could be found embellishing the arches, the walls, the bosses and the tops of every column, Letty had stopped to study a charming lizard eating a bunch of grapes which was carved on the far side of an arch through which they had passed. When she looked up, the group had gone. Untroubled, she continued her rambles quite contentedly. Near the door to the cloisters, she discovered to her delight a number of little sculpted scenes depicting rather unusual subjects. One was of a man scowling at a thorn in his foot. Another scene showed a man suffering with a toothache. She was studying a third, in which a man appeared to be stealing fruit, when a voice behind her made her jump. "Did you know that this scene is one of a series?" Roger was remarking pleasantly.

"Series?" she asked stupidly, trying to hide the turmoil which his sudden appearance caused in the pit of her stomach.

"Yes. Here he is stealing the fruit. In this next scene, he is being apprehended, and here in the last he's being beaten."

"Oh, dear," Letty said with a rueful smile, "I wish you hadn't told me that. It seems a cruel punishment for so small a crime."

"So it is. Perhaps we should turn our backs on the whole scene and take a moment's respite out there in the sunshine. I see an ivy-covered wall that looks quite inviting."

"But . . . I've scarcely begun to see the sights—" Letty demurred.

"I know, but I've walked *miles* looking for the sight of you, and I'm exhausted," Roger countered, drawing her arm through his. "Besides, I've been waiting all day for the opportunity to talk to you alone."

Letty's heart began to beat in a disturbingly irregular fashion. "But, my lord," she said with a smile so broad she hoped it would cover her uneasiness, "what can you wish to speak to me about? *You* haven't composed a poem in my honor, have you?"

Roger grinned. "Well, no, I'm afraid not. But I would make the attempt, if it would please you."

"No, not today. One poem a day is quite enough. Any more would surely turn my head."

"No, we certainly must not have your head turned," Roger agreed, firmly leading her to the place he had indicated. "You've given me enough trouble with your head just as it is."

"Given you trouble, my lord? *I*?" she asked demurely.

"Don't play the innocent with me, my girl," Roger said, lifting her upon the wall and jumping up beside her. "You're quite well aware of the trouble you've been causing me."

"If the trouble to which you refer is related to a subject which is barred from discussion between us, you bring it on yourself, sir," Letty said with sudden seriousness.

"When do you think, *Miss Glendenning*," Roger demanded, "that you will feel friendly enough toward me to call me Roger? I find your endless 'my lords' very intimidating."

"Intimidating!" she said, outraged. "You wouldn't be intimidated if I had a . . . a . . . leopard alongside me!"

"You have a very flattering estimate of my courage, my dear," he laughed. "I think a leopard might well do the trick, if your object is to keep me at arm's length."

"Then perhaps I should investigate the possibilities of obtaining one," Letty said with a smile.

Roger's smile faded. "You needn't go to such lengths as that," he said, taking her hand in his and looking at her with sober affection. "I'm much more vulnerable to your slights than you think. One harsh word from you would be enough to send me to the grass."

Letty could not help but be touched. "I have no wish to . . . to send you to the grass . . ." she admitted in a tiny voice.

"I'm glad of that," he answered earnestly, his eyes fixed on her face. "I do love you, you know."

She felt her throat constrict. "Roger—!"

His clasp on her hand tightened. "Don't look so frightened. I know I'm being too precipitous again, but surely you can't be surprised. You must know how I feel. I've not tried to hide it from you—"

"No, no—!" Letty said tearfully, trying to remove her hand from his grasp. "I didn't think—"

"But you *must* have realized," he insisted. "And you must feel it, too. I cannot be so misguided as to have misunderstood—! Letty, dearest, what *is* it that makes you so afraid of me?"

Letty, her hand trembling in his grasp, stared up at him. How dear he looked to her now, how sincere and how deeply troubled. She longed to believe him, to trust him, to touch his face and soothe away the frown that creased his forehead. But she forced herself to remember that this very man whose eyes now searched hers with such tender concern had once shown quite another face. She had seen it at Vauxhall Gardens and she could not forget it. "It's not that I'm afraid of you, Roger," she said at last, "but that . . ."

"Yes?"

"That I am . . . promised . . . to someone else," she said hesitantly.

She saw his cheeks whiten. "*Promised—?*" He could barely say the word.

Letty nodded and removed her hand from his grasp

which had now grown slack. "Yes. I've been . . . betrothed for some weeks now."

"But you never . . . ! I had not heard a *word*—!"

"We've had to keep our plans secret. My family would oppose him, you see. They keep hoping that I . . ." She flicked a quick glance at his face.

Roger nodded in understanding. "That you will accept *me*," he finished for her.

Letty clasped her trembling hands together in her lap and lowered her eyes, aware that he was staring at her incredulously. "You know him, of course . . ." she said, to make sure he didn't doubt her word.

"Do I?" he asked in surprise.

"Yes. Brandon Peake."

"Brandon!" His voice was shocked.

"You needn't sound so surprised," she said defensively. "You'd find him an intelligent and thoughtful person, once you grew to know him."

"Yes, of course he is. I know that already," Roger assured her with perfect sincerity. "I find him a most admirable and likable young man. I . . . most earnestly wish you every happiness."

Letty murmured a thank-you and kept her eyes fixed on her hands. She had never felt so completely miserable. "F-forgive me for . . . for not telling you before," she said lamely.

"There's nothing to forgive. You owe me no explanations or apologies. It is *I* who should apologize for forcing my attentions on you."

Unwittingly, Letty's hand went out to him. "No, please," she said gently, "you mustn't think . . . I have never felt that you've been in any way . . . displeasing. You've always shown me the utmost courtesy and . . . and . . ."

"Thank you, my dear," Roger said with a wry smile, "but I have a very clear recollection of at least one time when my . . . er . . . attentions must have seemed in excess of what a betrothed young lady could consider desirable."

Letty, remembering that her *own* reactions to that kiss in the curricle were in excess of what would be considered desirable in a betrothed young lady, colored to her ears. But Roger, who was jumping down from the wall, did not notice. He stood in thought for a while and then seemed to pull himself together. Turning to her, he grasped her by the waist, lifted her gently and set her on the ground. For a moment he held her against him and smiled wistfully down at her. "Your Brandon is a damnably lucky fellow," he murmured and then abruptly let her go. He took her hand and led her to the chapel where they found Gladys Summer-Smythe on the arm of Mr. Woodward, examining with feigned interest the magnificent vaulted ceiling. Leaving Letty in Mr. Woodward's charge, Roger made a bow and left them. He was not seen by them again that afternoon.

More than an hour later, having somewhat dissipated his disappointment and frustration by striding through the narrow lanes and byways of the tiny city, Roger began to feel more in command of himself. Thinking longingly of the solace of a glass of good brandy, he made his way back to the inn where he bespoke a private parlor and a glass of the best brandy in the house. The innkeeper complied in the leisurely style of country service, remarking as he poured the brandy that, "'T'other young gent ain't come down from 'is room as yet."

"Other young gent?" Roger asked, puzzled. "Whom do you mean?"

"The gent 'oo come in with your party," the innkeeper explained. "The one wi' the bad leg."

"Bad leg? I can't imagine—" Then Roger realized that he had not seen Brandon all afternoon. "Are you speaking of a rather short young man with spectacles?"

"Yessir, that's the very one."

"You say he had a bad leg? You'd best take me to him at once," Roger said, rising hastily, his brandy forgotten.

He found Brandon stretched out on the bed, his brow

wrinkled in pain, his arm thrown over his face. "Good Lord, Brandon," Roger said, dismayed, "what's amiss here?"

Brandon, startled, sat up abruptly and attempted to smile. "Oh, are you all back already? Don't look so troubled. It's nothing to speak of. I only twisted my ankle and decided not to march about the cathedral on it, that's all."

Roger took note of the whiteness of his lips and the tension in his face and was not taken in. "We are not *all* back, only I. So you needn't play the hero for my benefit. Let's have your boot off so that I can have a look at that ankle of yours."

Brandon was tremendously relieved to share his problem with someone as purposeful as Lord Denham, but he nevertheless was reluctant to make a fuss over what he knew was only a minor injury, the pain notwithstanding. "I don't think we should remove my boot," he demurred. "We won't be able to put it back on again, I'm afraid, and then everyone will see and make a great to-do—"

Roger had been feeling the ankle through the boot and shook his head in kind but firm disagreement. "I'm afraid you'll have to withstand a to-do, my boy. You've been subjecting yourself to needless suffering by keeping the boot on. Much as I admire your courage, I see no reason for you to endure unnecessary agony."

"But taking the boot off will be worse than anything," Brandon admitted fearfully. "Can't it wait until I get home?"

"Taking the boot off will be impossible now, I fear. Your ankle has become so swollen, we'll have to *cut* the boot off. But cutting it off won't cause you much discomfort, I promise, and the relief of removing it will be a positive blessing." With those comforting words, he turned to the landlord and ordered the necessary implements and the bottle of brandy.

When the innkeeper returned, Roger urged Brandon to

drink a good quantity of brandy before he set to work cutting off the boot. But Brandon, not accustomed to drink, was reluctant. "I can bear it," he said manfully. "I don't need spirits to give me courage. Go ahead and cut."

Roger grinned at him. "Quite the hero, aren't you? No wonder Letty prefers you to me."

Brandon shot a startled glance at Roger's face. "Oh," he said with an agitated tremor in his voice, "did she . . . tell you about that?"

"Yes, she did. Do you mind?"

"Well, I had hoped she wouldn't have to—" Brandon began.

"But she *did* have to. I was forcing my attentions on her again, you see."

Brandon worriedly studied Roger's face, but Roger seemed to be quite calm and unconcerned. Nevertheless, a pervading sense of guilt depressed Brandon's spirits. Roger Denham had always been more than kind and generous to him, and even now was doing his best to help Brandon out of this fix that his ankle had caused. To repay Roger with a lie—to let him believe in this false betrothal to Letty—was beyond anything. He regretted with all his heart that he had given his word to Letty. But there was nothing he could do now. With a hopeless sigh, he reached for the brandy. "I think I *will* take that drink after all," he said.

By the time the others returned to the inn, Brandon was seated downstairs in the private parlor, his leg freed from the constricting boot and his ankle neatly bound with strips of cloth and propped up before him on a cushioned stool. The high color of his face, the foolishness of his smile and the brandy glass in his hand gave instant evidence that he was, if not quite cast away, at least gloriously tipsy. As he had predicted, a great fuss was made over him, especially by his mother who, when they went to the carriages for their return to Bath, insisted that he sit next to her in the barouche to permit her to administer whatever aid he should require on the journey.

Since the only aid she offered was to wring her hands and make repeated comments on the Peake family's tendency to adversity and misfortune, Brandon wisely turned away from her, closed his eyes and fell into a stertorous sleep.

The occupants of the other two carriages were not much more cheerful. Roger was forced to drive the vapid Miss Summer-Smythe in his curricle, and after responding to her inanities for half-an-hour he found himself gritting his teeth in impatience. As a result, he urged his horses into a wild gallop, frightening poor Miss Summer-Smythe into a frozen tension and completing the more-than-three-hour journey in less than two.

In the phaeton, Mr. Woodward and Osbert were at first overjoyed to find themselves squiring the two Misses Glendenning, but they soon noticed that their quips and pleasantries fell on deaf ears. The two girls sat side by side in a dismal, abstracted silence. Prue's thoughts were completely occupied with guilt and self-loathing. She had caused Brandon to sprain his ankle. She remembered saying to Letty one morning that she hoped he'd broken a leg. She hadn't meant it, of course, but it was as if she'd put a curse on him. And tonight, at the inn, when she'd tried to apologize to him, he'd turned away from her. She had ruined everything. Brandon, so serious, so sensible and reliable, was the only man whose good opinion she desired. For him, she would enjoy curbing her impetuosity and controlling her flirtatious behavior. But she had pushed him from the carriage and injured him. How could she expect him to forgive her when she could not forgive herself? She had lost forever the chance to show him what a truly lovable girl she could be if she tried.

Letty, too, was wrapped in misery. She could hear Roger's voice saying, "I do love you, you know." Even in her dreams she had not permitted herself to imagine his voice saying those words to her. But he'd said them. It had happened in a reality more wonderful and more terrible than any dream. His eyes had been lit with such warmth and confidence, and she had snuffed out that light with a couple of words. With a lie. It would have been so easy—so easy!—to have told him the truth, that she loved him to distraction, that she had never loved anyone else, that she wanted nothing more than the feeling of his arms around her. How different this ride home would have been if she had let herself say those things! At this very moment she would have been sitting beside him in the curricle, her head on his shoulder, his arm around her waist, blissfully whispering the sweet things that she imagined lovers say to each other when they are alone together.

But she could not let herself dwell on the might-have-been. She had thought the matter through clearly when she'd been calmer and more sensible. She had made what she was certain was the wisest decision under the circumstances. Everything had gone as she had planned. He would not ask her again. If the price she had to pay to see her plans fulfilled meant living in this utterly abject misery, well, she must pay it.

Thus three carriages returned from a pleasure trip with all the passengers disgruntled and more than half their number sunk in deep despond. When the goodnights were finally said, there were not many among them who did not secretly vow to stay closer to home in the future.

Chapter ELEVEN

ROGER HAD BEEN at home an hour when Lady Denham wearily entered the house after the seemingly endless journey back from Wells. The first sight to greet her eye as she stepped in the door was Roger's man, Trebbs, climbing the stairs carrying a portmanteau and a small campaign trunk. "What on earth are you doing with those, Trebbs?" she inquired.

"Good evening, my lady," Trebbs said, turning and setting down the luggage. "I am carrying these up from the storeroom so that I can have them packed by morning."

"*Packed?* What for?"

"His lordship's orders, ma'am. He wishes to leave shortly after breakfast."

"Is his lordship leaving? He said nothing of it to me," the dowager said, puzzled. "Has he gone to bed?"

"No, my lady. He's in the study, I believe. Would you like me to find him and send him to you?"

"No, never mind, Trebbs. I'll find him myself."

Roger was indeed in the study, a glass of brandy in his hand and a half-empty bottle on the table at his elbow. Although he seemed to be staring at the glass with more-than-ordinary concentration, there was no other evidence that he had been imbibing too deeply. His mother stared at him for a moment with a troubled frown. "What's this Trebbs has been telling me?" she asked when it became apparent that he was not going to look up from his fascinated contemplation of the contents of his glass.

"Do you truly intend to leave tomorrow?"

Roger looked up at her with a rather unfocussed gaze. "Oh, there you are, Mama. Should stand up, o' course, but can't seem to use m' legs."

"Roger!" his mother said disapprovingly. "You're *foxed*!"

Roger nodded. "Drunk as a lord," he declared, and laughed. "Very appropriate saying, that. Drunk 's an earl might be even better. Tha's it. Drunk 's an earl."

"Well, if you're drunk, you should *not* be making decisions. Tell Trebbs to stop packing and to get you to bed. In the morning, when you're more yourself, you won't want to leave at all," Lady Denham said firmly, relieved that Roger's decision to depart was only the result of an alcohol-induced whim.

But Roger shook his head. "No. Made m' decision before I shot the cat. Cold-sober decision. No point staying here, y' know. She won't have me."

"What are you talking about? You aren't making a bit of sense. Roger, you sot, we can't have an intelligent conversation while you're in this condition."

"Nothing to discuss, Mama. 'S all very simple, really. She won't have me. Betrothed already. May 's well take myself back to London, see? Won't do any good staying here and brooding."

Lady Denham was beginning to understand. Her plan had apparently fallen apart. But she was too tired to probe further into the matter now—especially with Roger in this condition. "Take yourself to bed, my boy. That's my advice to you. We'll talk about this in the morning." She went to the door, but before she left the room, she stopped to give him one last warning. "Don't you try to steal away before I see you in the morning! Do you hear me, Roger? I want your word that you'll provide me with a coherent explanation before you desert me."

Roger lifted his glass in a salute. "Word of an Arneau. Promise. You may interog . . . inter . . . question me 's much 's y' like. But not now. In the morning."

Lady Denham shook her head compassionately. "Very well, my dear. In the morning."

Lady Denham had been awake for hours before her son made an appearance the following morning. It was after ten o'clock when she looked up from her coffee to find him looming in the doorway of the breakfast room, his eyes bloodshot, his brow furrowed and his mouth grim. But he was dressed for travel, and his mother saw at once that his present sobriety had not caused him to change his mind. She smiled at him over her coffee cup and beckoned to him to join her. Roger came in, bent to kiss her cheek and sat down. Before he uttered a word, he reached for the coffee pot and poured himself a cup with a hand that trembled slightly. Then he faced his mother with a rueful smile. "It seems that your son is a curst rum touch," he said. "I'm sorry you had to see it."

She patted his hand. "Don't underestimate me, my dear—or overestimate your own proclivities toward sin. I've lived a long time and seen a great deal worse."

He smiled at her. "Have you really? What a game old girl you are!"

"I suppose that is meant to be a compliment," she responded drily. "Roger, you do look awful. Do you feel well enough to travel today?"

"I feel like the devil," he answered bluntly. "I'm neither well enough to travel nor to answer the questions I know you're agog to ask me, but I intend to do both. Pluck to the backbone, that's the sort I am."

"Will you have time to see Brandon Peake before you go?" Lady Denham inquired. "He sent a message begging you to drop in for a moment this morning."

Roger raised his eyebrow. "Did he? Well, I suppose I..." He looked at his mother sharply. "Did he say anything else?"

Lady Denham looked puzzled. "No. Were you expecting something more?"

"I wasn't expecting anything at all. Now let's get to the

inquisition. What is it you want to know that I haven't already spilled out in my drunken stupor?"

"*My son* was not in a stupor! And I will not subject you to an inquisition. I only want to know why Letty refused you again."

"I'm sure I've told you. She is betrothed to someone else. I believe that is the sort of news which we must accept as final," Roger said flatly.

"Oh, dear. *Betrothed!* And under our very noses! I was so *sure* that the child was quite besotted over you."

"It seems that *we* are the ones who were besotted."

"*We?* Did *you* believe she cared for you, Roger?"

"Yes, I did. I would not have asked her, otherwise. It seems I'm quite a coxcomb after all."

"No, you're anything but that," his mother insisted. "Her behavior is inexplicable. I can't help feeling that there's more to this affair than we know."

"Don't start that again, Mama, please," Roger begged, putting a hand to his throbbing temple. "She is attached to someone else. Let that be the end of the matter."

"Attached to someone else? I can scarcely credit it. Who, pray, *is* the gentleman?"

"Sorry, but I'm not at liberty to say."

"I see. Not that it matters, anyway. If she won't have *you*, I don't much care *whom* she marries."

"That sounds a bit churlish, doesn't it? *I* at least wished her well."

"It's too much to ask of *me*, I'm afraid. I suppose I shall *have* to wish her well when she tells me about it openly and frankly," Lady Denham said grudgingly. "I only wish she had done so earlier."

"So do I. Although, to be fair, this fix is more our fault than hers. We should have accepted her word when she first refused me. I could have walked away *then* without a backward look. *Now*, however—"

Lady Denham peered at her son with an expression which combined dismay and pity. "Oh, my dear, have you learned to care for her so much?"

Roger merely studied the coffee in his cup.

His mother pressed her hands against her mouth. "To what dreadful pass have I brought you?" she murmured heartbrokenly.

"Don't be so tragic, Mama," Roger said with a smile. "You've always wanted me to learn what love is. And now I have." His smile broadened as he added reflectively, "I had never quite believed in the kind of love about which the poets like to rhapsodize. But now I feel almost like one of them—the new romantical ones who are causing such a stir. Don't be surprised if you discover that I am busily composing tragic love ballads during the dark hours of the night."

She sighed. "You may joke about it if you wish, but it's quite true that I've wanted you to learn about love. I never wished you to suffer, of course, but this experience may be good for you nevertheless."

Roger gave a snort of laughter. "How easily you are consoled, Mama! In less than a minute a 'dreadful pass' has become a 'good experience.' If I stay here and continue this conversation, another minute may bring us to celebrating this whole disaster with a drink of champagne! If you don't mind, I'd rather endure my poetic suffering alone than share your satisfaction at the broadening of my experience. If you'll excuse me, I shall trot out to see what young Peake wants of me."

Lady Denham didn't try to hold him. She knew better than to press him further. His wound was too raw to permit much probing. Perhaps, in time, when the entire experience was well behind him, they would be able to talk about it more dispassionately and come to some understanding of what had gone wrong. For the time being, she had no choice but to let him go.

Roger found Brandon ensconced on a chaise lounge before a sunny window, desultorily attempting to read the *Philoctetes*. At the sight of his visitor, Brandon's face brightened. He tossed his book aside and held out his hand. "I'm so glad you came, Roger," he said in greeting.

"I've been wanting to thank you properly for what you did for me yesterday."

"If that's why you asked me here, I shall go away at once. You must have thanked me at least a dozen times already," Roger responded in disgust.

"If I had, I don't remember it. All I remember is taking my first sip of brandy. Everything else is rather hazy in my mind."

"Yes, you were quite well to live by the time I'd gotten your boot off. I must say you look none the worse for it this morning," Roger said enviously. "I wish I could say the same for myself. My head feels as if someone had hammered a row of nails into it."

"Were you foxed too? I felt the same way earlier today, but I'm now feeling much more the thing," Brandon said cheerfully.

"Good. Then there's hope for me, I suppose. How's the ankle?"

"Fine, as long as I remain off my feet. I shall probably be hobbling around for weeks. But, please, let me say how very grateful I am for—"

"One more word of gratitude, my boy, and I shall walk out that door! By the way, Brandon, you never did tell me how you came to sprain your ankle. You obviously never went to the cathedral, so you couldn't have done it there. And you couldn't have done it while driving the curricle, so I can't imagine when or how it could have come to pass."

Brandon looked away in embarrassment. "I was hoping you wouldn't ask. It was the stupidest thing. I . . . I . . . er . . . fell off the curricle."

"Fell off the—? See here, old fellow, do you think to run sly with me? No one with sense would credit such a tale."

Brandon grimaced. "I was afraid of that," he said worriedly. "I've been avoiding the question so far—Mama has asked me at least fifty times how I came to do such a thing—but sooner or later I shall have to give some sort of explanation..."

"What's wrong with the truth?" Roger asked reasonably.

"The truth is rather awkward. I would be grateful for your advice, Roger, but as there is a lady involved, I...er...by your leave... will have to ask you—"

"Not to tell your story to anyone? You need have no worry on that score. Your secret will be absolutely safe with me, I promise you. There's a lady involved, you say? Are you referring to Letty?"

"Letty?" Brandon asked, looking at Roger in surprise. "Why, no. What made you think this has anything to do with *her*?"

Roger shrugged. "Nothing, really, except that I learned yesterday about your betrothal, so I assumed..."

"Oh, yes," Brandon mumbled, belatedly remembering his conversation on the matter with Roger the day before, "the betrothal. Yes, I see."

"But Letty had nothing to do with the accident?" Roger inquired curiously.

"No, oh no! Nothing at all. It was her sister, Prue," Brandon explained hurriedly, happy to avoid the subject of the betrothal. "She was in the curricle with me, if you recall."

"Yes, now that you mention it, I do."

"Well, the truth of the matter is..." Brandon began, then lapsed into awkward silence.

"Go on. The story can't be as difficult to tell as all that."

"No, I suppose not, but... Why don't you sit down, Roger? It makes me uneasy having you stand over me like this."

Roger smiled. "Like a disapproving schoolmaster, is that it?" He pulled over the nearest chair and sat down. "There, now, I'm seated. Can you find any other excuses to postpone your tale? If not, please proceed. You were driving with Prue. And then—?"

"Well, the truth of the matter is," Brandon repeated shamefacedly, "that she pushed me out of the curricle."

"*Pushed* you? Hang it, Peake, is this another hum?" Roger demanded, trying his best to hide his amusement.

Brandon looked at him askance. "Go ahead and laugh. It's true!"

Roger permitted himself to grin. "You're not seriously expecting me to believe that a tiny chit is strong enough to push a full-grown man like you out of a carriage."

"Well, I wasn't expecting it, you see . . ." Brandon said defensively.

"I should think not!" Roger laughed. "Why in earth did she want to do such a thing to you?"

Brandon sighed. "That's the hardest part to explain."

Roger cocked his brow with a sudden suspicion. "Brandon, you're not trying to tell me that you behaved in some sort of ungentlemanly way, are you?"

"Ungentlemanly?" Brandon asked in complete innocence. "I suppose you could call it that. I shook her."

Roger, who had begun to believe that Brandon had attempted to seduce the sister of the girl to whom he was engaged, had been almost ready to give Brandon a facer. But the answer to his accusation was so unexpected and naive that Roger gaped. "Sh-shook her?" he asked in confusion.

Brandon nodded. "I'm afraid so."

Roger put his hand to his forehead unsteadily. "All this is a bit beyond me today, Brandon," he said. "Perhaps you'd better begin at the beginning."

"I'm not sure where to begin. I suppose the best way would be to say that she hates me."

"Hates you? *Prue* does? But why?"

"Because I tried to tell her that her flirtatious behavior was . . . er . . . unseemly."

"Did you indeed? That was not very wise. If I were a girl, I wouldn't feel very kindly toward you myself," Roger said frankly.

"I realize that now. I could bite out my tongue. But I've

apologized and apologized, to no avail. She wouldn't say a word to me almost all the way to Wells!"

The tone of these remarks arrested Roger's attention. Until this point, Roger had assumed that Brandon had taken a brotherly interest in his betrothed's sister. But Brandon's concern was beginning to seem a bit beyond the brotherly. Observing Brandon closely, he remarked casually, "That must have been a bore."

"Not a bore, but a . . . a . . . strain," Brandon explained. "And then, when finally she *did* speak, it was only to criticize me."

"Oh? And what could she find to criticize?"

"You might better ask what could she *not* find to criticize! My speech, my manners, my . . . er . . . tendency to quote the classics, everything!"

"How very galling," Roger sympathized. "No wonder you shook her."

Brandon looked at him gratefully. "You *do* understand. But I didn't shake her until she . . . she . . . called me a . . . a . . ."

"A *what*, Brandon?"

"A stuffed prig."

Roger choked. "No, really? That was quite dreadful of her. I must admit she seems really to have *deserved* the shaking."

"Exactly!" Brandon agreed with satisfaction.

"And then she pushed you out of the carriage?"

"Yes. And *then* the vixen made off with the curricle! It must have been half a mile before she brought it to a halt. And I had to hobble after it on my twisted ankle, all the while terrified that she would do some damage to the grays!"

Roger shook his head compassionately. "Dreadful! I'd say she's a veritable hoyden."

"Well, not really," Brandon said hastily. "She only needs someone to give her a strong guiding hand, wouldn't you say?"

"I suppose so," Roger answered, watching Brandon

carefully. "It's fortunate, however, that you've chosen the *sister* to marry."

Brandon, his imagination dwelling on a vision of himself offering a firm, guiding hand to Prue, did not readily follow the turn in conversation that Roger had made. "Marry? What do you mean?" he asked innocently.

"I mean Letty. Prue's sister. The girl you intend to wed."

"Oh, Letty. Yes, of course. I'm very fortunate. Very," Brandon said, the feeling of acute discomfort which had assailed him before returning with even stronger pangs.

"Yes, you're a most fortunate fellow," Roger repeated. "Can you imagine the turmoil of your life if you had to marry the younger sister? If you dared to tell her one morning that you didn't like the breakfast biscuits, she might push you from the window!"

Brandon smiled, but Roger noted that the smile was wan and unconvincing. "I . . . don't like you to think that of Prue," Brandon said hesitantly. "After all, she only pushed me because I shook her so hard. You mustn't think she's a termagant. I didn't mean to malign her to you."

"Of course you didn't," Roger said agreeably, rising to leave. "Give it no further thought. There's no permanent harm done, after all. No doubt the whole incident will be forgotten in a month."

"I suppose so," Brandon said somewhat glumly. Then realizing that his guest was about to leave, he said quickly, "Wait, Roger. You mustn't go yet. I wanted, by your leave, to have your suggestion concerning the story—Oh, dash it, I did it again!"

"Did what?"

"Said 'by your leave.' I've been trying to break myself of the habit."

"Why? I see nothing wrong with it."

"Prue says I say it every time I open my mouth."

"Does she?" Roger asked, looking at Brandon

shrewdly. Then he turned to the door. "I think she exaggerates."

"You can't leave yet, Roger. You haven't told me what to say to people who ask me how I came to injure my ankle."

"Just tell them what you told me at first—that you fell out of the curricle."

"But... but *you* didn't believe me—!"

"They'll believe you if you tell it with conviction. And who cares if they don't? If I were you, I wouldn't give a hang if they believed me or not."

Roger walked to his mother's lodgings slowly. Brandon's artless story had given him much food for thought. The boy had spoken of no one but Prue. Prue seemed to occupy all his thoughts. Roger had tried repeatedly to bring Letty into the conversation, but Brandon had not seemed interested in discussing her. His embarrassment over the subject of Letty could, of course, be explained by his realization that he and Roger had been unwitting rivals for Letty's hand, but that embarrassment did not explain his inability to stop talking about *Prue*. If Roger's conclusions had any validity at all, Brandon was in love, *not* with his betrothed, but with her sister.

He began to recollect little signs that Prue had shown—unobtrusive glances, eyes which brightened when Brandon appeared in a doorway, overly animated flirtations with other men when his eyes were on her, and exaggerated indifference when he spoke to her—all indicating that she, too, was feeling the early pangs of love. If Brandon and Prue were, as he suspected, attracted to each other, what place had *Letty* in the situation? Was Letty about to be hurt?

The more Roger thought about the matter, the more convinced he became that Letty's heart was not involved in her betrothal. He was not a schoolboy, and he did not believe himself to be so foolish as to have mistaken Letty's response to his kiss or the look in her eyes whenever he came upon her unaware. He also was quite sure that she had an inexplicable but deep-seated fear of him. There was something havey-cavey about the entire business, and the more he thought about it, the more curious he became. He had to get to the bottom of it.

When he arrived at the lodgings, he found Trebbs in the hallway, dressed for travel and surrounded by a pile of neatly packed luggage. Roger winced. "I'm afraid you'll have to unpack again, Trebbs. We're not leaving after all."

Trebbs had been well schooled in the impassivity which was deemed appropriate for the demeanor of a gentleman's man; therefore, he merely nodded, murmured a soft, "Yes, my lord," picked up a piece of luggage and headed for the stairs. Lady Denham, however, who chose just this moment to make an appearance, was not so schooled. She gaped.

"What is going on *now*?" she demanded. "Why are you taking that portmanteau upstairs, Trebbs?"

"His lordship has asked me to unpack, my lady," Trebbs said with a barely noticeable quiver of disapproval in his tone. Before continuing up the stairs, he permitted himself to flick an accusing look at his lordship, who stood just inside the doorway rubbing his chin sheepishly.

Lady Denham wheeled about to face her son. "Unpack? But why?"

Roger grinned, shrugged and walked quickly to the stairs. "I've decided to stay after all," he said and quickly started up.

"Just a minute, jackanapes. Come down here! I want an explanation," his mother demanded.

Roger came down again. "The only explanation I can give you is that I've changed my mind," he said, kissing her cheek.

"But *why*?" she insisted curiously.

"Mama," Roger said with his most charming, winning

smile, "you know you are my dearest love, so I hope you will not take offense when I tell you that I think it would be best if you permitted me to manage my own affairs from now on."

"B-but, Roger—" she began, "you know I never—"

He placed his hand gently on her mouth. "Don't say anything for a moment, please, and listen to me. I agreed to permit you to find a suitable lady for me to marry. That was a mistake, and it has not ended well. Oh, I don't blame *you*—not at all! The mistake was all mine. I intend to rectify that error by taking the matter back into my own hands, as I should have done from the start. So, if you don't mind, I'd prefer not to discuss the matter with you. I promise that, when I find a girl and she has accepted me, you will be the very first person to be told." With that, he removed his hand.

"But Roger, my dear," she said as soon as she regained her breath, "I only want to know—"

"Mama!" he said warningly.

"But I can tell that something's happened. Have you found another girl already? Is that it? Just answer *that* and I promise to ask nothing else."

"I have nothing to tell you, ma'am," Roger said firmly. "And I want you to say nothing else but that I'm welcome to remain."

"But, Roger—" she pleaded.

Roger frowned at her sternly. "Very well, my dear," he said, "I shall tell Trebbs to repack and find lodgings elsewhere." And he started up the stairs again.

"Roger—!" Lady Denham cried.

He turned. "Yes, Mama?"

She raised her hand and opened her mouth to scold, hesitated, made a little helpless gesture and closed her mouth again. She drew in her breath and let it out in a long sigh. "Very well, my dear, you are welcome to remain," she said, defeated.

Chapter TWELVE

THE NEWS HAD reached Bath that Charles James Fox had died, and the subject of his loss to Parliament and to England was discussed in the Pump Room, on every street and in all the drawing rooms of the city. But the members of Lady Upsham's domestic staff had something closer to their interests to discuss. Miss Tristle had taken Katie-from-the-kitchen under her wing! This surprising turnabout caused such endless expression of surprise and speculation that the topic drove all other matters from their conversation. All of the servants—even the butler—had felt a touch of Miss Tristle's spleen from time to time, but none of them had had to endure the verbal slights, the frequent criticism, the constant interference and the venomous disparagement which she had vented on poor Katie. Her sudden about-face on the subject of the rival abigail was nothing short of sensational. The death of Fox, famous though he was, had no power to drive from their minds and their tongues the subject of Miss Tristle's change of attitude toward the girl who she had once said was an ignorant and vulgar urchin trying to encroach on her position in the domestic domain.

Ever since the morning Katie had prepared a herb wash for her toothache, Miss Tristle had begun to look upon the girl with new eyes. The wash had been surprisingly efficacious. For the first time in days, Miss Tristle had found herself free of pain, and repeated rinsings with Katie's concoction had virtually cured the problem. She began to feel a new respect for Katie. She suddenly began to see the native intelligence and shrewdness which lay beneath Katie's unpolished surface. Everything Katie said made good sense, and she had somehow acquired an astonishing fund of interesting and useful information on all sorts of subjects. Miss Tristle was impressed. Grudgingly at first, but soon more readily, she began to ask the girl's opinion on matters she would never have deigned to ask before. Did Katie prefer the fichu or a Norwich shawl for Madam's plum-colored evening dress? Did the London ladies still lean toward tight curls hanging over their ears for daytime wear? Could Katie recommend a recipe for removing freckles? For all these, Katie had a ready—and usually original and sensible—answer.

By the time three days of this testing had passed, Miss Tristle had been won over. She made what was, for her, an amazing condescension—she invited Katie to spend the evening in her room so that they both could do their mending while enjoying a companiable coz together. Since it was much discussed among the servants that Miss Tristle's room was one of the largest and best lit of the servants' rooms, and that she kept it well supplied with tea, cakes and sherry, Katie readily accepted. The evening proved to be a great success. The two abigails discovered that they each had something to teach the other—Katie could teach Miss Tristle all manner of recipes for medications and cosmetic lotions (useful secrets she had learned from her many relatives in service) and Miss Tristle could teach Katie the rules of proper speech. They discovered, too, a shared interest in the strange and ever-fascinating doings of the *ton*, and when the educational part of the conversation had begun to pall, they turned to gossip.

Here, too, Miss Tristle found Katie surprisingly knowing. Her retentive memory stored away such interesting tidbits as the number of husbands that Lady Hester Houghton had managed to acquire before she passed away; the name of the fancy piece currently under the protection of the Marquis of Atherton; and the exact cost of the jeweled pendant the Prince had presented to Princess Caroline when he married her. In fact, Miss Tristle could rarely offer a juicy morsel that Katie did not already know.

However, she did manage to do so once or twice. One bit of news in particular seemed to be of great interest to Katie. Miss Tristle said she had heard that the elegant, vacant house on the Paragon had been let to a lady from London.

"Really?" Katie asked. "And who might she be?"

"I think Mrs. Besterbent said the name was Brownell," Miss Tristle said, knotting her thread and cutting it off with her teeth.

Katie eyed Miss Tristle with interest. "Brownell? Not Mrs. *Kitty* Brownell?"

Miss Tristle looked up with arched eyebrows. "Well, yes, I believe that was the very name. Why? Do you know of the lady?"

"Blimey if I don't," Katie said darkly. "I'd go bail that this means there's trouble brewin'."

"You don't say," Miss Tristle said eagerly, leaning forward with her mouth agape. "Why? Who is she?"

"I don't like bein' a chaffer-mouth, so I best not say nothin'. However, I don't think nobody what knows 'er 'll be glad she come'd."

"Came, my dear, *came*," Miss Tristle corrected condescendingly.

"Oh, is she 'ere a'ready?" Katie asked.

Miss Tristle was not gifted with a sense of humor, and so she merely looked at Katie with a confused expression. "No, I don't think so," she answered seriously. "Mrs. Besterbent said she's not due to arrive for yet a fortnight."

Katie leaned her elbows on the petticoat she had been trying to mend and propped her chin in her hands. "It queers me what 'er lay is," she muttered thoughtfully.

"I don't know what you're saying with those dreadful street words," Miss Tristle said testily, bursting with curiosity about Mrs. Brownell's identity but too proud to ask, "but you're making a mess of that petticoat. Here, give it to me. I'll finish it for you."

Katie, who had a distinct distaste and lack of talent for sewing fine stitches, gave over the petticoat with alacrity. "I'm only puzzlin' over what she's comin' 'ere for," she explained.

"Well, I can't help you, since I never heard of the lady."

"Kitty Brownell ain't no more lady 'n me! Less, in fact," Katie declared with disgust. "I'll tell you 'oo she is if you promise not to tattle it about."

"I can keep my mouth shut as well as you," Miss Tristle declared with an offended sniff.

"Then keep this tight under y'r bonnet," Katie said dramatically. "Mrs. Brownell is none other than Lord Denham's game pullet."

Miss Tristle's busy needle stopped. "You don't mean—?" she asked, aghast.

"Yes, I do. She's 'is bit o' muslin, 'is doxie, 'is *ladybird*!"

"No!" breathed Miss Tristle in popeyed fashion. "How shocking!"

"So it is," Katie agreed. "I'd give a yellow-boy to get wind of 'er game."

The two lapsed into silence, absorbed in contemplation of the problem, but since no solution presented itself to either one, they put the question aside. A fortnight would soon pass, they told themselves, and then they would see what they would see.

Unaware of the impending calamity about to descend upon their lives with the arrival of Mrs. Brownell, the Glendenning sisters were making preparations to attend a small dinner party arranged by Mrs. Peake to cheer her housebound son. Mrs. Peake's guest list was small and select. She had invited Lady Upsham and her nieces, Lady Denham and Roger, and a Mr. Eberly, a wealthy gentleman who had been associated with her husband in some business ventures and who now resided in one of the elegant apartments in Bathwick.

Letty had dressed early on the afternoon of the dinner party and then went to her sister's room to see if she could be of assistance to Prue. She found her sister in a state of high-strung nervousness, pulling off a gown with angry impatience. Katie stood beside her with at least half-a-dozen discarded gowns thrown over her arm. Katie greeted Letty with relief. "I'm so glad you come'd . . . *came*, Miss Letty. This sister o' yours can't make up 'er mind what to wear."

"Everything this goosecap of an abigail has brought me is too . . . too garish!" Prue burst out, tossing the dress she had just removed at Katie crossly.

"Garish!" Letty said in bewildered amusement. "Is this the same Prue who said to me not long ago that it is better to be stared at than ignored?"

"Did I say that? Well, never mind. Tonight I want to look . . . subdued."

"Subdued? Whatever for? You couldn't look subdued with that hair of yours if you were dressed in mourning," her sister told her flatly. "Here, Katie, let me see what you have there."

"I told 'er this 'ere rose-colored one is bang up to the mark," Katie suggested.

"No!" Prue shouted, grimacing at Katie. "It makes my hair look too glaringly red."

"Then how about this blue silk? You quite swooned over it when we chose the pattern," Letty reminded her.

"The bodice is cut too low."

"Too low? What's the matter with you, Prue? You nagged Mama incessantly until she agreed to permit the dress to be cut this way."

Prue hung her head. "I don't care," she pouted. "I'm not in the mood for it today."

"I know!" Letty said with sudden inspiration. "Katie, bring her my lilac lustring. The color is so dusky, she's bound to find it subdued."

Prue's face brightened. "Your lustring would be perfect!" she cried, throwing her arms about her sister in gratitude. "Oh, Letty, you're an *angel*! But . . . you're so much taller than I . . . Don't you think it will be too long?"

"Perhaps? But if Katie pins it up at the shoulders, and you hold up the skirt just a bit when you walk, I think it should serve."

Prue's borrowed dress proved to be an excellent choice, for Brandon's eyes brightened perceptibly when she entered his mother's drawing room that evening. He was standing beside his mother, leaning on a sturdy stick and greeting her guests with an eager welcome. When Prue came up to him, he smiled at her uncertainly. "Good evening, Miss Glendenning," he said shyly. "By your leave, I'd like to say how lovely you l— Oh, hang it all!"

Prue looked up at him startled.

Brandon colored. "I do apologize. I didn't mean to say it, you know."

"Say what?" Prue asked, beginning to bristle. "That I look lovely?"

"Of course I meant to say *that*. It was the by-your-leave. It slipped out."

"Oh," said Prue. It was now her turn to blush. She turned away in embarrassment. She should never have said those cruel things to him. Now he would have to guard his tongue every time he spoke to her. Nevertheless, she was pleased to see that he apparently approved of her appearance. The look in his eyes when he saw her gave her the courage she needed to proceed on the course of action she had planned to undertake this evening; she had determined to find an opportunity to speak privately to him and apologize for causing his injury.

Roger, who had arrived some minutes earlier, did not fail to note Brandon's expression when he welcomed Prue. Roger was standing on the far side of the room engaged in conversation with the one unfamiliar guest, Mr. Eberly. Eberly was not much older than Roger, but he appeared to be many years his senior. He was a heavyset, imposing gentleman who had lost much of the hair on his head and seemed to make up for it by the great amount of hair on his face. His eyebrows were remarkably thick and he sported a large and bushy mustache. He and Roger were discussing with approval the news which had just reached them of the passage in Parliament of a law which abolished the slave trade. Roger had managed to keep the conversation going while he observed Prue and Brandon in the doorway, but when Letty appeared, his concentration failed him.

Letty was indeed breathtaking this evening. Her thick auburn hair was loosely bound and fell in a soft curl over her shoulder. Her face glowed from the reflection of her burgundy-colored Belladine silk gown which rippled gracefully as she moved. Mr. Eberly, following Roger's eye, smiled appreciatively. "What a lovely woman," he remarked.

"Yes," Roger said, the casual tone of his voice giving no indication of the pang the sight of her had caused in his chest. "Very lovely."

"She must be the Miss Glendenning I've been hearing so much about."

"Well," Roger explained with a smile, "she's one of them. She is here with her sister, who also has been turning the heads of the young Bath bucks."

"Do you mean that charming child over there with the red curls? I've noticed her myself. She seems always to be about to trip over her skirt."

"Yes, she's the one. Come along and let me introduce you to them."

When the introductions had been made and the guests had had their sherry, they moved into the dining room where, for more than two hours, they lingered over an excellent dinner, the highlights of which were a delectable veal ragout and a gooseberry trifle. The trifle was a culinary masterpiece concocted of cream, cake, wine, jam and almonds, but although the guests ate it with relish, they did not remark on it, so interested were they in the conversation which enlivened the dinner. Led by Roger and Mr. Eberly, the discussion centered on the part played by the late Mr. Fox in pushing the abolition bill through Parliament. Roger held that Fox had been a man of tremendous talent and great personal charm, while Mr. Eberly contended that Fox was basically a man of pathetically poor political judgment. Both Lady Upsham and Lady Denham agreed with Mr. Eberly, giving examples of many irresponsible acts Fox had committed in his political life. But Letty, who had been listening quietly through most of the talk, finally felt impelled to speak her mind. "You may be right about Mr. Fox's other failings," she said earnestly, "but I cannot help but feel that he deserves most of the credit for the abolition bill's passage, and I deem it a tragedy that he didn't live to see this fruition of his most commendable efforts."

"I think, Miss Glendenning," said Mr. Eberly, raising his glass to her, "that you've evaluated the matter most sensibly. I drink to you, my dear. As far as I'm concerned, you have quite won the day."

"Hear, hear!" Brandon added with enthusiasm, raising his glass as well.

Letty blushed at the unwonted attention and, quite despite her will, her eyes flew to Roger's face. His eyes were fixed on her, and they held a look of such unmistakable warmth and pride that her heart lurched. She quickly looked away and tried firmly but vainly to keep from glancing at him for the duration of the meal.

After the ladies had left the room, the men did not long linger over their port. When they rejoined the ladies in the drawing room, they found that Letty had been prevailed upon to play the piano. They took seats quietly and sat back to listen. Letty had chosen to play a simple country air to which she added impromptu variations, the sort of music with which she often entertained her young sisters. The small group of listeners enjoyed the unpretentious charm of the music as much as her sisters had. Prue, however, did not attend the music. Instead, she moved unobtrusively to the sofa where Brandon had seated himself and slipped into the seat beside him. "There's something I must say to you," she whispered.

"Is something the matter?" he whispered back.

"Yes, there is. *I'm* the matter. I'm terribly headstrong and thoughtless. It's all my fault that you're injured, and I just have to say how sorry I am that I pushed you out of the carriage."

Brandon reached impetuously for her hand. "You don't have to be sorry," he said, close to her ear. "It was more my fault than yours. I never should have shaken you like that."

"Well, I never should have been so rude and criticized you so dreadfully," she whispered into his ear, her breath tickling his neck and causing exquisitely agonizing bumps to form down his back and along his arms.

"Oh, Prue," he murmured with a catch in his voice, "I—"

But she was not to learn what he intended to say, for the music ended at that moment. He dropped her hand and they jumped apart, applauding enthusiastically for Letty's music as if they'd been listening as attentively as the rest. After that, Brandon, although incapacitated, had nevertheless to perform the duties of a host, making sure to give his attention to each of his guests and see that they were entertained and wanted for nothing. No further opportunity presented itself for him to complete the sentence he had started with such a burst of earnest feeling.

Roger, meanwhile, came up to the piano before Letty could leave and, leaning on the instrument, smiled affectionately at her. "You are full of surprises, my dear," he said. "I didn't know you were so accomplished a musician."

"You are surprised, my lord, only because you had prejudged me before we were fully acquainted and arrogantly decided that I *had* no accomplishments," she answered saucily, feeling more confident with him than she had before she was protected from him by her supposed betrothal.

"That is grossly unfair," he protested. "Experience had taught me that beautiful young women have little need for other accomplishments, and therefore don't trouble to develop them. How was I to know that you are the exception?"

"Stop, please," she said with a smile. "It is not like you to stoop to such wanton flattery."

"Do you think I offer you Spanish coin? Far from it, I assure you. Your playing was truly delightful. And your comments on Fox were quite impressive, too. I had no idea that you take an interest in politics."

"Any person of sense takes an interest in politics, my lord," she said, "although you must not conclude from one little remark of mine that I'm really knowledgeable."

"I insist on being permitted to draw my own conclusions, Miss Glendenning," Roger stated with a twinkle and helped her to rise from the piano stool. They turned and joined the others. Like Brandon and Prue, they found no other opportunity for private conversation.

Prue was feeling rather pleased with herself by the time Lady Upsham rose and indicated that it was time for them to take their leave. The entire evening had passed without a single instance of indecorous behavior on her part. She had sat politely beside her aunt, smiling and nodding and saying polite things to anyone who addressed her. She had neither giggled nor laughed loudly; she had not flirted; she had not drawn any attention to herself. In short, she had been a model of decorum, and she was sure that Brandon had noticed. Every time she'd met his eye, he had smiled at her approvingly.

Brandon rose and, leaning heavily on his stick, went to the entryway to bid the guests goodnight. Prue went up to him and held out her hand. "Do you truly forgive me, Brandon?" she asked in an under-voice.

"You know I do," he answered feelingly, squeezing her hand tightly.

She met his eye and felt a strange flutter inside her. Hurriedly, she turned to the door to join her aunt and Letty. In her confusion, she forgot to hold up the skirts of her borrowed gown. She stepped on the too-long hem and tripped clumsily. She would have fallen flat on her face had it not been for Mr. Eberly who was standing nearby and swiftly reached out for her. She fell heavily against his chest and looked up at him in mortification. "Oh, how... how clumsy of me," she gasped. "I'm so sorry!"

Mr. Eberly laughed jovially and set her on her feet. "No need to be sorry," he said with a booming heartiness. "I quite enjoyed that! It's not every day that I can play the gallant to a charming young girl."

Prue glanced quickly around the foyer. Everyone was watching. She had made a fool of herself, and everyone had witnessed it. Her quick glance took in a glimpse of Brandon's face. He was frowning. In despair, she turned and ran to the door. She had made a spectacle of herself again. Her evening was ruined!

Lady Upsham and Letty, unperturbed at what Prue thought was a dreadful scene, said cheerful goodnights, and the three departed. Mr. Eberly stood in the hallway smiling after them. "Charming little chit, Miss Prudence, don't you think?" he asked Brandon in a jolly man-to-man tone. He had no idea why Brandon chose to glare at him for saying it.

Chapter THIRTEEN

ROGER HAD BEEN an interested observer of the little scene played at the doorway. The whole evening had done much to reinforce his feeling that, whatever tie had bound Letty and Brandon, it was not love. Brandon had been whispering in *Prue's* ear and had held her hand in a most lover-like fashion all the while that Letty had been at the piano. In Roger's view, Letty had looked so charming that any man who really loved her would not have been able to tear his eyes from her. And in addition, when Eberly had caught Prue in his arms (when the girl had tripped on her skirts), Brandon had looked as if he would like to call the fellow out. Brandon's interest in Prue was obvious. On the other hand, as far as Roger could tell, Brandon and *Letty* had not spent a moment in each other's company, nor had they exhibited an inclination to do so.

Of course, it was possible that Brandon and Letty had agreed to behave in this way to throw Lady Upsham off the scent, that they and Prue had conspired to enact a charade to confuse observers. But Roger's instincts told him that it was unlikely that Brandon's and Prue's behavior could be feigned. He was quite convinced that the two were strongly attracted to each other.

What he needed to ascertain was Letty's feeling for Brandon. He had never observed their behavior when they were together in private conversation. But he had a plan. He would arrange to take Brandon for a drive the very next day.

Brandon's gratitude to Roger for his invitation was so sincere that Roger felt a pang of guilt. Brandon, delighted to be freed from his imprisonment indoors on this beautiful late-September day, felt compelled to express his thanks all the while Roger helped him into his rented phaeton and during the first few minutes of the ride. But the subject of gratitude was completely forgotten when Roger suggested that they stop at Lady Upsham's to see if Letty would care to join them on the drive.

"Letty?" asked Brandon, taken aback. "But... Well, won't it be a bit awkward?"

"Awkward? Not at all. That's why I've rented this phaeton instead of taking out my curricle. I'll climb up on the box and leave you two lovebirds alone."

"That is most...er...thoughtful of you, Roger, but...I was thinking of Lady Upsham. She...er... mustn't see Letty and me together, you know."

"Oh, don't worry about that," Roger said airily. "I won't mention that you're here. You'll remain outside waiting in the phaeton. I'll allow her to believe that I've come alone. Lady Upsham won't permit Letty to refuse me."

"I see..." Brandon said nervously. This situation was not at all to his liking. It was bad enough to have had to acknowledge Letty as his betrothed when it was not true, but it was even worse to have to enact a lover-like role before a witness. Especially before Roger. The fact that Roger was behaving in this excessively kind way made this predicament doubly painful. Besides, he had no skill at dissembling. He was sure to make a mull of it. He was being pulled deeper and deeper into an abyss of dishonesty and deceit. His mind searched desperately for a way of escape. But he could think of nothing except...Prue! Perhaps, with the addition of another person, he would not be forced to play the 'lovebird' role. "Er...Roger, do you think, perhaps, that you ought to ask Prue to come along too?" he suggested hesitantly.

"Prue?" asked Roger innocently. "I don't think so. I

planned this so that you and Letty could have some time in each other's company. Prue would spoil everything. Besides, Lady Upsham never permits Prue to come along when Letty and I go riding."

Brandon could think of nothing else and relapsed into a worried silence. Roger whistled cheerfully until they drew up in front of Lady Upsham's residence. Promising Brandon a speedy return, he jumped down from the phaeton and went inside. In a few minutes he returned leading a puzzled-looking Letty to the carriage. She started at the sight of Brandon. "There!" Roger said in a self-satisfied way. "I told you I had a surprise for you."

"B-Brandon," Letty stammered uneasily, "what are you—? That is, how v-very nice to see you."

Roger helped Letty into the phaeton beside Brandon and vaulted up to the box. "It seems to me such a shame that a betrothed couple cannot spend any time together, so I made up my mind to give you both the opportunity to do so. You needn't mind me, you know. I'll just drive and think my own thoughts. Just pretend I'm not here."

Brandon and Letty exchanged helpless looks behind Roger's back, and Brandon shrugged to indicate that he couldn't have done anything to avoid the situation. Letty tried to fill in the dismaying silence by asking loudly how Brandon's ankle was getting on. Brandon answered in such complete detail that Letty could find nothing more to say on the subject, and another interminable silence ensued. Finally Letty asked brightly if Brandon had had any time to pursue his studies. To this Brandon responded that he'd had little time since his accident to spend on his books because of all the callers who had come to pay their condolences and because of the assistance his mother had required in preparation for her dinner party. "However," he added, "I did manage to read the translation of Horace that Roger was good enough to lend me."

"Oh, yes," Letty said with sudden interest, "you *did* tell me that Lord Denham is a scholar of the classics. I didn't think you had interests along those lines, Lord Denham."

"Are you speaking to me?" Roger asked guilelessly, turning around to look at them.

"Yes, I am," Letty said. "Brandon tells me you've studied the classics. I was surprised to learn that you have interests in that direction."

Roger's eyes twinkled maliciously. "You are surprised, Miss Glendenning," he said, parroting her words of the night before, "only because you had prejudged me before we were fully acquainted and arrogantly decided that I had no accomplishments."

Brandon was appalled. "Oh, I say, Roger," he objected vehemently, "you can't call Letty arrogant! That's coming it a bit too strong, isn't it?"

Letty laughed and put a restraining hand on Brandon's arm. "He's only teasing, Brandon. That's what I said about *him* last night. And besides, I can now toss his reply to *me* right back at him."

"What reply was that, Miss Glendenning?" Roger asked.

"Experience has taught *me*, my dear sir," she replied archly, "that noted Corinthians like yourself, who spend their time in gaming, in sporting pursuits or in . . . er . . . other adventures, have little time for books."

"Touché," Roger admitted with a grin. "It would seem, ma'am, that we *both* have been guilty of misjudgment."

Roger turned back to his horses, leaving Letty and Brandon with the problem of finding something else to talk about. They succeeded in finding only the merest commonplaces, and both of them took every possible opportunity to draw Roger into the conversation. The halting and stilted exchanges were so amusing to the eavesdropper on the box that he had a difficult time keeping his shoulders from shaking.

After a while, Roger discovered that he'd taken a wrong turning. Seeing a cottage near by, he excused himself and climbed down to seek assistance from the inhabitants. Letty seized the moments of privacy to ask Brandon how this terrible state of affairs had come about.

"I don't know," Brandon said miserably. "He acted as if he were doing me the greatest favor. I didn't know how to refuse him."

"Do you think he's testing our story?" Letty asked worriedly.

Brandon shook his head. "Confound it, Letty," he groaned, "I wish I'd never agreed to your silly scheme. He's the best of good fellows, and I hate to play him false in this way."

Letty couldn't dispute him. "I know," she said disconsolately. "I don't like it either. But we've gone too far to deny it now. There's nothing for it but to play the game out."

"Very well, if we must. But Letty, I don't even know what to say to sound like a man betrothed to a girl. What do betrothed people talk about to each other?"

"I don't know," Letty said, chewing a nail nervously. "How much they love each other, I suppose. Fulsome compliments, dreams and plans for the future... But Lord Denham will not expect us to talk about such things when he's seated right there within earshot."

"Then what *can* we talk about to each other?" Brandon asked in desperation.

"Well, I have an idea. There's to be a ball at the Upper Rooms next week. Ask me if I intend to go and suggest ways that we might be together without calling attention to ourselves."

"But, Letty, I can't attend a ball with a sprained ankle," he objected.

"There comes Roger now," Letty said hurriedly. "You *can* attend if you don't dance. There's no time to think of anything else. Please, Brandon, do the best you can!"

The conversation between them, after Roger's return, did not differ in quality from their earlier attempts. Although they discussed the ball at great length, Brandon showed rather too much un-lover-like politeness in his oft-repeated request that Letty spend some time at the ball sitting out the dances at his side. Letty, realizing that the conversation between them lacked the sparkle of a couple in love, cast a number of agitated glances at Roger's unresponsive back, but in truth, Roger had long since given up paying any attention to what his passengers were saying to each other. The lack of intimacy in their tone of conversation had already convinced him that his estimate of the situation was correct—their betrothal was not based on love. His mind was grappling with a more perplexing problem.

Now that he was convinced that their betrothal was not a love-match, he had to determine what had brought it about. The most obvious solution was that it was nothing but a ruse, designed to keep *him* from pursuing Letty. He spent the remainder of the ride trying to understand why a girl whose eyes brightened when she looked at him, whose mind seemed closely attuned to his, who so delightfully responded to his quips, his tastes, and even his kiss, should go to such lengths to keep him at a distance. He could find no answer.

But one fact was glaringly, upsettingly clear. Letty was firmly fixed on preventing him from making her another proposal of marriage. The girl, for all the signs of her attraction to him, did not want Roger for a husband. He sighed in discouragement and wondered how he had permitted himself to occupy this position of humiliation—the position of *an unwanted suitor who has not the sense to take himself off.* Perhaps he should oblige Letty and restore his self-esteem by giving up the pursuit. With every day that he lingered in her vicinity, he found himself more deeply attached to her. The longer he remained, the greater would be the pain if he ultimately failed to win her. Perhaps now was the time to give up the struggle and return to London.

They drew up outside Lady Upsham's lodgings. He jumped down from the box while Letty said her goodbyes to Brandon. Then he reached for her hands to help her down. She paused on the carriage step and looked down at him, her eyes searching his face for a clue to his thoughts. For that moment, time seemed to stop for him. What was it he read in her expressive face? Fear and uncertainty, surely, but just as surely there was something else. Without conscious awareness, Roger smiled comfortingly at her and was rewarded by a sudden glimmer of luminescent gratitude which sprang into her unbelievably speaking eyes. Confound it, he thought, why did he always feel that they could converse with eyes alone? Fool that he was, he knew that he would not go away just yet. He would play out the game until the bitter end.

As if she had read his thoughts, her eyes dropped, her cheeks crimsoned and she withdrew her hands from his clasp. Without a word, she ran to the door and disappeared inside. He stood there staring after her long after she'd gone, and it was not until Brandon gave an awkward cough that he was brought back to consciousness of where he was.

"My very first ball, and I don't even want to go," Prue said glumly to her reflection in the mirror as she sat brushing her curls into a sophisticated hairstyle known as the *Sappho*. Katie stood behind her, watching admiringly and making herself useful by handing Prue hairpins and combs as they were called for. "'Course you want to go," she said sensibly. "You'll be in high leg soon as you're tiffled up and see how pretty you look."

"I *won't* be in high leg, as you call it. I'm in the dismals and will probably remain there all evening. The ball is bound to be deadly dull. I know every young man in Bath, and none of them is capable of brightening a girl's disposition."

Katie looked at her archly. "Not even a certain Mr. Peake?" she asked with brazen insolence.

Prue frowned at her. "You go too far, Miss Katie-from-the-kitchen. One of these days, I'll box your ears and send you back to the scullery."

Katie, having heard those threats many times before, merely ignored them. "If you know'd what I know'd," she said tauntingly, "you'd be took out o' the dismals like a shot."

"What's that?" Prue asked curiously.

"That Mr. Peake will be there this night."

"Don't be silly. He can barely walk with a stick, so why would he come to a dance?" Prudence asked logically.

"'E'll be there. You ain't never knowed Katie to bamboozle you, 'ave you?"

Prue stared at her abigail suspiciously. "How do you know? Who told you?"

"Oh, I 'as my ways," Katie said superciliously, having learned to enjoy her reputation as a 'knowing one.'

Prue, convinced, found that, as Katie had predicted, she was rapidly becoming quite cheerful about the prospects for the evening. The blue silk, which had been rejected on the night of Mrs. Peake's dinner party because of its low *décolletage*, was deemed suitable for a ball, and by the time the dress had been donned, Prue's mood had changed from dismal to radiant.

Letty, on the other hand, saw no prospect of anything but a dull evening. She had determined to spend a good part of it at Brandon's side, for she was sure the two of them would be observed by the omnipresent Lord Denham. She knew that *she* could summon up the spirit to smile and flirt with Brandon with enough enthusiasm to confound Roger, but she had no confidence in Brandon's ability to be equally convincing. Brandon had no ability to act a role. Naive, innocent and straightforward, Brandon's discomfort when forced to practice deception was obvious to any observer, and a man of Roger's perspicacity would never be fooled.

The two sisters arrived at the Assembly Rooms in completely opposite states of mind. Their eyes searched the room for the same young man, but one looked with eyes of eagerness and the other with eyes of dread.

Brandon, even with the assistance of his mother, was not able to make his way to the Upper Rooms easily. Therefore, it was quite late when they made their appearance in the ballroom. Mrs. Peake helped her son to a vacant chair and left him to join the elderly ladies who spent their time at dances watching and gossiping. Brandon sat back as comfortably as he could on the spindly chair and looked at the dance floor. The first thing to attract his eye was Prue's red-gold hair. She was spinning by on the arm of Sir Ralph who was whirling her around the floor in a waltz with rather unexpected expertise. The waltz, while still restricted at Almack's in London to couples under the sanction of the patronesses, was indulged in quite freely in the more limited society of Bath. Brandon had never thought about it before, but now he was struck with disapproval. It was, he decided, a tasteless, indecent display, and Prue should have known better than to permit herself to indulge in it.

When Letty came up to him a few moments later, he greeted her with a strong reproof, blaming her for neglecting her sisterly duties. "How could you have permitted your sister to make a spectacle of herself on the dance floor?" he demanded.

Letty, taken aback, responded with annoyance. "You are being positively gothic, Brandon," she told him shortly. "*Everyone* dances the waltz in Bath. Even my aunt sees nothing objectionable in it, so I don't see why you should disapprove. Of what concern can it be to you, in any case?"

Brandon, having no answer, lapsed into a glum silence. Letty would have liked to walk away from him, but she caught a glimpse of Roger across the room, talking to Mr. Eberly but looking directly at them. She pulled up a chair and sat down beside Brandon with a sigh. "Don't glower so, Brandon," she begged. "Roger is looking at us."

"Bother Roger and bother this ball," Brandon said pettishly. "I wish I hadn't let you talk me into coming. By your leave, Letty, I'm bound to tell you that every time I let you persuade me to do anything, I soon regret it."

"Of all the ungallant things I've ever heard you say," Letty said in chagrin, "that is the worst. I never thought,

Brandon Peake, that you could be so churlish and unkind. I thought you were my *friend*!"

Brandon, completely unequal to feminine attacks, completely unable to withstand their flashing eyes and quivering voices, subsided at once. "I... I'm sorry, Letty," he mumbled uneasily. "I didn't mean—"

"For heaven's sake, don't look so miserable," Letty said uncomfortably, keeping her eye on Roger as she spoke. "How can Lord Denham possibly believe that we're lovers when you look so glum in my company."

"Lovers!" Brandon groaned. "How does one look like a lover?"

"Stop asking me those silly questions. Just look at me and *smile*. Talk to me! Say something... anything! We used to have very interesting conversations when we first met. Can't we do so now?"

"I don't know," Brandon said bitterly. "We weren't involved in such deception then. How can I concentrate on anything when I know we're being watched?"

"Can't you forget that we're being watched? Can't you tell me about your precious Greeks? Once you spent *hours* telling me about Thucydides!"

"Well," Brandon said, grasping at a straw, "I *had* once planned on talking to you about Catullus. He's not a Greek, of course, but a Roman."

"Oh, Brandon," Letty laughed in relief, "as if *that* matters."

"I don't have the book with me, however. I don't know many of the verses by memory. But he'd make an excellent subject. He wrote love poetry, you see."

"Then we'll manage without the book. He'll make the perfect subject," Letty said encouragingly, leaning close to him.

By the time Prue extricated herself from the attentions of the Rabbit and came up to them, Letty and Brandon seemed quite happily absorbed in conversation. At the same moment, Roger approached the little group. After the greetings were exchanged, he turned to Letty. "Would you care to stand up with me, Letty? A set is just now forming for a country dance."

"Thank you," Letty answered pleasantly but with a negative shake of her head, "but I don't wish to leave Brandon sitting here alone."

Prue, with full realization that she was behaving in an unladylike manner, spoke up brazenly. "I'll keep Brandon company, Letty, if you wish to dance."

Letty cast a look of irritation at her sister. Why couldn't Prue mind her own business? But she knew she was being unreasonable. Prue had no idea of what was going on. So she smiled brightly at Prue but said in a determined voice, "No, thank you, Prue dear. Brandon has been reciting to me the love poetry of Catullus." Here she flashed a challenging glance at Roger. "I've been finding it delightful. Besides, I've *promised* this dance to Brandon, so to speak, haven't I, Brandon?"

Brandon cast a glance at Prue and nodded miserably. Prue, feeling the rejection like a sudden douse of cold water, recoiled. Roger, on the other hand, merely smiled jauntily. "I can quite understand your preferring Catullus to my dancing," he said, "but I don't think 'delightful' is the right word for his poetry. 'Passionate,' or 'frenzied,' even 'bitter,' but *not* 'delightful.'" With that, he made a little bow and left.

Prue gave a stammering, incoherent little apology and backed away. Unfortunately, she did not notice that Mr. Eberly had come up behind her, and she blundered into him. She lost her balance and fell against him, but he held her easily and restored her to her feet. She looked at him in agony and mumbled. "Oh, Mr. Eberly! I'm so sorry . . .!"

Mr. Eberly smiled down at her fondly. "My dear girl," he said in playful admonition, "have you blundered into me *again*? What am I to make of that, may I ask? Can it be that you are endeavoring to attract the attention of an old bachelor like myself?"

This flirtatious raillery did much to restore Prue's

self-esteem. She threw Brandon a triumphant glance and smiled winningly at her rescuer. "Old bachelor, pooh!" she said with an enchanting giggle. "You are just the right age."

"The right age for what, you little minx?" Mr. Eberly inquired.

"For dancing with clumsy little minxes," Prue answered with a rather too-loud laugh. "Don't you agree, sir?"

"I most certainly do," Mr. Eberly said warmly and drew her arm through his. They walked off without a backward look, and only a toss of her head in Brandon's direction gave any sign that she had given him another thought.

"Did you mark that?" Brandon demanded of Letty as soon as they were out of earshot. "Is *that* the sort of behavior of which your aunt approves?"

"What are you talking about now, Brandon?" Letty asked, perplexed.

"Is it now considered permissible for a young lady to ask a gentleman to dance with her? It was my understanding that it is the gentleman's place to do the asking."

"If you are referring to Prue's suggestion that she sit here with you while I dance, I find nothing reprehensible about that."

"I am not referring to that at all. I am referring to her behavior with Eberly just now!" Brandon said in disgust.

"Oh, that," Letty said, dismissing it curtly. "That was only a bit of innocent flirting. Anyone with half an eye could see he was delighted with her."

"That's just it!" Brandon insisted. "She shouldn't be permitted to encourage an elderly man like Eberly to leer at her in that odious way."

"He's not elderly. And he did not leer. Really, Brandon, you are becoming quite tedious. I'm beginning to wish that we *were* betrothed, so I could have the pleasure of breaking it off!" And she walked away and left him to mope alone.

Prue, her self-esteem restored by the flattering attentions of Mr. Eberly, returned to Brandon's side when the dance ended. She had made up her mind to try again. Finding him alone, she dropped into the chair vacated by Letty and smiled at him brightly. "It's good to sit down," she said cheerfully. "My feet positively ache."

"I'm not a bit surprised," Brandon muttered sullenly. "What else should one expect when one has been bouncing around the floor as you've been doing?"

Prue blinked at him in surprise. "Whatever do you mean, Brandon? I can't say I like your tone."

"I can't say I like the way you *danced*, either," Brandon could not restrain himself from saying. He was feeling used, abused and neglected. He had sat in lonely misery, watching the dancers whirl about the room happily oblivious of his discomfort. He felt very, very sorry for himself.

Prue drew herself up stiffly. "What was wrong with the way I danced?" she asked, her voice taking on an ominous formality.

"The way you waltzed around with Sir Ralph was unquestionably the most tasteless, indecent exhibition I've ever seen," Brandon said heedlessly, his sullen mood driving him on, "and the way you encouraged Eberly to ogle you must have caused any observers to turn away in acute embarrassment!"

Prue whitened in fury. "How dare you!" she gasped in a horrified whisper, her lips trembling. "How *d-dare* you speak to me in such a way! I wouldn't permit my own b-brother to say such th-things to me! *Indecent?* A little waltz? And accusing Mr. Eberly of *ogling* me? I have a good mind to tell him what you've said! He'd probably call you out and *horsewhip* you. If only I were a man, I'd do it *myself*!"

She got to her feet and glared down at him, biting her

underlip to keep back her tears and clenching and unclenching the hands held stiffly at her sides. Brandon looked up at her in shock. He had gone too far, and he knew it. He had no idea what had made him say those dreadful things. He didn't even believe those accusations himself. Disregarding his ankle, he struggled to his feet. "Prue..." he began pleadingly, "Prue—!"

"Don't speak to me," she said between clenched teeth. "Don't *ever* speak to me, Brandon Peake. I don't want to see you, or hear you, or know anything about you from this day forward! Do you hear? From now on, as far as I'm concerned, *you don't even exist*!"

She turned on her heel and walked rapidly away. He sank back on his chair and let his misery envelop him. This time, the misery was not self-induced. It came from the destruction of his dreams, and its painful reality made his earlier self-indulgence seem positively pleasurable in comparison.

Chapter FOURTEEN

LADY DENHAM, in response to an urgent note from Lady Upsham, met her friend at the library on Milsom Street on an afternoon three days after the ball. As soon as the ladies had greeted each other, Lady Upsham embarked on the problem which occupied their thoughts. Circumstances beyond the knowledge or control of either one of them seemed to be destroying their hopes, and Lady Upsham wondered aloud if there was not some action they should take.

Lady Denham had confided in Lady Upsham earlier that, although Roger had masterfully taken matters out of her hands, she had every confidence that he would manage successfully on his own. Roger, she had said, was a man of amazing perception, competence and charm—facts which, of course, were obvious to anyone, not only his mother—and she had assured Lady Upsham that it was only a question of time before the entire affair would be settled. But now, Lady Upsham reported, there were unmistakable signs that matters were not going at all well. Both Letty and Prue were sunk in the doldrums. They remained abed until late, and when they finally made their appearances, they both looked hagged. Their eyes were circled, as if they'd not slept well. They resisted her repeated suggestions to visit the Pump Room or meet with their friends. They seemed to prefer to mope about the house. It was only with the strongest urging that she could prevail upon them to take the air briefly by strolling about in the Parade Gardens opposite their lodgings.

Lady Upsham had no idea what had happened or why the doldrums seemed to beset both girls at once.

With arms linked, the two friends strolled up Milsom Street abstractedly. Each put forth various theories to explain what might have happened, but these were rejected. There was only one encouraging note in their entire conversation: Lady Denham noted that Roger did not seem unduly depressed. His mother could not go so far as to say that he actually was cheerful, but he was active, went riding daily, attended some of the evening functions at the Upper Rooms and, most significant of all, made no reference to returning to London. If Roger did not have expectations of success, why was he remaining fixed in a place which he normally abhorred?

With this slight bit of encouragement, the ladies considered what action they might take to move things forward. "Our first objective must be to find a way to shake my nieces from their lethargy," Millicent said shrewdly. "Nothing will happen while they remain hidden away at home."

They walked on in silence. Suddenly, Lady Denham stopped and smiled. "I think I have a suggestion," she said. "The fireworks."

"Fireworks?" Lady Upsham asked, regarding her friend with an arrested look. "Are you speaking of the display in the Sydney Gardens?"

"Yes, exactly," Lady Denham answered. "I hear that a display will be held tomorrow. I have not previously attended, but I understand that they are quite breathtaking. I shall make up a party for tomorrow evening. We shall have an al-fresco dinner right there in the park. With the promise of music and merriment, and a most attractive fireworks display, your nieces will not be able to resist my invitation."

Lady Denham's prediction did not turn out to be quite accurate. Both girls looked decidedly dubious when Roger appeared at the house on the North Parade bearing his mother's invitation. In fact, they showed every indication that they intended to resist vigorously. Roger, recognizing the signs, remarked that the party would be very small—Lady Denham was inviting only Lady Upsham, her two nieces and himself—and that, under those circumstances, their absence would be disastrous to her plans. At this, Letty weakened perceptibly, and Prue looked thoughtful. After he left, Aunt Millicent made it quite plain that they would face her severe displeasure if they refused. So, in the end, the two sisters wrote a gracious note to Lady Denham accepting her kind invitation with thanks.

If the truth were told, it was the information that Brandon would not make one of the party that had decided the matter in the minds of both Letty and Prue. Letty would have been hard-pressed to spend another evening in Brandon's company. It was not that she was angry with him any longer, but she had had quite enough of dissembling. She could not have endured spending another evening pretending closeness to Brandon while Roger watched them with his shrewd and ironic eyes. She was quite relieved at the prospect of a temporary respite from the problems which her deceit had caused. She could look forward, instead, to an evening relaxed and at peace, knowing that Brandon would not be present to remind her of her foolish trickery and that Roger's friendship could be enjoyed without concern that he would press her for anything more.

As for Prue, she would not have agreed to go to the Gardens at all if Brandon had been included in the party. Her pain at his cruel and unjustified criticism of her behavior had not abated, and her determination to avoid him at all costs remained firm. As it was, however, she could look forward to a comfortable, if not a joyous, evening.

Of course, there was nothing to prevent their running into Brandon at the Gardens. The fireworks and gala festivities were open to the public, and often the entire population of Bath turned out for the display. There was no certainty that they would not come face-to-face with him. But since he was not to be one of their party, they would be under no obligation to associate with him.

Once the objections to their attendance at the Sydney Gardens were rationalized away, the mood of both girls brightened perceptibly. For the three days since the disastrous ball they had, each for her own reasons, been indulging in bouts of depression. But it is not in the nature of healthy young women to steep themselves in depression for very long. Their natures are amply supplied with qualities like hope and anticipation which gather strength like antitoxins to fight the gloom. These hopeful feelings had lain dormant under the depression, waiting for an excuse to burst forth into the open. The prospect of the evening at the Gardens provided just such an excuse. What healthy, pretty, spirited young lady could remain gloomy with the prospect of a gala evening of music, lights and spectacular fireworks before her? Both Letty and Prue quickly became aware that their dismals seemed miraculously to disappear, and the world suddenly became a much more cheerful place.

On the afternoon of the gala, Lady Upsham ordered them both to return to their rooms for a nap before dressing. The fireworks would not begin before complete darkness had fallen, she explained, and they were bound to be out until late. Therefore, a nap in the afternoon was advisable. The girls complied, but neither one could sleep. Prue dug her face into her pillow and concocted daydreams in which she received elaborately worded offers of marriage from Osbert, the Rabbit, Mr. Woodward and Mr. Eberly, all of which were overheard by a jealous and tortured Brandon who gnashed his teeth and clenched his fists in helpless agony.

Letty's mind was occupied with even more nonsensical fancies. She dreamed that she had become Roger's *cher amie* in place of Kitty Brownell, and she tried to imagine what it would be like to be with Roger in such a situation. She would, no doubt, have to appear before him quite scantily clad, and to permit him to handle her with disrespectful and passionate abandon. She covered her face in shame, but try as she would, her thoughts refused to take a more proper course, and she finally admitted to herself that, deep down, she was convinced that it was more appealing to be a man's mistress than his wife!

She was roused by a knock at the door, and Katie came in with two white dresses laid carefully over her arm. The abigail had decided that white was the most effective color without bothering to discuss the matter with either Letty or Prue. Letty took her dress from Katie's arm without objection. But Prue, when Katie delivered the other dress to her bedroom door, set up an instant outcry. She would wear a bright color—crimson, perhaps—no matter what *certain people* would say if they saw her. It was better to be stared at than ignored. Hadn't she always said so? But Katie was adamant. This was the dress she had prepared, and this was the dress Prue would wear.

When Lady Denham and Roger called for them in the barouche, Letty and Prue looked fresh, bright and lovely in their gowns of crisp white cambric. Their eyes sparkled in anticipation, their complexions glowed and their smiles were bright. No one would have guessed that they had spent the last few days sunk in gloom.

But Letty's high spirits seemed to disappear as soon as they entered the Sydney Gardens. The carriage had brought them to the entrance at the foot of Pulteney Street, and no sooner had they descended and entered the main pathway when Letty uttered an involuntary gasp. The Sydney Gardens had been completely transformed from their daytime appearance. There was music and singing everywhere, with the tinkle of high laughter combining with the music. The fountains and cascades sparkled, and the illuminations were superb. It was another *Vauxhall*! She shivered as the memory of that other night struck her with an almost tangible reality.

Lady Denham noticed the shiver. "Letty, my dear, you're cold," she said with concern. "Here. Take my shawl and put it over you." And she draped a magnificant green fringed shawl over Letty's shoulders. Letty, noticing with horror that it was the same bright green of her domino, wanted to snatch it off, but she merely shook her head and let it slip from her shoulders. "Th-thank you, Lady Denham," she said hastily, handing it back, "but I'm not at all cold. Please keep it for yourself."

Lady Denham's butler had set up the table on a grassy knoll protected from the breeze by a row of trees. The pickled salmon, the cold chicken and ham, the Highland creams were all delectable and served with the same elegance that would have marked the service in her ladyship's dining room. The champagne, chilled to perfection, had a beneficial effect on Letty. Her spirits rose again, and she and Roger indulged in light-hearted badinage with all the comfort and intimacy of old friends, while Lady Denham and Millicent watched with satisfied smiles.

After the dinner had been consumed, Lady Denham and Lady Upsham turned their chairs about to watch the parade of passersby. Although full darkness would not fall for another hour or more, the elderly ladies intended to pass the time seated comfortably where they were. The younger people, however, were more eager for activity, and Roger offered each girl an arm, suggesting that they stroll about the gardens to admire the illuminations. This they agreed to eagerly. Lady Upsham warned them absently to stay together, Lady Denham insisted that Letty take her green shawl, and the three set off.

After spending more than half-an-hour exploring the once-familiar paths which had been so stunningly transformed by the ingenious lights, they came upon the entrance to the labyrinth. Although illumination had been provided here and there, the paths inside seemed rather frighteningly dusky in the gathering gloom. "Well, ladies," Roger said challengingly, "are you courageous enough to walk through these paths in the dark of night?"

"Oh, yes! Let's!" Prue responded eagerly.

"I don't know," Letty said hesitantly. "I've been told that, with all the ins and outs, one must walk half-a-mile before finding the way out. We may be late for the fireworks."

"I don't think it will take as long as that," Roger assured her. "But you must both agree to hold on tightly to my hands. I don't want us to separate. We *will* be late if we have to waste time looking for each other."

The labyrinth proved to be even greater fun in the darkness than it had been in daylight. They ran down the pathways hand-in-hand, turned the dark corners with a great pretense of fear and a great deal of sincere laughter, pulled poor Roger in opposite directions at each intersection, and indulged in many boisterous arguments over directions. When the sisters were in disagreement, Roger asserted his authority as the eldest of the three and made the final decision. At one point, however, he sided with Letty when Prue was convinced that she was right. "I *know* the exit is down there to the right," she declared stubbornly. She twisted her hand out of Roger's grasp and ran to the right. Calling over her shoulder, "I'll meet you at the exit," she disappeared around the bend.

"Prue, come back here!" Roger demanded, but she did not come. Letty and Roger exchanged helpless glances and turned to follow her. But when they rounded the bend, she was nowhere in sight. They called her name in vain. They peered into all the nearby paths of the maze but couldn't find her.

Prue, meanwhile, had run down the path she was convinced led to the exit, but it proved to be a dead end. Annoyed, but without real concern, she tried to retrace her steps, but the paths were confusing and not the same as they had seemed before. It was now quite dark, for the gardens' bright illumination could not penetrate the thick, tall shrubs which lined the paths of the maze. She called Roger's name, but there was no answer. Suddenly frightened, she called even louder for Letty. In response, she heard a raucous, drunken laugh. "'Ere, dearie, 'ere! I ain't no Letty, but won't I do?" came a drunken voice, and two hulking youths appeared from around a corner and stood blocking her path. From the look of their clothing she took them to be farmers, but they stood unsteadily on their feet and reeked of drink.

"Look, now," one of them said drunkenly, "we found oursel's a right pretty little straw-hat."

The other nodded enthusiastically, his tongue licking a slack, leering mouth. "For once you ain't bammin'," he grinned. "Come 'ere, little poppet, and give us a kiss."

Prue, her heart hammering in her chest and her blood turning to ice, drew herself up proudly. "Stand aside, sir, and let me pass," she demanded with as much dignity as she could command.

The two men laughed. "Well, well—will y'listen to the dolly? Givin' 'ersel' airs like a lady," said one of them, coming a step closer to her.

"Ain't never know'd a dollymop what didn't want to pass fer a lady," the other said scornfully.

The first man reached for Prue and pulled her to him. Prue, in desperate fear, pushed against him with all her might. Already unsteady with drink, the fellow fell backward and dropped to the ground heavily. The other man grasped Prue's arm and laughed heartily. "You're as lushy as an old elbow-crooker," he said to his friend on the ground. "Go put your noddle under the pump and leave this 'ere morsel fer—" But he never finished his sentence, for Prue bit his hand and went flying down the path. The sounds of their grunts and shouts followed her, and she ran even faster, rounding a turn without slowing her step. A large pebble in her path caused her to lose her balance, and she fell flat on her face. She could hear the heavy pounding of their footsteps, and she jumped to her feet and ran on.

Rounding the next corner, she found to her intense relief that she had come to the exit. She noticed as she stumbled out of the labyrinth that the path was reassuringly bright, but to her dismay, Letty and Roger were not there. Somewhere just inside, she could still hear the shouts of her attackers. Would they follow her even here on the open path? Breathless and exhausted, she lifted her skirts and ran down the path, hoping to find safety among the crowds that must be milling about somewhere. At that moment, a sound like a cannon shot broke through the air, causing her to scream out loud. The boom was followed by a burst of light. She looked up in alarm to see a cascade of colored sparks wheeling about in the sky above her head, and she realized that the fireworks had begun. The unexpected display seemed eerily frightening, and the terrified girl continued to race down the path. Suddenly, just ahead, she saw a familiar figure leaning on a walking stick, his eyes turned up to the sky, absorbed in the spectacle now dwindling into darkness above them. "Mr. Eberly! Oh, Mr. Eberly!" she cried out in intense relief.

Mr. Eberly looked round abruptly and gaped in alarm as Prue, her hair disheveled and falling about her shoulders, her dress torn and covered with dust, came stumbling down the path. "Why, Miss Prue! What has happened to you?" he asked, holding out his arms to catch her. She tumbled into them, gasping and trembling, unable to speak. "There, there, child," he said soothingly, patting her back with avuncular kindness, "you're quite safe now."

The awkwardness of his gestures and the fatherliness of his voice were utterly comforting, and Prue responded with a flood of tears. Slowly and haltingly, she managed to convey to him an account of her ordeal, and after repeated assurances from him that she was now safe, her sobs subsided. He withdrew a large handkerchief from the pocket of his coat and dabbed at her cheeks. She looked up at him with gratitude. "I d-don't know how t-to thank you, s-sir," she said tremulously. "You seem always to b-be on hand when I have need of rescuing."

At that moment, Brandon Peake came hobbling along the path, supported by the cane in his right hand and his mother at his left. The sight that met his horrified eyes caused him to stop in his tracks. There stood Prue in a public embrace! She was dusty, tousled and disordered from head to toe, yet she was standing there shamelessly, for all the world to see, in Mr. Eberly's arms. He could feel his mother's arm tighten as she, too, came to a comprehension of what she was seeing. Just as Mr. Eberly became aware of their presence and seemed about to step forward and greet them, Mrs. Peake gave him a curt, dismissive nod, clutched Brandon's arm and hurried him off.

"Did you ever see anything so shocking?" Mrs. Peake hissed as they turned onto another path. "Embracing in public that way! The girl looked a veritable wanton!"

His mother's words so appalled Brandon that their lack of justice—and the injustice of his own impression of what he'd seen—burst upon him. "That is not fair, Mama," he said coldly. "They were not embracing. She looked upset about something."

"How can you be so naive?" his mother demanded. "That was an embrace if ever I saw—"

"By your leave, Mama," Brandon interrupted firmly, "I would rather not talk about it. We blundered into what was meant to be a private matter. We do not know what was going on, nor is it any affair of ours. I wish you would refrain from referring to this matter again, either to me or to anyone else."

Mrs. Peake sniffed indignantly and relapsed into offended silence, leaving Brandon free to reflect on the mixture of feelings which warred within him. One part of him was furious with Prue for permitting herself to appear wanton, her hair unkempt, her dress soiled, her face streaked with tears. Another part of him rejected this interpretation of her appearance. Prue was headstrong, short-tempered and stubborn, but she was not a wanton. There was undoubtedly an explanation for her appearance. But this restrained and temperate feeling did not soothe the anguish that continued to wash over him. The source of that anguish was not hard to determine. It was the look on Prue's face as she looked up at Mr. Eberly. The anguish he was feeling was an emotion he had never felt before but had read of often. Homer had written of it. Sophocles had written of it. And Catullus too. It was jealousy—naked, ugly, raging, murderous jealousy. He would have liked to knock Mr. Eberly down with his bare fists for the pure joy of lifting him up to knock him down again. And when Mr. Eberly would be lying on the ground senseless, his blood slowly dripping into the grass, Brandon would have liked nothing more than to pull Prue into his arms, to have her look up at him with just such a look as he had seen on her face tonight.

Meanwhile, the subjects of his reverie were standing where he had left them, looking after Brandon and Mrs. Peake with expressions of startled embarrassment. "Well," said Mr. Eberly ruefully, "I believe Mrs. Peake and her son have given us the cut direct."

"So it would seem," Prue said in innocent bewilderment. "I wonder why."

"I believe they misunderstood what they saw," Mr. Eberly explained gently. "After all, I had been holding you in a position of . . . er . . . shall we say *intimacy*?"

Prue stared at him. "Intimacy? Do you mean they thought we were *lovers*?" she asked in astonishment. "Of all the . . . the . . . presumption! Why, you're old enough to be my *father*!"

If poor Mr. Eberly's recent encounters with the unpredictable Prue had encouraged any flights of fancy in his bachelor's heart, if he had permitted himself to dream of romance with a red-headed chit barely out of the schoolroom, if he had indulged in even the *merest* hope of the possibility of making this bewitching child his own, her blunt words were a sufficient set-down to kill those illusions forever. He looked down at her, not knowing whether to laugh or scold. But he merely smiled wryly. "Well, not your father, perhaps," he said in his gentle way, "but certainly your uncle." With a sigh, he took her arm and escorted her back to the knoll where Lady Denham and Lady Upsham sat waiting. When the exclamations and explanations had been made, Mr. Eberly accepted their invitation to watch the fireworks with them, but he admitted that his enjoyment of them was somewhat diminished from what it had been earlier.

Roger and Letty had searched the maze without success until the first burst of fireworks lit up the sky. "They've started," Roger remarked. "She cannot still be here. She must have gone back to your aunt by this time."

"I hope so," Letty said, troubled. "Do you think she can have found her way back alone?"

Roger smiled at her comfortingly. "She is quite resourceful. I'm sure she can." Seeing that Letty still looked dubious, he pulled her arm through his and led her to the exit of the maze. When they came out to the open pathway, there was no one to be seen. A second burst of fireworks crackled in the air, causing Letty to jump nervously. Roger turned to her, took the green shawl from her arm and draped it over her shoulders. "Come along, my dear," he said. "I'll have you back with our party in a moment, and you'll see for yourself that Prue is safe and sound and undoubtedly enjoying the fireworks without a care in the world for *you*."

They hurried along the pathway and turned into the brightly illuminated lane which led to the knoll where their party waited. This lane was crowded with people moving in both directions, laughing, carousing and looking up at the sky. Passage was difficult, and even with Roger's expert maneuvering, their progress was slow. At one point, their way was completely blocked by three people who walked abreast, preventing any passage around them. The three persons, a tall woman wearing a poke bonnet trimmed with enormous feathers and a gentleman on each side of her, were proceeding so slowly that Roger became impatient. Tapping one of the gentlemen on the shoulder, he begged pardon for disturbing him, requested passage room, and guided Letty through the space he had arranged between the bonneted lady and the gentleman.

They walked on for only a step or two when the lady's voice stopped them. "This is fine treatment, I must say, Lord Denham," she said with a ringing laugh. "Is this the way you treat old friends?"

Roger seemed to stiffen at the first words, and he and Letty turned around. "Kitty!" he said, his voice shocked and edged with steel.

The lady was indeed Kitty Brownell. Ignoring the coldness in his voice, she came purposefully toward him, a bright smile fixed on her face, her hand extended for him to kiss. But a choked gasp from Letty diverted Roger's attention, and he quickly turned to her. Her face was white, and as he watched, her trembling hand flew to her mouth as she stared at the approaching woman with horrified eyes. For the briefest of moments, Roger was puzzled. She didn't know Kitty—they *couldn't* be acquainted! Then why was Letty reacting so strangely to the sight of Kitty? He glanced quickly at Kitty, who had heard Letty's gasp and was looking at her with cool curiosity, and then he looked back at Letty. A glimmer of a memory struck him. But even before his *mind* was able to grasp what it was that he'd remembered, his *feelings* grasped it. He felt a sharp contraction in his throat. There was something terribly disturbing about this scene. Disturbing and *familiar*. Letty's horrified eyes... her green shawl... the bright garden lights all around them... Kitty. He had seen all this before. *Good Lord*! he thought, gasping audibly, *the girl at Vauxhall*!

For a frozen moment they all stared at each other. Then Kitty, her eyebrows raised quizzically, turned to Roger. "Really, my dear, what—?" she began.

But Roger did not heed her. He was staring at Letty

agonized. With an urgent movement of his hand, he took a step toward her and clutched her shoulder. "Letty—?" he asked, pleading.

But Letty took a step back, shaking off his hand and leaving only the shawl in his grasp. With one last, horrified look at him, she turned and fled, brushing by the startled strollers without stopping, blundering into people like someone blind, on and on down the path until at last she was lost from his view.

Chapter FIFTEEN

KITTY BROWNELL SURVEYED ROGER CURIOUSLY. He was staring down the road after the disappearing girl, his brow furrowed, his mouth in a tight line, his eyes unreadable. The fist in which he clutched the green shawl was clenched so tightly that the knuckles showed white. "Who was that peculiar girl?" she asked bluntly.

Roger forced himself to attention. "Good evening, ma'am," he said with cool formality, "I had no idea that Bath still had attraction for the fashionable set."

"You, my lord, are the attraction. I had intended to surprise you," she said with a teasing smile. "I seem to have succeeded beyond my expectations."

Lord Denham ignored the hints of intimacy in her tone and asked in a businesslike manner, "Are you fixed in Bath or just passing through?"

"Oh, I'm quite fixed. I've taken a house in the Paragon," she answered. "Number twelve," she added, her voice lowered. "Perhaps you would care to call on me there tonight."

Roger made a gesture toward the two gentlemen who escorted her. They had stepped aside as soon as they had become aware that some private drama was being played, but remained waiting for Mrs. Brownell to acknowledge them. "I see you are well provided with company for the evening. You won't have need of me."

"The gentlemen with me tonight? Oh, my dear, you're not going to pretend to be jealous of *them*," she said archly. "They are old friends who insisted on accompanying me on my journey from London. We only arrived today, you know."

"No, I'm not going to pretend to be jealous, ma'am," Roger said shortly. "Nor am I going to pretend to be pleased at your decision to take up residence here—a decision which I consider greatly lacking in both propriety and taste."

Kitty's smile grew strained. In an attempt to change the subject, she said hurriedly, "May I present my escorts to you?"

"Spare me, Kitty, please," he said in an undertone that brooked no argument. "I'm in quite a hurry and must instantly take my leave of you."

Unmindful of observers, she clutched his arm. "You can't go like this, Roger. Do you think I've come for any reason but to see you?"

"I will call on you," he said stiffly.

"Tonight?" she pressed.

He frowned at her in irritation. "Not tonight. You did notice, did you not, that I am otherwise engaged this evening?"

"Later tonight, when you have finished with that strange creature?"

"Damn it, Kitty, not tonight," he said between clenched teeth.

"Tomorrow, then."

He bowed in cold acquiescence and walked off quickly. She watched him for a moment with eyes that smoldered. Then, taking the arm of each of her escorts, she favored them with a smile as vivacious as it was false.

Roger hurried away down the path, dismissing Kitty from his mind. She presented a problem that he knew he must solve, but a solution would not be difficult to find. He would deal with her in due course. It was this new revelation about Letty that worried him. He needed time to think, to remember, to understand what he had done to her and how to make amends. He looked down at the green scarf in his hand. For a moment it had seemed to be a green domino.

The incident at Vauxhall was merely a blur in his memory, but he had no doubt that it was the clue to Letty's fear of him and to those occasional moments when she seemed to view him with aversion. He must have treated her dreadfully if the incident had lingered in her mind with such painful intensity. He flushed with humiliation to think that he could ever have used his lovely Letty as if she'd been nothing more than a bit of muslin! Gentle, sweet, sensitive Letty. What had he done to her?

The sky above him burst into spectacular brightness and the air boomed with the sound of dozens of fireworks being set off at once. The display had no doubt reached its climax and would be ending shortly. There was no time for him to think. He needed solitude and quiet in order to prod his memory. But there would be no solitude until he returned his guests safely to their home. And there would be no quiet until he could calm the turmoil inside him. At the moment, nothing was clear except that he loved Letty with an aching certainty. He had the terrible feeling that his whole life was falling down around him, and the falling shower of sparkles from dozens of fireworks only seemed to add to that illusion.

Letty had run down the path in heedless misery, not knowing where she was fleeing or what she was to do. It was only when she almost blundered into a tree that she stopped running and began to return to awareness of her surroundings. She was gasping for breath and sobbing. People on the path were looking at her curiously. She knew she must contain her emotions and return to her aunt. She moved around the tree so that it hid her from the lane and leaned against it until her breath was regained. Pressing her hands tightly against her chest, she forced her sobs to cease. What was there to cry about? she asked herself. She had known for a long time that Roger had a mistress. She had even seen Mrs. Brownell before. Of course, she had had no idea that Roger had installed her *right here in Bath*! That fact was indeed shocking, but certainly not something to cry about.

She realized bitterly that she had behaved like a child instead of a woman of sense and dignity. She should have pretended to be ignorant of Kitty's identity, permitted Roger to introduce them, and continued the evening as if nothing had happened. Instead she had behaved as if the world had come to an end. She had embarrassed Roger, made a fool of herself, and now had to face the others looking red-eyed and distraught.

She sighed tremulously and a fresh spring of tears spilled from her eyes. She had really believed he loved her. During these past few weeks in Bath, Roger had been so attentive, so charming, so . . . loving. When he had sat beside her on the churchyard wall and said those beautiful words, she would have sworn he was utterly sincere. What a fool she was. He had probably had his mistress conveniently established in Bath *all that time*!

But she could not dwell on the matter now. She had to compose herself. No matter how difficult, she was determined to pass off the rest of the evening with some vestige of self-respect and dignity. She wiped her eyes, forced herself to breathe deeply and evenly, and hurried off down the path to find her party.

When she came to the place where the Lady Denham and her guests were ensconced, the first person she laid eyes on was Prue, sitting beside Mr. Eberly, gazing up at the fireworks with childish absorption. Letty felt a twinge of shame. *Prue*. . . She had completely forgotten her! "There you are, Prue," she said with all the cheerfulness she could muster. "We looked all over the maze for you. You alarmed us greatly, you naughty puss!"

"Don't scold me, Letty," Prue pleaded. "I've had the most dreadful time. You see, as soon as I'd left you—"

"Before you hear the tale," Lady Denham interrupted,

"please tell us what has become of my irresponsible son. It was unforgivable of him to permit you both to go about alone!"

Letty, living up to the promise she had made to herself, answered pleasantly, "He was not irresponsible, ma'am, I assure you. Prue ran away from us—you cannot blame Lord Denham for that. And as for me, I have only walked on ahead of him. He met a . . . a friend a little way back on the path and stopped to exchange greetings."

Satisfied with Letty's explanation, Lady Denham allowed Prue to relate the horrifying tale of her misadventures in the labyrinth, a tale to which Letty reacted with consternation and sympathy. Roger made his appearance shortly thereafter. His eyes immediately sought Letty's face, but she did not look at him. He was greeted eagerly by Prue and the others, so he concluded that Letty had not revealed anything about Kitty's appearance. Following her example, he pretended to a nonchalance he was far from feeling and turned to Prue demanding an accounting of her whereabouts. The story was then repeated for his benefit with all the dramatic details included. While Prue told it, he moved unobtrusively behind Letty and put the shawl around her shoulders. She shuddered and pulled it off, but gave no other sign that she was aware of his existence.

At the conclusion of Prue's tale, Roger admitted to being much abashed by his failure to care for her properly. He thanked Mr. Eberly profusely for his aid to Prue in those dire circumstances. "No need for thanks," Mr. Eberly said, smoothing down his mustache in a deprecating manner. "I've been thanked quite enough by the young lady herself. To be cast in the role of rescuer is quite a romantic adventure for an old codger like myself."

Roger looked at him askance. "Old codger? You can't be more than eight and thirty."

"Thirty-seven, actually," he sighed. "I didn't consider myself elderly, either, until Miss Prue pointed out to me that I'm old enough to be her father."

"Oh, I see," Roger said, smiling at him with quick and sympathetic understanding. "So that's the way it was."

Mr. Eberly's eyes met Roger's, and he shrugged ruefully. "I'm afraid so."

"You shouldn't let it weigh with you, you know. The perspective of seventeen years is a distorted one when it looks toward thirty."

"Oh, it doesn't weigh with me, my boy. Not at all," Eberly assured him with a wry smile. "The fact that I'm suddenly quite tired and shall have to lean heavily on my cane on my way back to my bedroom does not signify at all." He bid his goodnights to the ladies and, with a wink at Roger, hobbled off leaning on his cane in an exaggeratedly elderly manner.

To Letty's relief, Roger did not go to her but sat down next to Prue. He spent the rest of the evening trying to explain to that heartless young vixen that telling a man he is old enough to be her father was a worse than tactless way of thanking him for his gallantry. Prue merely shrugged and said that since he *was* old enough to be her father (or at least *looked* so) she had only spoken honestly.

Not long afterward, Lady Denham led her guests back along the path to the waiting carriage. In the brightness of the illuminated lane, Prue noticed the redness of Letty's eyes. "Letty," she cried in another tactless act, "have you been *crying*?"

"Of course not, silly," Letty said quickly, trying with a quelling glance to silence her sister. But both Lady Denham and Millicent had heard. In the carriage, the strained silence between Roger and Letty was noticed, and the redness around Letty's eyes could easily be discerned by Aunt Millicent's sharp eyes. "I hope you will find time to meet me at the library on Milsom Street tomorrow," Millicent said to Lady Denham in discouraged tones when the carriage arrived at her door.

Lady Denham nodded with the same feeling of despair.

Somehow her party had become a dismal failure. "Yes, of course, Millicent," she said with a deep sigh.

Something forbidding in Letty's eyes kept Aunt Millicent and Prue from prying further into the cause of her red eyes and strained expression, and she was permitted to retire without delay. She hurried upstairs to her bedroom, only to find Katie waiting for her. Turning away so that Katie would not get a good look at her face, she said, "Please, Katie, go to Prue. I don't need you, but she's had a difficult evening and will be very grateful for your assistance." And she sank down on the edge of her bed.

Katie did as she was bid, but after she'd heard Prue's story, helped her wash the dirt away and tucked her into her bed, she returned to Letty's room and peeped in to see if anything needed doing. To her surprise, Letty was still sitting on the edge of her bed. She apparently had not moved for almost an hour. Her hands lay slackly in her lap and her eyes were fixed on the middle distance with an unseeing stare. Katie crept in, shut the door gently and knelt down before her. "Miss Letty, nothin' in the world can be bad enough to make you look so," she whispered worriedly.

Letty focused her abstracted eyes on Katie's face. The abigail was looking up at her with unmistakable affection and concern. It was the first sign of real sympathy Letty had had since Roger had come into her life. Because she had so determinedly kept her problems secret, the warmth and compassion that normally would have been offered by her mother, her sisters, and probably her Aunt Millicent had not been given. For months she had had to keep her own council and to weep into a lonely pillow. There had been no ear into which she could pour her troubles, no shoulder on which she could find comfort. So the troubled look on Katie's face undid her. "Oh, Katie," she whispered tremulously, the tears spilling from her eyes. The tiny abigail did not need to hear more. She jumped up beside her mistress and put a supporting arm around her. Letty's head dropped against the girl's shoulder, and she wept in great, gulping sobs. Katie rocked her gently, cooing soft, comforting sounds into Letty's ear. She continued her gentle rocking until Letty's sobs had worn themselves out. Then she washed Letty's face, undressed her and put her to bed. She blew out the candles and sat at the side of the bed until Letty had fallen asleep. She had asked no questions and had learned nothing of the cause of her mistress' anguish. But Katie had, as usual, learned *something* from the experience; she hadn't realized until tonight that anyone but scullery maids could cry that way.

Lady Denham kept silent until she and Roger had returned home and dismissed the servants. "I suppose you're going to tell me now," she said to her son furiously, "that you did nothing tonight to upset Letty. Do you intend to tell me that you exchanged nothing but the merest commonplaces again tonight?"

"I am not going to tell you anything tonight, Mama," Roger said wearily, "except to wish you a very good night."

She glanced up at him, ready to make a sharp retort, when she caught sight of his face. He was quite pale, his lips compressed, the line of his jaw tight and tense. Mother-like, she immediately softened. She reached up, drew his head down and kissed him lightly on the cheek. "A very good night to you, too, my dear," she said gently and went off to bed.

Roger dropped onto his bed without bothering to undress. He needed to think, to reconstruct that evening at Vauxhall, and he wanted to do it without delay. It must have occurred more than a year ago. He doubted if he could remember.

Lying in the darkness, he stared unseeing at the ceiling and tried to reproduce the evening in his mind. There was to be a masquerade at the gardens, he recalled, and even weeks before, Kitty had teased to be taken. But he disliked Vauxhall and he disliked masquerades. He had given in to her wishes, of course, but with ill grace. And he'd refused to wear a costume. A domino would suffice, he had told her with finality. Strange how it was coming back to him. He remembered that she'd decided to dress as Little Bo Peep. She had beautiful ankles, and the costume would give her an opportunity to display them to the world. The costume had been copied from a picture in a book of nursery rhymes and had looked quite charming. But when it had arrived from her dressmaker's, and she had put it on to show it to him, she had looked at herself with disgust. The very high waist and the short, full skirt had not flattered her. "I look as if I were *breeding*!" she'd said in revulsion. In the end, she'd worn a domino—a bright green domino.

He tried without success to remember the color of his own domino. It was not important, but he wanted to remember every detail. He didn't think it had been green. Whatever the color, he'd been wearing it when they'd arrived at the gardens. He had put on the mask, but he now remembered that he'd found it annoying—it was somewhat too narrow for his face and his vision had been partially blocked because of it. His groom had set up a table in a pleasant, Grecian-like alcove set within white pillars. Kitty had complained that the situation was not to her liking—too far from the bustle—but he'd ignored her complaints. Thinking back on it, he realized that he'd been a most ungracious host. She'd wanted him to take her to the rotunda to dance, but he'd refused. He was not overly fond of dancing, even in the best of circumstances, but to be milling about in the throng at the rotunda struck him as the very *worst* of circumstances. She had flounced off in annoyance, threatening to take up with the first familiar face she could find.

He remembered sitting alone for a long time, his feelings alternating between a desire to throttle her and guilt that he'd been so surly. But when more than half-an-hour had passed, he had begun to feel concerned. While it was true that Kitty was not a simpering little innocent and could easily take care of herself, this was a place which attracted all manner of ruffians, and the lady *was* there under his protection. He'd roused himself from his musings and had gone off to look for her.

Here Roger tried to envision every detail. He had come to the rotunda and looked over the crowd. At first, he'd been dismayed by the number of revelers who thronged the area. He'd feared that he never would find her in the mob. But almost at once, he'd seen the bright green domino and the auburn curls peeping out from under the hood, and he'd felt a wave of relief. Like a worried parent who finds a lost child, his relief had been followed by an explosion of fury. A parent would shout, slapping the child's face, "How *dared* you to be so naughty!" His feelings were quite the same. He would have liked to beat her! Instead, he'd dragged her ruthlessly behind him all the way back to the table.

But—good God!—*that* had been *Letty*! The memory of it made him groan aloud. The poor child had stumbled along behind him, terror-stricken, and he had callously ignored her cries. He had been completely convinced that it was Kitty whose hand he clutched. He'd thought that her cries were *play-acting*—in fact, the choking sounds he'd heard behind him had seemed like suppressed laughter and had only increased his fury.

He closed his eyes and tried to imagine Letty's feelings. The girl was being abducted by a complete stranger and dragged to God-knew-where. Perhaps even to rape and murder, for all she knew! Roger felt sick with self-revulsion. But he knew there was more to remember, and reluctantly he forced himself to recall the rest.

They had returned to his table, and he had unceremoniously dumped her into a chair. She had said something about a mistake—*I am not the lady you think me*, or some such expression. He had not paid attention. He'd believed that Kitty was being coy—teasing him out of his anger. He'd said something curt to prevent her from continuing the nonsense. What had he said? He couldn't recall it at all. Try as he would, he could recreate none of the conversation that must have passed between them. He remembered only that she'd made a rather pretty, pleading speech, in a voice much lighter than Kitty's, and he'd been struck by what he thought was Kitty's talented acting. *Acting!* Lord, what a fool he'd been! The 'acting' had seemed to give Kitty an unexpected charm, and he remembered feeling a surge of desire for her. He'd tossed off his mask to see her more clearly. She'd stood up before him, the curves of her body smooth, lithe and enticing under the domino, and he'd pulled her into his arms.

He shut his eyes in pain. How roughly had he handled her? He could not—or would not—recall. But he remembered how she'd felt in his arms. She had been unexpectedly light and soft, and for a moment he'd enjoyed the sensation without thought. Then he'd kissed her. She'd been pliant and unresisting, but also unresponsive. It was the unresponsiveness which had set off the warning bell in his head. He suddenly became aware that the girl in his arms was trembling from top to toe. That could *not* be Kitty!

The rest was easy to recall. Kitty had arrived, the two women had looked at each other carefully, and it was clear that both had understood what had happened. Then the girl—Letty—had darted off into the underbrush and made her escape. He'd tried to find her—to apologize—but she'd disappeared. He had felt guilty and uneasy for a brief while, but (he admitted to himself with shame) he had soon forgotten her. He'd returned to Kitty. That lady, probably because of an instinctive jealousy, had suddenly become so enticingly complaisant that the entire incident had gone completely out of his mind.

Lying there in the darkness, Roger felt himself flush hotly in mortification. He pulled off his neckcloth and tossed it to the floor. He pulled himself to his feet and strode about the room. But he could not shake off his feelings of humiliation and self-disgust. Damnation, he thought, I should be horsewhipped! Letty had a brother, hadn't she? Why hadn't *he* come looking for Roger, demanding satisfaction? London was supposed to be civilized—men could not go about abducting and abusing innocent girls without castigation! If he'd been properly taken to task at that time, he wouldn't now be in this impossible muddle.

It was clear that he'd taken off his mask and that Letty had recognized him. Why, then, had her family done nothing? And why, one year later, did they encourage him to pay his addresses to the girl he had so abused? The answer was obvious. *Letty had never told anyone.* The family did not know. The realization that she had confided in no one—not even Prue—made him sink down on the bed, his brow furrowed in deep speculation. She had kept the whole terrible story to herself. Why? His spirit leaped up at a ray of hope. Had Letty cared enough about him, even then, to protect his name?

No, the thought was ridiculous. They had barely been acquainted at the time. And after his gross mishandling of her at Vauxhall, it was scarcely likely that she could have any feeling for him but the deepest loathing. She had probably kept her peace and told no one because she wanted to forget the whole sordid affair. It was no wonder that she later refused to marry him. She had seen a side of him that no innocent girl should see. Letty had been gently reared—a sensitive, chaste, refined, obedient, ingenuous girl. How could she agree to wed a man she knew to be a vulgar, lustful, brutish lout?

He lay back on the bed and threw his arm across his forehead in a gesture of despair. At last he understood the nature of the obstacle which he had sensed lay between them from the first. But it was a sizeable obstacle indeed. He had badly botched his hopes. He'd done it unwittingly, but, he feared, irrevocably. Even if he were to assure her that he would never again treat her with anything but the most gentle understanding, would she be likely to believe him? Of course she wouldn't, he realized with a jolt, sitting up abruptly and staring out into the darkness in chagrin—she'd seen Kitty again tonight! She must have thought—good Lord!—that *he* had brought her here! If he had in any way softened her resistance to him during all these weeks in Bath, the meeting with Kitty would surely have hardened it again to a rock-like, impenetrable solidity.

No, she would never take him now. Feeling drained and empty, without hope, and moving with the abstracted air of a somnambulist, he bent down and removed a boot. How ironical, he thought, that the artificial relationship he'd had with Kitty should appear to Letty more real than the agonizing genuineness of the love he felt for *her*. In a burst of anger at the helplessness and futility of his position, he stood up and flung his boot to the far corner of the room. Furiously, he repeated the act with the other boot. This conduct failed to relieve his frustrations but only succeeded in making him feel quite foolish. Without undressing further, he threw himself upon the bed, folded his hands beneath his head and stared up at the ceiling. Dawn would come eventually. In the meantime, he permitted himself an unaccustomed indulgence in self-pity, during which he glumly rejected even the small comfort his mother had once offered—when she'd said that a bit of suffering over a love affair would be good for his character. He very much doubted that this agony was good for anything—not his character, not his future, not even his immortal soul.

Chapter SIXTEEN

THE MORNING SHOULD have dawned in gray and drizzly gloom, but Mother Nature, with her usual callousness and lack of sensitivity to human moods, brought forth a day of such sparkling brightness as to be considered singularly inappropriate by a good number of Bath's inhabitants. Roger, for one, buried his head in his pillow when Trebbs came in and threw back the curtains. "Shut those things!" he muttered hoarsely. "And Trebbs, be a good fellow and take yourself off. Don't come back until I call you. Sunshine! Faugh!"

Prue observed the sunlight spilling into her bedroom window and making lopsided rectangles on her carpet with a frown. "Doesn't it ever rain in this benighted place?" she asked no one in particular.

Her sister stood before the window in *her* bedroom studying her face in a hand mirror. The puffy redness of her eyes was quite unmistakable in the revealing glare of the sunlight. A grayer day would have made the morning—and the sight of her face—a little more bearable. She, too, drew the curtains against the relentless brightness.

Brandon also viewed the day with distaste. He stood leaning his forehead against the windowpane, watching two children play a game of hopscotch on the walkway below. He envied them their agile limbs and carefree hearts. From his window, he could see a bit of Union Street which was already busy with strollers. That meant that the square before the Pump Room would by now be thronged with cheerful crowds, and he envied them, too. Only *he*, he felt, burdened with an injured leg and a bruised heart, was isolated from the laughing world and bereft of even the comfort that drops of rain upon the glass would have offered him. On a rainy day, one was less apt to be aware of a bustling, cheerful world outside one's window. Brandon realized that his thoughts were selfish and petty. He tried to turn them in a nobler direction. "Waste not tears over old griefs," Euripides had written. "No human thing is of serious importance," Plato had said. Why, today, did he feel that his Greeks were not as wise as he once had thought?

Even Mr. Eberly found the sun irritating. While he stood at his shaving mirror, a ray of sunshine, reflected in the glass, found its way to the left point of his mustache, emphasizing the fact that an increasing number of gray hairs lodged among the brown. "I'm well aware of them," he said to the streak of light in disgust. "I don't need you to point them out to me!" With a glance at the window and the glorious day which lay beyond, he sighed and asked whatever gods might be listening in, "Don't you think the time has come for a little rain?"

The morning was quite well advanced when Letty knocked at the Peakes' door. Her knock was answered by the elderly butler, who informed Miss Glendenning that Mrs. Peake was not at home. Letty, who had already peeped into the Pump Room to make certain that Mrs. Peake was there and therefore surely not at home, pretended to be disappointed. "Oh, dear, that *is* too bad. However, you may announce me to *Mr.* Peake if you please. I have found a book I feel sure will amuse him during his convalescence and am most eager to show it to him."

The butler pursed his lips in disapproval, but Letty put up her chin and stared at him firmly, and the old man, shaking his head in a manner which clearly revealed his low opinion of the manners of the younger generation, led her to the library. There they found Mr. Peake, seated in a wing chair, a book unopened on his lap, staring moodily into space. At the sight of Letty his eyes brightened perceptibly, but they quickly took on a look of wary concern. He struggled to his feet. "Letty! How . . . how nice," he said awkwardly.

The butler showed an inclination to linger in the doorway. Letty glanced at him over her shoulder, wondering what to do to arrange a private conversation with Brandon. It was not *her* place to dismiss the man. She smiled weakly at Brandon and said in as cheerful a voice as she could summon up, "Good morning, Brandon. Look at the book I found for you at the library. It's the Thomas Bowdler edition of Gibbons' *Decline and Fall of the Roman Empire*. I thought it would be of interest to you."

Brandon made a face. "Thank you, Letty. That was quite thoughtful, but I'm familiar with the edition, and, by your leave, I think it silly beyond anything. Mr. Bowdler is a womanish old prude who becomes distressed with any word even vaguely connected with the human body. Why the word *body* itself offends him. He goes through the texts and changes it to *person*!"

"That does sound silly," Letty agreed absently. "I'll take it back and change it for something else." She looked back at the butler watching them in the doorway and threw Brandon a helpless look. Brandon, at last realizing that Letty wanted to talk to him, and that the book was just a ruse, told the man to close the door. With raised eyebrows and definite reluctance, the butler did as he was bid.

"Sit down, Letty, sit down. By your leave, I don't know where my manners have gone." Letty sank gratefully into an armchair and Brandon took his seat in the wing chair. "You wish to see me about something? I should have realized that old Bowdler was only a stratagem."

"Yes," Letty nodded, "and when you dispensed with him so quickly, I didn't know what to do!"

"I'm sorry. It's hard for a man to realize, sometimes, how difficult it is for a lady to pay a call on a gentleman when she's unaccompanied. What did you want to see me about? I hope you're not going to ask me to lie to Lord Denham again."

Letty bent her head. "I'm going to ask you something much, much more difficult, Brandon," she said.

Brandon eyed her warily. "See here, Letty," he said bluntly, "I don't wish to be rude, but, by your leave, I may as well be honest with you. I don't like deception. I most sincerely feel for you, and you know I would help you if I could, but I cannot—will not—lie any more."

"But . . . no deception will be necessary, I assure you," she said earnestly, meeting his eye with a level gaze.

"In that case," Brandon said with relief, "I'll be glad to listen."

"First, I need some information from you, and I want you to be as frank and honest with me as you can."

"Fire away," he answered promptly. "I don't mind being truthful."

"Well, then," Letty said with some hesitation, "what I want to know is how . . . how you plan to spend your life."

This was unexpected. "Spend my life?" he echoed. "What do you mean?"

"Do you plan to live always with your mother? Do you plan to remain at Oxford? And most important, do you intend to marry, and if so, have you some young lady in mind?" Noticing how he gaped at her, Letty colored slightly. "I know these questions are most impertinent, but we *are* friends, after all, and the answers have great significance in determining how I shall proceed."

"I see," said Brandon, frowning. "Well, I suppose there can be no harm in discussing such things with a lady—"

"A friend," Letty emphasized.

"A friend, then. Let's see now. First, I do *not* plan to live with my mother. As for Oxford, my studies there will be concluded within a few months. I plan to take lodgings in London, to continue my studies, perhaps to publish some translations if they are good enough. I have friends, an adequate competence from my father and some property which comes to me when I'm twenty-five which—"

"I didn't mean to pry into your financial affairs," she cut in, blushing.

"No, no, I don't mind. I only want to explain that my income will be more than adequate for me to live comfortably in London and to travel abroad from time to time—something I've always wanted to do."

"With a . . . a wife?"

Brandon looked at her in surprise, looked away and sighed. "Once I dreamed . . . of . . . of marrying. But no longer. I think I'm more suited to a bachelor life," he said grimly.

"Oh." Letty regarded him thoughtfully. "Are you *sure*, Brandon? You are very young, you know, and probably know very little of love."

"I know as much about it as I need," he declared bitterly, "and I don't want to feel it ever again!"

"I see. Then there *was* a young lady whom you loved. Is there a possibility—even a very remote one—that you may change your mind and wish to marry her after all?"

"No, none," he said flatly. "She is in love with another. I've no doubt an announcement of their betrothal will be forthcoming very soon."

"But, Brandon, if they are not yet betrothed, you may still have a chance—"

"No, I tell you! Even if she does *not* marry him, she is not for me. She is very volatile . . . and irresponsible . . . and would not be a suitable wife for a scholar. I want a quiet life, a withdrawn life. I have no great liking for balls and parties. Oh, the theater and the opera and small dinners with one's friends are pleasant enough, but the rest bear 'the evils of idleness,' to quote the great Seneca."

"Oh, Brandon," Letty breathed in relief, "that is exactly the sort of life *I* want! I shall make a very good wife for you, really I will!"

"Letty!" Brandon gasped. "What are you *saying*!"

Letty's eyes flickered up at him and then fell. She gave him an embarrassed smile. "Oh, dear, I didn't mean to say it so abruptly. It isn't easy to make a proposal of marriage, is it?"

"A proposal of *marriage*? Letty, have you lost your mind?"

"Brandon, hush! You are making me feel as if I'd said something *indecent*! You are not Thomas Bowdler, after all. You don't want me to think *you* a womanish old prude, do you?"

"No, but... but asking me a thing like that! It's not... it's not *done*!"

"How do you know? When people become close, they can say things to each other that may be unacceptable in the highest social intercourse. I would not be surprised to learn that *many* marriages were suggested by the woman of the pair!" Letty declared with conviction.

Brandon was not convinced. "I won't believe it," he said stubbornly.

Letty sighed. "Well, now that I've done it, shall I go on? Or are you so shocked that you want to call your old butler and have me shown the door?"

"Of course I don't," Brandon said impatiently. "I'm not such a prude as you seem to think. But this subject is—"

"This subject is why I came," Letty said bravely. "I must find a husband, and quickly! Lord Denham does not seem to take our betrothal very seriously. I thought he would return to London as soon as we told him about it, but he has remained here, persistent as ever. And everything has become worse! I'm at my wit's end, I can tell you, and I must do *something*!"

"I wish you could think of something to do that does *not* involve *me*," Brandon muttered ungraciously.

Letty looked at him with troubled eyes. "I'm sorry,

Brandon, truly I am. But I believe my plan would be good for us both. I really *would* be a good wife to you. We have always got on well together. I could keep house for you in London and help you with your work. I could look things up for you and copy manuscripts and organize your library. And you could teach me Latin and Greek! I would love to learn. And we would be company for each other at the opera. And would it not be more cheerful to travel with a companion than to take your first look at the Acropolis alone?"

He leaned back and studied her with amazement. "Would you truly like to do those things?" he asked.

"Yes, I would. Truly." She leaned forward and reached out a hand to him. "Oh, Brandon, I'm sure we would learn to be content."

"Would you really like to study Greek?" he asked, moving to the edge of his chair and taking her hand. She truly was a lovely young woman, gentle and soft-spoken most of the time. She'd always shown an interest in his studies. It might be amusing to teach her the classics, to show her the famous shrines of Greece, to recite the great poems to her, to mold her mind. Prue would only have tortured him, led him a merry dance, laughed at his work, flirted with strangers under his very nose, teased him to take her to balls and festivities. She would have made an impossible wife. Yet he still felt a sharp sting of pain at the very thought of her. Perhaps Letty could help him ease that pain.

Letty watched him, her breath arrested. She had not really believed that he would seriously consider her proposal, but now it seemed that she had struck the right chord. She waited silently, her hand in his, for him to speak.

But after a moment, Brandon shook his head. "No, Letty, I don't think your plan will work. You are even younger than I, and know less of love. I would not wish to bind you to a loveless marriage."

Letty smiled sadly. "You're mistaken, Brandon.

Women learn about love much sooner than men. I didn't ask you about the love you have put aside, and I hope you will not ask me about mine. But I can assure you that I am not more likely to succumb to love again than you are."

With this assurance, Brandon capitulated. They became betrothed in earnest. The only things remaining to be discussed were the details of the nuptials. In this matter, poor Brandon was to have another jolt.

"What? *Elope!* Letty, you cannot mean it!" he cried in alarm.

"Please, Brandon, don't be difficult. It's the only way. Think of the obstacles an elopement will avoid. We won't have to fight my family. I won't have to face Lord Denham ever again. And don't try to convince me that *your* mother will be happy about this. I have had the impression that she disapproves of my entire family."

Brandon colored. His mother would prove to be more difficult than even Letty's aunt. She had a point there. An elopement *would* permit them to escape family censure. Once the deed was done, their opposition would be pointless.

They finally agreed on Gretna, and, after much more persuasion by Letty, the date was set for dawn on the following morning. "It's an excellent time," Letty said with a teasing smile as she rose to leave, "for it gives you no time to reconsider."

Brandon hobbled to the library door with her and kissed her hand gallantly. "What a poor sort you must find me," he said ruefully. "But you needn't worry. We are truly betrothed now, and I am not likely to cry off. In fact, Letty, I'm rather looking forward to our marriage. I've had more adventures since I met you than ever before in my life. I suspect that our life together will not be dull."

"Thank you for saying that," Letty said gratefully. She leaned over, kissed his cheek, and with a quick reminder that she would watch for his carriage at dawn, she took her leave.

* * *

Lord Denham finally brought himself to face the day, and in the early afternoon, dressed impeccably in buff-colored breeches and a coat of blue superfine, he entered a jeweler's shop on Milsom Street. He emerged ten minutes later and slipped a small package into an inner pocket of his coat. Then, squaring his shoulders, he made his way to Number 12 on the Paragon.

He was admitted by a simpering maid and found Kitty standing before the window, the sunshine filtering through the sheer curtains and making dazzling highlights on her auburn hair and the curves of her white breast which were tantalizingly revealed by the loose, low *décolletage* of her gown. She made a striking picture, as well she knew, but Denham was strangely unmoved. He smiled, took a step into the room and waited for the maid to close the door behind him. Then he carefully placed his hat and gloves on a table near the door, looked up at her and said admiringly, "You look like a painting by Van Dyke, my dear. Very sumptuous."

Kitty, having made the impression she wanted, walked quickly across the room and threw her arms around his neck. "Roger, you beast! You gave me a sleepless night with your coldness."

"Did I?" he asked coolly, removing her arms. "You look none the worse for it, I assure you. Come, sit down here with me. I want to talk to you."

She shook her head and slipped her arms around his waist. "But, love," she whispered into his ear, "we can talk later. I haven't seen you for almost a month."

"You are not trying to tell me that you've missed me, are you?" he asked, freeing himself from her embrace and leading her firmly to the sofa.

"But *of course* I've missed you, dearest. I've been so bored and lonely that I fell into flat despair! That's why I decided to come here. I was quite beside myself without you." She spoke with quavering sincerity and put her head on his shoulder.

Roger raised an eyebrow. "Oh? Then the news that I've

had from London was no doubt false."

Her head came up abruptly. "News? What news?"

"The news that you were seen frequently in the company of your duke."

"*My* duke?" she exclaimed, drawing herself erect. "Roger, are you trying to pick a quarrel? If it is Eddington you are speaking of—"

"Oh? Have you *another* duke as well?"

"Really, my dear, you are being quite ridiculous. You cannot be jealous of Eddington! He is half bald, has a stomach as big as a barrel and is the greatest bore in Christendom."

"I am no more jealous of him than I was of your escorts last evening. I will admit that, in the past, I found it irksome to share your affection with other men while you openly declared that you were living under my protection. However, I no longer wish the right to feel irked. I think the time has come, my dear, to sever our connection."

Kitty whitened. "You can't mean it! Is it because I followed you?" She put a hand on his chest. "You cannot blame me, love. I *did* miss you so."

"I think it much more likely that you heard a rumor of my interest in matrimony. You *did* hear some gossip, did you not?"

"Well, I may have heard—"

"And you came to see if you could dissuade me, isn't that it?"

"Nonsense, Roger," Kitty said, getting to her feet and beginning to pace about the room. "I always knew you would marry eventually. What difference can it make to me? To us?"

Roger leaned back on the sofa and watched her agitated pacing unperturbed. "You always knew what my marriage would mean to us. I made my intentions quite plain. I never intended to play a wife false."

She halted her stride and stared at him. "Then you *are* to be married?" she asked tensely.

"I don't know," he answered frankly. "It seems

unlikely." With a rueful smile, he added, "Not every woman finds me so good a catch as you do."

"Oh?" Kitty asked, brightening. She returned to the sofa and sat down close to him. "Is your courtship proving difficult?" She ran a finger affectionately along his jaw and the side of his face. "The girl must be a fool," she said in a low, provocative voice.

"Kitty, stop playing," he said brusquely, brushing her hand away. "Let's talk with gloves off. Whether I marry or not, it is *over* for us. It's been over for some time. Don't shake your head. You know it as well as I. Let's end what has become nothing more than a charade. Take your duke while you still can."

"No!" she said furiously, jumping up and turning her back on him. "He never meant anything to me! Your friends are *vicious* to have sent such gossip. You *know* you have always been first with me."

Roger rose and stood behind her. "First, perhaps, but never *only*," he said meaningfully. He reached into his pocket and took out the box. Turning her to face him, he placed it in her hand. She flicked him a sullen glance and then opened it. Against the black velvet lining of the box lay a magnificent diamond bracelet.

"Do you think to *buy* my complaisance?" she asked furiously, tossing the bracelet at him. It fell to the floor where it lay unheeded.

"I have no need to buy your complaisance or anything else," Roger said gently. "I offer the gift to you only as a gesture of thanks for some pleasant memories." He went to the door, picked up his hat and gloves, and looked back at her. She stood in the middle of the room, her eyes stormy, her fingers clenched. "Try not to be angry," he said soothingly. "I think you and your duke will get on famously, especially now when you need no longer concern yourself about keeping that—and your other liaisons—secret from me. Goodbye, Kitty."

Kitty's color rose to an almost apoplectic red as the finality of his words struck her. A vase, filled with fresh flowers, was close at hand. She picked it up and hurled it against the door which he had just closed behind him. It crashed noisily to the floor, spilling water and blooms in all directions. She next picked up a lovely and expensive Sèvres bowl and was about to send it crashing to a similar fate when her eye fell on the bracelet. It was truly a magnificent piece. She replaced the bowl and knelt down. She picked up the bracelet and held it so that the light shone through. Her high color faded and her eyes narrowed as she observed the dazzling highlights of the multi-faceted jewels. She sat back on her heels with a resigned sigh. He was right, of course. Everything he'd said was true. And even now, knowing her duplicity, he'd been more generous than she had any right to expect. With a shrug of acceptance, she began eagerly to count the diamonds.

Chapter SEVENTEEN

LADY DENHAM SENT round a note to Lady Upsham begging her forgiveness for being unable to keep their appointment for the afternoon. She was beset with a painfully nagging toothache, she wrote, and had taken to her bed. *I have learned nothing whatever from Roger,* she added, *about what transpired last night. Perhaps my discomfort with my tooth is the cause of my present mood, but I'm afraid, my dear Millicent, that I feel very little hope that our plans will ever come to fruition. I am much inclined to wash my hands of the entire matter. The young men and women of that generation behave in ways quite beyond my understanding.*

Lady Upsham read the note with sinking spirits, although the contents didn't really surprise her. She had been feeling, of late, that a match between Letty and Roger was not to be. Some serious impediment, the nature of which she could not guess, lay between them, and since neither of them saw fit to permit an outsider to assist them in overcoming it, the match was undoubtedly doomed. She knew she should accept that fact with resignation. But what she really felt was irritation.

To relieve that feeling, she sat down at her writing desk and penned a scathing letter to her sister-in-law. *Your daughters,* she wrote, *are quite impossible, and I seriously doubt if you should persist in the hope that they will make beneficial marriages. Letty remains unmoved in her position vis-à-vis Lord Denham. All our exertions in that direction have proved useless. And as for Prue, she continues to frustrate my hopes. She had attracted the attention of a mature and wealthy bachelor named Mr. Eberly. I was in transports, I can tell you. But last night the silly child blithely told him that he was old enough to be her father, and the poor man scurried off without a backward look. Although the little flirt has all the young men of Bath hanging at her heels, none of them can be considered marital prizes. The one ray of hope I can offer you is the prospect of a better choice when I bring Prue out next season. If, in the meantime, we can teach her to control her tongue—*

Her writing was interrupted by a tap at the door, and Miss Tristle came in to tell her that Lord Denham had called and was waiting below. "Lord Denham?" Millicent asked in delight. "Tell him I'll be right down." Hope sprang alive in her breast. If Lord Denham still cared to call, all was not lost. Perhaps her letter to Lady Glendenning had been hasty. She tore it up, straightened her hair and hurried downstairs.

Lord Denham had called to ask her permission to take Letty for a drive. This she gave with alacrity and sent Miss Tristle to fetch Letty at once. Miss Tristle returned alone and whispered in Lady Upsham's ear that Letty had sent her regrets to Lord Denham—she was feeling indisposed. Millicent could not permit Letty to ruin this opportunity. "Excuse me, Lord Denham," she said firmly. "Letty and I will return in a moment."

Millicent's resolve almost failed her when she entered Letty's room and confronted her. The expression in Letty's eyes was like that of a trapped rabbit. "Don't order me to go, Aunt Millicent," she pleaded. "I am not feeling at all the thing today."

"Of course I won't order you, my dear," Millicent said, offended. "I am not an ogre or the wicked stepmother in a fairy tale!" She took a seat and looked up at her niece in concern. "I only wish you would explain to me what it is about Lord Denham that makes you so eager to avoid him. Perhaps if I understood, I would refrain from giving him further encouragement," she said in as patient a tone as she could muster.

Letty shook her head and turned away. "It is not . . . There is nothing I can speak of, Aunt," she said in a muffled, quivering voice and went to the window.

A dreadful thought suddenly occurred to Millicent and caused her to rise quickly and follow Letty to the window. Putting her hands affectionately on Letty's shoulders, she asked gently, "Oh, my dear . . . It is not . . . Lord Denham cannot have behaved improperly toward you! Is that it? I should never forgive myself if—"

But Letty didn't let her finish. "No, no!" she said fervently. "You must not think such a thing! Lord Denham has never been anything but gentlemanly and proper in my company, I promise you. There is no blame to be placed on him or on you—or indeed on *anyone*!"

Millicent, much relieved, could not help but pursue her goal. "Then, Letty, what can be the harm of a little drive in his company?"

Letty turned away and stared out the window at Roger's curricle waiting below. "Tell him . . . tell him I'll ride with him *tomorrow*," she said in sudden inspiration.

Millicent smiled. At least her renewed hopes need not yet be dashed. "Very well," she said agreeably, and then added shrewdly, "but I would be obliged if you could go down and tell him so yourself."

Letty wheeled around, the frightened-rabbit look returning to her eyes. "No, please, don't ask me to do that!"

Millicent hardened her heart to Letty's look. What could be so dreadful about speaking briefly to Lord Denham? The girl was being too missish. Millicent told herself that such foolishness should not be encouraged. "I *do* ask it," she said coldly. "I am much too tired to climb down the stairs again. I'm going to my room to lie down."

"Then couldn't Miss Tristle—?" Letty asked desperately.

"Miss Tristle?" Millicent said in horrified accents.

"Surely you cannot suggest that we treat Lord Denham in such cavalier style. Go down at once, and don't make a to-do over nothing."

With those quelling words she marched from the room. Letty had no choice but to obey.

Lord Denham was standing before the high, paned windows of the sitting room, his manner calm and cool, the picture of the impeccable and elegant Corinthian from the top of his curly hair, cut with a casual-seeming artistry, to his gleaming top boots which gave a subtle emphasis to the excellent shape of his legs. The sight of his sartorial splendor reminded Letty that she had not even checked her appearance in the mirror before she had left her room, and her hand unwittingly flew to her hair which she had loosened when she'd returned from her visit to Brandon and which now hung in unkempt abandon around her face. Her careless appearance gave her a decided feeling of disadvantage until she noticed that he was twisting his curly-brimmed beaver rather nervously in his hands.

His whole face brightened when he caught sight of her. "Letty!" he said in a voice vibrant with hope. "Are you coming with me, then?"

She gave him no answering smile but merely shook her head. "I hope you will forgive me, my lord," she said with excessive formality, "but I find I am rather indisposed this afternoon."

"I see," he said, deflated. There was a moment's pause. "Thank you for taking the trouble to inform me of your indisposition," he said carefully. "I hope it will not be of long duration. But since you're here, I wonder if you might spare me a moment or two. I have some matters of urgency to discuss with you."

Letty took a deep breath. "Lord Denham," she said with what she hoped was crushing dignity, "I don't believe there is *anything* which must be discussed between us."

"Letty, for heaven's sake!" he burst out impatiently, "must we hide behind these artificial attitudes? We've passed far beyond these formalities, you and I. You *know* there are matters to be discussed."

"You are mistaken, sir. The matters to which you refer are not my affair and of no concern to me."

He took a step toward her and looked at her intently. "Are you sure, my dear?"

She met his eyes unwaveringly. "Quite sure," she said.

They stared at each other, both of them pale and strained. His eyes fell first. Wordlessly, with a quick bow, he turned and went to the door. But there he hesitated. Without turning, he lowered his head and asked in a choked voice, "May I not even be permitted to apologize for . . . for Vauxhall?"

She felt her breath catch. "I . . . It is not at all necessary, my lord."

He turned and looked at her steadily. "It is necessary to me."

A pulse in her neck was beating wildly. Her knees felt weak and her determination to prevent any sort of intimate communication between them was weakening, too. But honest or meaningful conversations between them in the past had sometimes ended with an embrace, and she was well aware what his embrace could do to her resolve. "I am truly not up to exchanges of this kind today," she said helplessly.

Instantly he was struck with remorse. "I don't mean to press you," he said quickly. "Forgive me. Perhaps another time . . . ?"

She nodded. "Tomorrow," she said, her eyes downcast. "I'll . . . drive with you tomorrow."

His look of gratitude smote her like a blow. Then he bowed and was gone. She flew to the window and watched as he climbed into the curricle and drove off. By this time tomorrow she would be well on her way to Gretna Green. If she ever saw him again, it would be as a married woman, safely protected by wedlock against the temptations he represented. With her forehead pressed against the glass, she watched until the curricle had disappeared. Then she went up the stairs feeling hopeless, empty and enveloped in a misery so acute it was beyond tears.

Lady Upsham stood behind her bedroom door, listening for the sound of Letty's step on the stairs. When she heard it, she opened a crack in her door and peeped out at her niece's face. What she saw was intensely discouraging, and she closed the door with a deep sigh. Perhaps she should not have sent the girl down after all. Deflated and worried, she sank down on a chair, completely absorbed in her concern for Letty. For several minutes her speculations occupied her attention, but soon she became aware that Miss Tristle was bustling about with her walking clothes. "What *are* you doing?" she inquired irritably.

Miss Tristle looked up in surprise. "Laying out your clothes, my lady. Are you not going out to meet Lady Denham this afternoon?"

"No, no. Put those things away. Lady Denham is laid up with a toothache."

"Oh, the poor dear," Miss Tristle murmured sympathetically, her own recent experience with the toothache fresh in her memory. "You should send Katie to her."

"Katie?" Lady Upsham asked, mystified.

"She's a wonder when it comes to concocting medicines and potions."

"Is she?" Lady Upsham asked with interest.

"Indeed she is," Miss Tristle said with enthusiasm. "She gave me an herb wash took my toothache off like *that*!"

"Is that so? Then you may be right—perhaps we should send her to Lady Denham." Lady Upsham paused thoughtfully. "But not today. Miss Letty may have need of her today. Remind me about it tomorrow."

The morrow brought the rain. In the early morning hours the downpour began. Nature, in her contrary way, was responding to the wishes expressed by so many the day before—but much too late. Brandon in particular was struck by the spitefulness of the weather. He had risen before daybreak, dressed, picked up his packed cloak-bag and stolen from the house, to be greeted by the heaviest rainstorm he had known since his arrival. The air had a decided autumn rawness, and by the time he had limped to the stable he was thoroughly chilled and drenched. It was then he realized that he couldn't use his phaeton. Its light hood would be small protection against such a deluge. The only carriage in the stable which would be suitable was his mother's ponderous coach, and he could not in good conscience make off with that. Resigning himself to another soaking, he made his way as quickly as his slowly mending ankle permitted to the nearest livery stable where he was forced to spend almost an hour under the narrow eaves waiting for the proprietor to make an appearance.

Letty viewed the rain with equal distress. It prevented her from seeing the road clearly from her window, and as the hour grew later, she wondered if it would be better for her to creep outside with her things and wait for him at the side of the road. While she vacillated, she heard the first stirrings of the servants in the hallway. She knew she had better leave at once.

She peeped out to make sure the hallway was clear. Then she lifted her overstuffed bandbox, took an umbrella and crept out. As she passed Prue's door she stopped in horror. She had left no word for Prue or anyone else in the family. Her thoughtlessness appalled her. She tiptoed back to her room, pulled off her gloves and found a pen and paper. *Dearest Prue,* she wrote hastily, *by the time you read this, I will be on my way to Gretna Green. I know that you, at least, who have been closest to me and have been most aware of my unwillingness to marry Lord D., will understand why I take this step. It will not be the sort of wedding I would have wished for myself, and I know Mama and Aunt Millicent will be very shocked at my reprehensible behavior, but I can find no other way. Do not tell Aunt Millicent where I've gone until you can hold back no longer. Tell her that I am truly grateful for all she has tried to do for me and that my most painful regret is that I am forced to serve her what I am sure she will think is a backhanded turn. Tell Mama the same, and that I love her above all. And tell them that they will become more resigned to my marriage when they have learned to accept the fact that it is better so. They will grow to feel kindly toward Brandon, I am sure, once they recognize his admirable characteristics. Until we meet again, dearest, I remain your loving sister, Letty.*

She folded the letter carefully, put on her gloves again and turned to go. But to her consternation, the door was opening. Katie stood in the doorway, gasping at the sight of her mistress who was fully dressed and packed for a voyage. "Miss Letty! Wha—?"

"Hush, Katie," Letty whispered frantically, pulling the girl into the room and shutting the door.

"But, Miss Letty, what is it y're up to?" Katie demanded, her hands on her hips and her arms akimbo.

"I'm eloping," Letty said briefly. "And now that you've found me out, you can help me."

"I ain't helpin' till I know more about it," Katie said firmly. "Don' know yet if I hold wi' it."

"Oh, Katie," Letty laughed weakly, "you're impossible. You must take my word that what I'm doing is for the best."

"So *you* say," Katie replied sceptically. "Is it 'is lordship?"

Letty gave Katie a wondering glance. "What do you know of his lordship?" she asked.

"I ain't no slow-top. I know'd 'oo you was cryin' over that night."

Letty frowned at her. "Never mind that. I'm going to marry Mr. Peake."

Katie's brow wrinkled worriedly. "You're bammin' me! Tell me you're bammin' me!"

"It's true. So don't delay me further. Promise me you'll tell *no one.* And give this note to Miss Prue when she wakes."

"Does Miss Prue know what y're doin'?" Katie asked, looking at her narrowly.

"I've told her in the note."

Katie shook her head. "It's not right, Miss Letty. Y're makin' as big a mistake as a body can make."

Letty smiled at her indulgently and gave her a quick hug. "Don't worry, Katie dear. I know what I'm doing. Just be a good girl and do as I ask." She picked up her bag and ran out. Katie stood where Letty had left her, shaking her head in concern. "You don' know the 'alf, Miss Letty," she murmured. "You don' know the 'alf."

The rain had not abated when Letty came out, and by the time the hired coach came down the street, her bandbox and her shoes were sadly soaked. Brandon made profuse apologies for his lateness and tried his best to put on a cheerful aspect, but the bad start seemed to auger ill for their future, and though neither would admit it, they both were inwardly very depressed. Brandon could not help thinking of Euripides' words: *A bad beginning makes a bad ending.* And Letty, looking out the back window at her aunt's house, rapidly disappearing from view behind a thick curtain of rain, found that a little phrase kept repeating itself ironically in her brain: *Happy the bride the sun shines on.*

Chapter EIGHTEEN

KATIE WENT ABOUT her morning duties with an abstracted air. Miss Letty's note to her sister Prue was stowed in her apron pocket, ready to be delivered as soon as Prue should waken, but Katie dreaded the chore of delivering it. She knew that Prue would take the news hard. Mr. Peake seemed to occupy all Miss Prue's thoughts and dreams, and Katie knew that the news that he was to be her *brother-in-law* would be painful for the girl to bear. But half the morning went by without a sign of stirring from her bedroom.

On many mornings, Lady Upsham would ask Katie to wake the girls, but on this rainy day, her ladyship evidently had decided to permit the girls to stay abed. Katie paced the corridor outside Prue's bedroom anxiously. When the clock struck half after nine, she could bear it no longer. She opened the door and tiptoed in. Prue stirred and snuggled deeper into the pillows. "Are you awake, Miss Prue?" Katie asked tentatively.

"Mm. 'S raining," Prue mumbled.

"Yes'm, rainin' somethin' fierce. I never seen such a downpour," Katie said briskly, taking matters in hand. She pulled open the drapes and went over to the bed. "Do y'know it's half after nine?"

Prue yawned. "Is it?" she asked, stretching lazily.

"More'n time you turned yourself out," Katie said brusquely.

Prue sat back among the pillows and regarded Katie balefully. "You needn't sound so quarrelsome. I don't see why I should hurry to rise and dress on a morning like this. Is Letty up?"

Katie bit her lip. "Yes. Got up hours ago, she did. She's... gone out, y'know..."

"Gone out? In this weather? Where?"

"Can't say," Katie said shortly, "but she give'd me this for you." With a surreptitious glance at Prue's face, she handed over the letter.

"What on earth—?" Prue asked, perplexed, and opened the note. Her mouth dropped open as soon as she'd read the first sentence. "Gretna!" she gasped. "She must have lost her senses!" She looked up at Katie accusingly. "Do you know anything of this?"

Katie shrugged. "Is that all she says? That she's made off to Gretna?"

Prue scanned the rest of the letter quickly. Not until she'd read the last line was her eye arrested. "Oh, my God! Brandon! She hasn't gone off with *Brandon*! She *couldn't*...!"

Katie said nothing but watched Prue with concern. Prue had paled, and the hand holding the letter had begun to tremble. Prue turned to Katie suspiciously. "Is this some sort of hum? Is Letty trying to hoax me?"

Katie shook her head. "I ain't whiddled the whole scrap, but she's took off with Mr. Peake for sure. It ain't no whisker. I seen 'em leave."

"You *saw* them? Then for God's sake, why didn't you *stop* them?" Prue demanded in a choked voice.

"It ain't my place to stop 'em, even if I could," Katie said reasonably.

"Then you should have called *me*," Prue said furiously. "I would have found a way."

Katie looked dubious, and Prue, meeting her eye, was about to argue the point further when suddenly her face seemed to collapse, and she burst into tears. "Why did L-Letty do it?" she asked despairingly. "She d-doesn't even c-care for him!"

"Are you certain sure o' that?" Katie asked pointedly.

Prue angrily dashed the tears from her cheeks. "Yes, I'm sure! And he doesn't really c-care for her, either!"

"Then why did 'e go?"

Prue hesitated. "I . . . I don't know," she said pettishly. Then, with an angry hitch of her body, she cast herself down into the pillows, turning her head away from Katie's level-eyed, rational stare. "And I don't *care*, either!" she flung back over her shoulder. "Let them go. Let them marry. They m-made their beds . . . let them lie in them!"

"If you really think they mistook theirsel's," Katie suggested, "why don't you tell your aunt? Maybe they can be cotched . . ."

"No, I won't! I don't care if they're caught or not. I won't lift a *finger* to stop them! If Brandon wants Letty instead of . . . of . . . well, he can have her." She crushed the letter in her hand and threw it away.

"Miss Prue," Katie said soberly, sitting on the edge of the bed and patting Prue's shoulder, "Don't you think you should say *somethin'*? It ain't right to run sly about a thing like this."

"I don't care. Letty said not to tell until I must. I'll stay here as long as I can and say nothing till I'm asked. That's what Letty wants . . . and Brandon, too . . . so that's what I'll do. As far as I'm concerned," she added vehemently, her underlip quivering and two large tears forming in the corners of her eyes, "I w-wish them h-happy!"

Katie tried to reason with her, but Prue dismissed the abigail coldly. Katie picked up the crushed letter, put it back in her pocket and left the room. Something told her to show the letter to Lady Upsham, but she could not bring herself to do so. "I ain't a tattlin' old chubb," she said to herself and, at last, she tore the letter to shreds and threw the pieces on the fire.

No sooner was this decision made than she was told by Miss Tristle that Lady Upsham wanted her to go to the Denham lodgings to help Lady Denham cure her toothache. With an unshakable feeling that she was going from the frying pan into the fire, she flung a shawl over her head and scurried off.

When she told Lady Denham why she had come, the dowager eyed her dubiously. Lady Denham had been seen by the most respected medical man in Bath, and the medication he had prescribed had not proved efficacious. Why, then, had Lady Upsham believed that this little maidservant, whose language reeked of the streets of London, would be of more help than the doctor?

Katie, with a professional air that belied her diminutive stature and humble position, took off her shawl and approached her patient, touching the swelling on Lady Denham's cheek with gently probing fingers. "What 'ave you took for it?" she inquired.

"This," Lady Denham said, handing a bottle of muddy-looking liquid to the girl and watching her with interest.

"What's in it?" Katie asked.

"I don't know," Lady Denham said with a shudder. "All I know is that it was too strong for my tooth to bear. I didn't even *try* to use it after the first experience."

Katie sniffed the liquid, then wet her finger with it and licked the finger with an exploring tongue. "I know'd it. Honey!" she declared.

"Honey?" Lady Denham repeated. "Is something wrong with that?"

"Everythin'," Katie declared with assurance. "Don' know why the doctors like this potion. It's made of juniper root, alum and honey, and maybe one or two other things. But honey ain't nowise good for bad teeth, ma'am. Take my word on it."

"I don't doubt you're right," Lady Denham said with a smile. The girl's air of authority had a winning charm and seemed to inspire confidence. "Doctors can be fools, you know. This silly man told me to soak my feet in hot water and rub them in bran at bedtime. I can't imagine how soaking my feet will be of any help to my tooth, can you?"

Katie grinned. "Sounds a queer start to me," she agreed.

The girl was given free rein. She made her herb wash, brought it to the patient, and after several applications a grateful Lady Denham was feeling some relief. Roger, entering his mother's bedroom in the early afternoon, was surprised to see her out of bed. She was sitting on a chaise, looking comfortably relaxed, while Katie applied cold compresses to her still-swollen cheek.

"Well, Mama," Roger greeted her, "you seem better this afternoon."

"Thanks to this child here," Lady Denham told him. "Lady Upsham sent her here to doctor me. Her name, she tells me, is Katie-from-the-kitchen."

Roger turned curiously and found himself regarded with equal interest by a pair of shrewd, bright eyes. Katie had heard a great deal about the fascinating Lord Denham and had even seen him once or twice from a discreet distance. This was the first time, however, that she could really look at him closely enough to make an evaluation. Roger could not help smiling at the intense scrutiny to which she was subjecting him. "How do you do, Katie-from-the-kitchen? How do you come by such a strange name?"

Katie curtsied awkwardly. "Miss Letty and Miss Prue like to call me that," she explained. "It's only a lark, y'know. That's where they come'd to find me."

"And a very good find it was, too," Lady Denham said affectionately. "I shall miss you when you leave me this afternoon. If ever you want a new place, child, come and see me."

Katie bobbed again. "Thank you, m'lady, but I like my place well enough." And she turned away to wring out a fresh compress.

Roger sat down beside his mother. "I've come to ask if I might use your carriage this afternoon," he said. "It's still raining too hard to permit me to use the curricle."

"Of course you may," Lady Denham said, "but I can't

imagine why you should wish to drive out on such an afternoon."

"Because, my dear, I promised to take Letty for a drive," he told her with a smile.

Katie, who had heard every word, turned around abruptly. She had looked closely at this man for whom her sweet Miss Letty had sobbed so bitterly. If she was any judge—and Katie had no doubts of the perspicacity of her own judgment—this man was the one for Letty. Perhaps it was not too late to save Letty from the folly of her impetuous elopement. "Beg pardon, m'lord," she said bravely, "but if y're meanin' to drive Miss Letty today, you'll be bum-squabbled."

Roger looked at her sharply. "Why? Is she ill?"

"No, sir. She ain't at 'ome."

"Oh?" Roger asked, his eyebrows raised. "But I'm sure she'll return in time for our drive. We had an arrangement..."

"Yessir, but she's gone, you see."

"No, I'm afraid I don't see. Gone where?"

It took all Katie's courage to answer. "To Gretna Green, m'lord."

Roger stared at the girl, the color draining from his cheeks. His mother sat upright with a cry. "Katie, what are you saying? Has Letty eloped?"

Katie nodded humbly.

"I don't believe it!" Lady Denham declared, thunderstruck. "Not Letty. She has always been the most well-mannered, beautifully behaved—"

"Do you know with whom she has gone?" Roger asked intently, not even aware that he'd interrupted his mother's words.

"Yes, sir, I do. She went wi' Mr. Peake."

For a moment the two stared at Katie motionless. "Brandon?" Lady Denham gasped. "It's not possible!"

Roger got to his feet and went to the window. "Yes, it *is* possible," he said in a flat voice. "She *told* me they were betrothed."

"Roger! Are you saying that you *knew* something like this would happen?"

Roger stared out at the relentless rain. "No, for I refused to believe it. What a fool I've been! I could have *sworn* she didn't care a fig for him!"

"She don't," Katie said decidedly.

Lady Denham looked at Katie with disapproval. She had forgotten the girl was there. It was most improper for them to discuss the matter before a servant, and even more improper for the girl to interject her views. But Roger turned and was eyeing the girl with interest. "What do you mean, Katie? Explain yourself."

"I hardly think, Roger," his mother said in gentle rebuke, "that it is at all seemly to discuss this matter with Katie."

"Let's forget the proprieties, Mama. This is too important for me to worry about trivial conventions. Go on, Katie."

Katie looked at Lady Denham hesitantly, but Lady Denham shrugged and waved an approving hand at her. "My son is right, girl," she said. "Go ahead and tell us."

"I think Lord Denham 'ad the right of it," Katie explained. "Miss Letty never talked about Mr. Peake, nor thought about 'im, neither." She met Roger's eye and added challengingly, "She cried o' nights for some *other* gent, not 'im."

Roger's gaze wavered under Katie's forthright challenge. Lady Denham asked, "How do you know, Katie, that it was some 'other gent' for whom she cried?"

"She 'adn't no reason to cry over Mr. Peake," Katie said bluntly.

Roger gave a short, mirthless laugh. "You're quite a knowing one, aren't you, Katie?"

Katie smiled broadly. "That's what everyone says."

"And you didn't tell us all this just to poke bogey, did you, girl?"

"No, sir. I ain't no blabbin' chaffer-mouth."

"Then, if you didn't say all this to tell tales, you had

another reason. You want something of me, isn't that it? Well, what is it you want me to do?"

"*Stop* 'er, o' course!"

"And how am I to do that?"

"It's a longish ride to Gretna, ain't it? And I don't suppose they call you a bruisin' rider for nothin'."

Roger rubbed his chin speculatively. "I have no rights in this—no claims," he murmured, half to himself. "She's given me no right to interfere—"

"Who's worried about trivial conventions now?" his mother asked, her eyes dancing in excitement.

"Mama!" Roger said in surprise. "Are *you* telling me to go after her?"

"Are *you* the 'other gent' who made her 'cry o' nights'?" Lady Denham countered.

Roger looked from his mother to the abigail. They were both watching him intently. He colored. "I *think* I am," he admitted.

"Then stop her, Roger, before it's too late," his mother urged warmly.

"Come on then, Katie-from-the-kitchen. I'll take you back to Lady Upsham and tell her my intentions. Mama, I hope you can manage without your carriage for a day or two. This expedition may take quite a while." With a quick kiss on his mother's cheek, he strode out the door, pulling little Katie firmly behind him.

Lady Upsham's household was in a turmoil. Her ladyship had discovered the absence of her niece by late morning and had sent for Prue. The two had repaired to the sitting room where, for more than an hour, Prue had had to endure an emotional harangue. The word had spread among the servants that some crisis of an extremely delicate nature was transpiring, and each of them managed to find some excuse to linger about in the corridor outside the sitting room until Miss Tristle and the butler took stations at each end of the hallway and kept them away. In the midst of this *contretemps,* an agitated Mrs. Peake had made her appearance. She had been ushered into the sitting room, and from then on the sounds of her shrill and hysterical outbursts could be heard all the way down the corridor, making a dramatic contrast to the low, ironically bitter tones of Lady Upsham's voice.

It was at this awkward moment that Lord Denham and Katie arrived at the door. The butler tried to discourage his lordship from entering, but Lord Denham ignored him and demanded to be announced to Lady Upsham at once. The butler tried to tell him that Lady Upsham was already engaged. "With Mrs. Peake, I presume," Lord Denham remarked drily, and walked past him into the sitting room, with Katie close behind.

The tension in the room was almost tangible. Lady Upsham stood near the fireplace, her cheeks pale and her lips compressed. Pacing about the room nervously was Mrs. Peake, her entire expression revealing the utmost agitation. In the corner farthest from the door sat Prue. Her hair had not been dressed, her eyes were stormy and red-rimmed, her face was strained and she twisted a handkerchief tightly through her fingers. Lady Upsham did not take kindly to the sight of the intruders. She fixed a cold eye on Roger and said curtly, "Lord Denham, I'm afraid you find me occupied with Mrs. Peake on pressing business. I must beg you to excuse us. I shall be happy to receive you at some future time."

"Forgive this intrusion, ma'am," Roger said, undeterred, "but your pressing business is also mine. I have some information for both you and Mrs. Peake and must advise you of it *at once.*"

Lady Upsham recognized the determination of his jaw and promptly waved the butler away. Then turning her eye on Katie, she tried to dismiss her as well. But Roger suggested that she might prove useful in their talk, and the girl was permitted to remain. "I stopped in to tell you, ma'am, that you need not worry about Letty. I leave immediately to follow the pair, and I hope to restore her to you safely before long."

Mrs. Peake gasped audibly. "How did you know?" she asked in a high, horrified voice. "Did Brandon tell you?"

"No, Mrs. Peake. It was Katie who brought me the information."

Lady Upsham's eyebrows shot up. "How dared you, Katie? Have you no loyalty? Is this how you repay Miss Letty's kindnesses to you—by spreading this terrible tale all over town?"

"No, Lady Upsham, you're out there," Roger intervened. "The girl is no gossip. She told only my mother and me, and you may surely count on our discretion."

"But she shouldn't have told *anybody*!" Lady Upsham said unyielding. "Why didn't you come to *me*, you ninny?"

Prue spoke up from her corner in a tone of sullen disgust. "What good would it have done to come to *you*, Aunt Millicent? What could you have done about it?"

"That's exactly the point," Roger agreed. "You could not have ridden after her. That's why Katie thought of me."

"I don't see what *you* have to do with all this," Mrs. Peake said petulantly. "These Glendenning girls have a way of embroiling outsiders into their affairs in a manner I cannot like."

"I'm afraid, Mrs. Peake, that this whole bumble-broth is more my doing than Miss Glendenning's. I suspect strongly that it was I who drove Letty to this pass. But I'm sure that I can straighten it all out, one way or another, and bring Letty back unharmed. Have I your permission to try, Lady Upsham?"

Lady Upsham looked up at him with such intense relief that her eyes became misty. Not given to sentiment, however, she did not shed a tear. She merely favored him with a tremulous smile and asked hopefully, "Are you sure you can catch them, Lord Denham? I believe they set out more than five hours ago."

"I'll catch them," Roger said reassuringly, "and before nightfall, too. So you may rest easy, ma'am." And with a quick bow to Mrs. Peake, he went quickly to the door. There he found his way blocked by a determined Prue.

"You shan't go," she declared. "Not without me."

"I'm touched by your concern for your sister," Roger said with gentle irony, "but there's no need for—"

"My sister? Do you think I'm concerned for my *sister*? You and Aunt Millicent have enough concern for her to make mine completely unnecessary. Letty, Letty, Letty—that's all I've heard! She's the only one you're worried about. What about *Brandon*? Has anyone given any thought to what *his* feelings might be when you ride up and wrest Letty away from him?"

"Well, *really*, Miss Glendenning!" Mrs. Peake declared coldly, "I fail to see how Brandon's feelings can be any concern of yours. I am his mother, after all, and *I* am convinced that a bit of humiliation will be an edifying lesson for him."

Prue stared, large-eyed, at Mrs. Peake and opened her mouth to remonstrate. Something made her change her mind. Brandon would not like it, she realized, if she engaged in a squabble with his mother. Ignoring her comment, she turned back to Roger and said in an urgent undervoice, "Please, Lord Denham, I *must* go! Take me with you!"

"I warn you, young lady, that it will not be a pleasure trip. We will not make any but the briefest stops, you will be jostled about unmercifully, and you will find me in no mood for idle conversation."

"Nothing you've said deters me in the least," she assured him.

"And I won't wait for you to change your clothes or dress your hair."

"I need only to put on a shawl."

Roger looked questioningly at Lady Upsham. Her ladyship, sore beset, put her hands to her forehead, sighed and made a helpless gesture of consent. Roger gave Prue a quick grin. "Come along then, minx. We've wasted too much time already."

Prue gave a little cry of joy and reached up to hug Roger gratefully.

"Lady Upsham," Mrs. Peake objected, "surely you don't intend to permit that child to involve herself in such a pursuit—!"

"Surely, Mrs. Peake, you do not mean to interfere with my judgment in—"

But Roger did not wait for more. With a wink and a wave to Katie, he grasped Prue's hand, and the two ran out to the carriage, leaving the ladies to continue their dispute without witnesses.

Chapter NINETEEN

IN HIS HURRIED planning for the trip to Scotland, Brandon had anticipated reaching Wolverhampton by nightfall. But the rain had turned some of the roads to mud, had slowed the horses and had so dampened the spirits of the driver that, by four that afternoon, they were only a short way past Worcester. By this time, Letty and Brandon were both regretting the rashness of their decision to engage in this enterprise. Brandon had been shivering in his damp clothes and soggy boots all day. He was now chilled to the bone. His head had begun to ache, his eyes were clouded, and there was a persistent and painful tickle in his throat. He knew the signs—he would, by nightfall, be very sick indeed.

Letty was also damp and cold. Her shoes had been so badly soaked during her wait in the rain that they were quite ruined, the inner lining cracking and curling and causing her additional discomfort. Even more disturbing was the growing doubt in her mind of Brandon's ability to see to the practical matters involved in a long journey. She was depressed by the prospect of her future—a future which now seemed considerably less bearable than it had appeared when Brandon had described it. He'd spent the first four hours of the trip telling her about the dramatic intrigue of the *Choephoroe*, but the Greek names had so confused Letty that Brandon had felt it necessary to lecture at length on the genealogy of the House of Atreus. This only confused her further, and her mind wandered to other matters. She was beginning to realize that, while

Brandon was brilliant on the subject of the classics, he was vague and absent-minded about the practical matters of life. At a toll gate, he had caused a considerable delay while he searched through all his pockets for a coin (which Letty finally supplied from her reticule), and he would, more than once, have taken the wrong road had not Letty been watchful. But he had gone on and on about Agamemnon and Clytemnestra and their impossible offspring until Letty was sorely tempted to tell him that it was time for school to be out. At length, however, even *he* had tired of the subject. They had lapsed into silence—a brooding, empty, isolating silence.

They had gone a little way north of Ombersley when Letty noticed that Brandon looked ill. Over his objections, she insisted that they stop at the nearest inn for the night. They both needed rest and warmth, she pointed out, and she would prefer to *sleep* through the rain than *drive* through any more of it. Brandon, too weak to argue, turned the carriage into the courtyard of a small, thatched inn whose lights had beckoned invitingly to them through the gathering shadows.

From the curious and somewhat discourteous glance of the innkeeper when they entered, Letty became uncomfortably aware of the shabby appearance they made. Their clothes were badly wrinkled and soggy, their hair matted, and even their luggage was meagre and unprepossessing. Brandon wearily requested two bedrooms for the night and, turning to Letty, asked if she would mind dreadfully taking her dinner alone. He was not hungry. A warm bed was all he wanted. Letty assured him that she would manage well enough on her own. Brandon bespoke a private parlor for her and limped tiredly up the stairs.

A young boy brought in their things. Letty followed him up the stairs to see to the distribution of their boxes and to make sure that fires were lighted in their bedrooms. She told the boy to give Mr. Peake assistance in his undressing, and after settling everything upstairs to her satisfaction, she went down again to procure some hot soup for Brandon to drink before he fell asleep. This time she was greeted by the innkeeper's wife. The woman was robust and red-cheeked, and Letty would have assumed her to be a cheerful, warm-hearted country wife except for her narrow eyes and thin lips which combined to give her a sour expression strangely inappropriate when combined with her apple-dumpling appearance. The narrow eyes surveyed Letty with obvious suspicion and disdain, taking due note of the wrinkled gown and ruined shoes. Letty requested the soup. The woman, after a moment's hesitation, nodded a surly acquiescence and went off to prepare it, her reluctance apparent in every step she took.

Letty herself took the soup to Brandon and sat beside him while he drank. His cheeks were flushed and feverish, and though she kept up a flow of cheerful conversation, her heart failed her. What would she do if Brandon became seriously ill? He handed the bowl to her with a grateful smile and slid down under the covers. He was asleep almost at once.

She tiptoed from the room and, having two hours to wait before dinner, went to her room, removed her damp clothing with relief and lay down to rest. She, too, was soon asleep. She woke with a start to find the room in darkness. She didn't know how long she'd slept. Quickly she dressed in a fresh gown, brushed and tied back her hair and went out. She opened the door to Brandon's room. He was still asleep, and she was relieved to hear his steady, unobstructed breathing. Perhaps he was not as ill as she had feared. A good night's sleep might be sufficient to restore him to health. If he were sufficiently recovered by morning, and if the sun shone at last, the prospects for the future might seem a little brighter.

With the return of more hopeful spirits, Letty realized that she was very hungry. She went down the stairs and found the innkeeper in the taproom where he was busily supplying tall mugs of home-brew to a surprisingly large number of locals. Evidently the weather had not deterred his patrons from seeking their nightly refreshment. She learned from the innkeeper that it was after eight. Requesting her dinner, she went to the private parlor where she took a seat before the fire and tried to relax. After only a moment there was a tap on the door, and the innkeeper came in, followed closely by his wife. The innkeeper, embarrassed, took only a couple of awkward steps into the room. He stood blinking at Letty wordlessly. His wife, however, came in purposefully, closed the door and, with a deeper frown than was usual with her, poked her husband in the back with an angry forefinger.

"Excuse me, ma'am," the innkeeper said hesitantly, "but we was wonderin'—that is, my wife here was wonderin—if you could see your way clear to . . . to . . ."

"Yes?" asked Letty encouragingly.

The innkeeper glanced dubiously at his wife. She glared at him in disgust and took over the matter herself. "We was wonderin' if you'd be so good as to pay yer shot now," she said grimly and shot a look at her husband which seemed to say that *that* was how to deal with suspicious-looking customers.

"Now?" Letty asked, nonplussed. "But . . . I don't understand. Is it customary to demand payment before the end of one's stay?"

"Well . . ." the innkeeper began.

"Don't care if it is or it ain't," his wife said flatly. "You come in 'ere wantin' two bedrooms 'stead of one and askin' fer the private parlor like you was a duchess. Well, how're we to know if you've so much as a copperjohn in yer pocket?"

"I can assure you, madam, that your reckoning will be paid in full," Letty said sternly.

"That's all well 'n good, but assurances don't ring near so good as brass," the woman said insolently. "A night like this'n is always busy fer us. We had *two parties* we turned away because you took the bedrooms, ain't I right, Joddy?"

The innkeeper nodded. "It *is* a busy night, ma'am," he said sheepishly.

"And now you want dinner, after I already let the fire die out," the woman complained. "This ain't the royal kitchen, y'know. We ain't inclined to 'ave dinner at all hours."

"There's no need to upset yourself over that," Letty said calmly. "Some cold meat and a piece of bread should do quite well."

"Cold meat or hot, I'd like to 'ear the clink o' yer guineas," she retorted.

"I'd be glad to oblige," Letty explained curtly, "but my . . . but Mr. Peake is not feeling well and is fast asleep. I would rather not disturb him just now. You shall have your money first thing in the morning."

The woman sneered and folded her arms across her chest adamantly. "It's now, my lady, or out you go," she declared.

Letty gasped and looked questioningly at the innkeeper. He shrugged helplessly. "Sorry, ma'am," was all he said.

Letty got stiffly to her feet and, with head erect, walked out of the room. She ran quickly up the stairs, tapped on Brandon's door and went in. He didn't stir. Reluctantly, she shook his shoulder. With a groan, he turned over and blinked up at her. "Letty," he mumbled hoarsely, "what—?"

"Sorry to wake you, Brandon, but I've just had a rather uncomfortable scene with the innkeepers. They want us to pay them *now*."

Brandon rubbed his eyes and reached for the spectacles he had placed on a table near the bed. He put them on and peered at her, trying to get his brain to function. "Pay them?" he muttered thickly. "Yes, of course. Just take the—" Suddenly he sat bolt upright, his eyes wide awake and staring in alarm. "Money! Good God, Letty, I've forgotten to take any money!"

Letty paled. "Oh, Brandon, no!"

He clapped his hand to his aching forehead, and a croaking sound came from his throat. "What a complete *fool* I am! What are we to do now?"

For a moment Letty stared at him in disbelief. How *could* he have been so disordered? She felt a wave of revulsion for so muddle-headed a man. But immediately, the injustice of her feelings became apparent to her. She had *begged* him to do this for her. He had been safe and comfortable and content with his life. It was *she* who had turned his world upside down, brought him to this miserable inn, sick and penniless. *She* was the muddle-headed one. Whatever had possessed her to involve him in her life, to *use* him for her own selfish purposes? If she had any character at all, she would release him from his promise and set him free.

But this was not the time for such thoughts. He was sick, and his eyes were desperately worried. She bent over him and put a cool hand on his forehead. "There, now," she said soothingly, "don't look so alarmed. I shall simply tell the man to trust us for a while." She took off his spectacles and helped him to settle himself into the pillows again.

"Do you think he will?" Brandon asked, eager to believe that they were not so close to disaster as he had feared.

"Of course he will," Letty said with a cheerfulness she was far from feeling.

"But what about money? Where can we procure some money?"

"Don't worry about that now. Let's get a good night's sleep. We'll think of something in the morning."

Brandon sighed. "Very well, Letty. Sorry I'm such an absentminded idiot. Goodnight, my dear."

Letty went out and closed the door. She paused for a moment on the landing to brace herself for the ordeal ahead. Then she went firmly down the stairs. The innkeeper and his wife were waiting at the foot. "I'm sorry," she told them without mincing words, "but I'm afraid we could not put our hands on the money tonight. You will have to trust us until tomorrow."

"*Trust* you? Do y'think we're loobies? You can pack yer things right now and take yerselves off."

"What are you saying?" Letty asked, trying to control her agitation. "You cannot mean to put us out at this hour . . . and on such a night?"

The innkeeper turned to his wife diffidently. "She's right, pet. It ain't human to send 'em off in this downpour."

His wife fixed him with a glare of such animosity that Letty quailed. "Keep yer sneezer out o' this if you've nothing better to say, you cod's-head!" she sneered at him. "We ain't in the business o' givin' charity. If this fancy-piece and her chap upstairs ain't out o' here in a quarter-hour, you can pick 'em up by their tails and heave 'em out the door!"

A gust of wind and spray of rain behind them caused them to turn their heads toward the outer door. It had opened. Impressively filling the dimly lit doorway stood the most elegant gentleman the innkeepers had ever seen. His tall, rain-spattered beaver, his driving coat with its six capes, the high boots which gleamed under a spattering of mud all proclaimed the Corinthian. The innkeepers gaped, and even Letty was struck by the imposing figure before her. It wasn't until he spoke that she realized who he was. "Mind your malignant tongue, woman!" he was saying to the innkeeper's wife in coldly imperious accents. "Apologize to the lady *at once*!"

"*Roger!*" cried Letty joyously and, completely without thought but with a sensation of glorious relief at the sight of him, she ran to the door and flung herself into his arms. "I've never been so glad to see anyone in all my life!" The terror of the last few moments vanished like the remnants of a nightmare, and she clung to him with the instinctive wisdom of a drowning child for his rescuer. She had been battling an antagonistic world all day, a world which had persistently presented her with larger and larger obstacles. She had pushed herself and Brandon into such deep waters that it had seemed they must drown, but Roger's sudden appearance had changed all that. Her prospects no longer had the power to overwhelm her. She was safe. With her head pressed against his shoulder, she surrendered to the tears that had been held just beneath the surface throughout this deplorable day.

Roger, amazed by the unexpected warmth of her welcome, held her closely to him in speechless gratification. He had no knowledge of the circumstances which had brought her to this pass, and he suspected that she would soon come to her senses and reconsider—with regret—her rash greeting. But in this brief, unguarded moment, she had revealed something of the depth of her feelings for him, and suddenly his prospects seemed brighter, too.

For an instant, he forgot his surroundings, the people who watched, the wind and the rain blowing at his back, and the reason why he came. His arms tightened around her, and he laid his cheek against her hair. Letty felt the movement of his arms and came to her senses with a jerk. She pulled herself from his arms and stammered guiltily, "Oh! I didn't mean to . . . that is I . . . I must explain why I—good God! *Prue*!"

Prue, who had been standing just behind Roger and watching the scene with fascination, could not help smiling. "I'm glad to find that *someone* has taken notice of me at last," she said. "I shall be drenched if I'm not permitted to come in out of the rain at once."

"Oh, indeed, come in, Miss," the innkeeper said hastily, ushering them all toward the private parlor with repeated and obsequious bows.

"I'm that upset that I disconstrued you, ma'am," the innkeeper's wife said to Letty with painful eagerness, "but I didn't know . . . I mean, if I'd know'd you was related to *this* gent 'ere . . ." But no one paid her any heed. With a great number of exclamations, gasps and half-uttered questions, they made their way into the private parlor.

"How did you find us?" Letty asked repeatedly. "And what are you doing here?"

Roger refused to discuss anything until he had disposed of the innkeeper and his wife, who remained at the door watching the goings-on with open-mouthed interest. "I shall leave Prue to explain how and why we're here," he said, "while I deal with our hosts and make arrangements for dinner and bedchambers. But when I return, my girl," he added, taking Letty's chin in his hand and forcing her to look up at him, "you and I are going to have a long, long talk." Letty was disconcerted by the unmistakable twinkle in his eye. It was there for no good reason that she could ascertain, unless he had exaggerated the significance of her greeting. She would have some arduous explaining to do.

As soon as the parlor door closed behind him, Letty turned to her sister and hugged her effusively. "I never *dreamed* you'd come after me," she exclaimed in astonishment. "Whatever made you do such a foolhardy thing? And why did you persuade Lord Denham to accompany you? That was beyond anything! I should really be angry at you, you know, except that I am so glad to see you that I shan't scold at all."

"Scold!" Prue said contemptuously. "You are in no position to scold anyone, Letty Glendenning! Eloping in that wild way! Whatever possessed you?"

"I refuse to answer any of your questions until you answer mine. Why did you bring Lord Denham with you?"

"I didn't bring him—he brought me," Prue said, taking off her shawl and settling near the fire. "He was coming alone, but I begged him to let me come along."

"But why did he wish to—? And how did he learn that I—?"

"Katie told him."

"Katie?" Letty asked incredulously. "But... *why*?"

"She thinks Roger is the perfect man for you... and so do I."

Letty's expression clouded over, and she frowned at her sister in annoyance. "My thanks to you both," she said tartly. "You know nothing whatsoever about the matter, either of you. Therefore, your opinions are worthless, and I'd be obliged if you both would refrain from expressing them."

"And *I'd* be obliged if you'd refrain from running off with a man for whom you care nothing," Prue retorted.

Letty gave Prue a startled glance. "What do you mean? Why do you say *that*?"

"I can tell. You've never even talked to me about him."

"I may not talk about him," Letty said, trying to convince herself as much as her sister, "but that doesn't mean that I don't think highly of all his admirable qualities."

"Well, *I* don't think of his 'admirable qualities' at all, and I—" She stopped, flushed and looked down at the floor.

Letty, arrested, stared at her sister. "Prue! What are you saying?"

Prue bit her lip. "I only mean that love doesn't have anything to do with *admirable qualities.* One can love someone without finding him so very admirable... I believe..."

Letty ran to her sister and knelt beside the chair. "Oh, Prue," she said softly, "you don't mean that you... you can't mean *Brandon*!"

Prue nodded and looked at her sister with a rueful smile. "Isn't it shocking? I know he's stodgy and stuffy and impossibly priggish, but... Oh, Letty, it's all midsummer moon with me!"

Letty looked up at her sister aghast. "But I had no *idea*...! Why did you never *tell* me?"

"I wanted to, Letty, truly, I *longed* to talk to you about him. But you've been so abstracted... so troubled... and you didn't seem to want to talk to me about it..."

Letty was deeply shamed. She'd been so self-absorbed, she'd taken no notice of what had been happening to her sister. She rose and turned to the fire. "I've been completely selfish," she said, deeply humiliated. "I never even *noticed*... and you must have had a difficult time of it! Can you forgive me, Prue?"

Prue stood up and joined her sister at the fire. "Don't be a goosecap," she said, slipping an arm around her sister's waist. "Just tell me truly if *you* care for him."

Letty grinned. "If today was an indication of the sort of life Brandon and I would have together, we neither of us could have borne it for a week! No, my dear. I've been completely foolish to have imagined that the two of us could make a match." She glanced at her sister cautiously. "But, Prue, are you sure that *you* would be happy with him?"

"You're asking if I could bear his by-your-leaves and his quotations and his endless prosings about his old Greeks, is that it?" Prue laughed.

"Yes, dearest, I am. And his absentmindedness, and his disregard for the practicalities, and... Prue, to be truthful, he is so *different* from you," Letty said with a worried frown.

Prue gave her an affectionate squeeze. "I know all that," she said with a reassuring smile, "but he doesn't dare prose on to *me* about Euripides and Catullus. He needs someone like me to enliven him, Letty, really he does. And I need him to... settle me down."

Letty stared at her sister with dawning admiration. The girl was right. Prue had always been practical and down-to-earth. She would enjoy seeing to Brandon's mundane needs—making sure that his hat was firmly on his head, his spectacles on his nose and his money in his pocket. She would tease him into displaying the charm that lay beneath his scholarly disposition, and she would bring enchantment to his hitherto ordinary existence. And *he* would curb the excesses of her volatile nature. They would undoubtedly quarrel and rub against each other frequently, but they would never spend a day of tedium such as *she* and Brandon had endured today. And it was Prue herself, not yet eighteen, who had realized all this. She had grown up these past few weeks, right before

Letty's eyes, and Letty, to her shame, had not noticed.

"What have you done with him, Letty?" Prue asked suddenly. "I haven't caught a glimpse of him. Why wasn't he with you while you were holding off that dragon of a woman at the door?"

"Oh, dear, I've forgotten to tell you. I'm afraid he's contracted a chill. He was quite feverish and went to bed immediately upon our arrival."

"Then I'll go to him at once," Prue said and started for the door.

But Letty suggested that this would not be the time for a meeting between them. He would be groggy, ill and bewildered. The morning would be soon enough, she reasoned, to confront him with the many surprises which he had in store. Prue, exhibiting the new maturity that had so amazed her sister, soon saw the wisdom of Letty's suggestion and agreed to curb her impatience.

Roger had been waiting outside to permit Letty and Prue to have their *tête-à-tête*, but now he entered and announced that all the arrangements had been made and that supper would immediately be served. Although the tiny inn contained no bedrooms other than the two that Brandon and Letty had taken, which meant that Roger would be forced to sleep on a narrow cot in Brandon's room and that Prue would share Letty's bed, Roger had managed to arrange a feast sumptuous enough to be worthy of a much grander establishment. The innkeeper's wife had evidently rekindled her fire without complaint, for she served them generously with steaming hot roast pork, a neck of mutton smothered in onions, a couple of small stuffed chickens, a currant pudding, a custard pudding and all the tea, hot punch and cool ale they could possibly want. These were served with such ingratiating smiles and affable manners that Letty could barely suppress her laughter at the woman's miraculous transformation.

When the meal was done, Prue tactfully excused herself and went to bed. Letty tried to follow, but Roger forcibly detained her. "I haven't driven all these miles to be cheated out of my chance to give you a proper scold, my girl," he said, taking her arm and leading her to the chair before the fire. "Why did you do such a shatterbrained thing?"

"It *was* shatterbrained, my lord. I'm most dreadfully sorry, and I can only express my gratitude to you for saving me from the consequences of my folly," she said carefully.

"Have we returned to 'my lord' again? If you really wish to express your gratitude, call me by my Christian name. You managed it quite beautifully, I thought, earlier this evening," he said with a mischievous gleam.

"As to that, my l—. Roger," she said, coloring, "I wish you will not refine on it too much. I was most sorely pressed, as you saw. It was so horrible to contemplate being forcibly ejected from this place, with Brandon feverish and the rain pouring down, that the sight of... of a friendly face was an overwhelming relief. I... may have passed the bounds a bit in my gratitude..."

Roger sighed. "Are you going to pretend that the look on your face was *gratitude*?" Discouraged, he turned away, leaned on the mantel and stared into the fire. "Letty, when will you bring yourself to speak your mind to me, honestly and openly?"

"There are some things that cannot easily be spoken between us. Yet I've tried to be as honest with you as I could, sir."

"*Anything* can be spoken of between us, Letty," he said, turning to her with a compelling look. "And now must be the time. We've been moving at cross-purposes for too long. Both of us have been guilty of some dishonesty and evasion, and the problems between us have not been resolved. Perhaps it is time to try some frankness."

"Very well, you may be right. Where would you like to begin, sir?"

"Shall we begin with Brandon? Do you want to marry him?"

Letty lowered her eyes. "No," she said in a small voice.

"I've behaved disgracefully in that respect. I made him lie to you about our betrothal. And this stupid elopement is all my doing. He never cared for me, except as a friend. In fact—" She looked up at him with a wry smile. "In fact, I shan't be surprised to learn that he has had a tendre for Prue all this time."

"I'm sure he does. I'm glad you've realized it. I didn't relish the idea of convincing you of the possibility."

"But, how did *you* realize it?" Letty asked in surprise.

"I watched and listened. I had to learn if you truly cared for him, you see. But when it comes to *you*, my wishes get in the way of my eyes. I was never certain. Tell me, my dear, *do* you care for him?"

Letty shook her head wordlessly.

"And I was right," Roger went on, "in assuming that the betrothal was concocted to keep *me* at arm's length?"

"Yes," Letty admitted shamefacedly.

"Don't look so miserable, my love," Roger said with an ironic smile. "The fact that you needed to trick me is more my fault than yours."

"Wh... What do you mean?" Letty asked falteringly. She knew that they now approached the subject that would be most painful for her to discuss. She didn't want to discuss it. She wanted, more than anything, to end this interview and go to bed. But she realized that there was no other way for her to make Roger understand that she could never marry him but to face the real reason for her refusal. So she clenched her hands in her lap and prepared herself for the ordeal to come.

"It is now *my* turn for honesty," he began. "I know the subject is a difficult one for a young lady as delicately reared and as sensitive as you, but you *must* let me explain my behavior." He turned back to the fire and spoke with some difficulty. "If, when I've finished, you still find the thought of marriage to me too... repellent, I shall not trouble you again."

For a moment he fell silent. She found that she was holding her breath. He didn't turn but spoke quietly into the fire, feeling that he could not face the look of revulsion he feared he might see in her eyes. "I didn't know you were aware that I had a mistress when I first asked you to marry me. I had no recollection of that night in Vauxhall, when you first learned of it. But you must believe that the liaison would not have continued once I had married. Kitty . . . Mrs. Brownell has always understood that my relationship with her would end when I married." He took a deep breath. "There is something even more important that I beg you will believe. I didn't bring her to Bath. Since my first evening here, I haven't given her a single thought. She arrived the day of the fireworks display and surprised me as much as she did you. And I didn't come to you again until I had severed all ties between us. The relationship never signified anything very important in my life, and its ending gave me great relief. It's not a thing I'm proud of, Letty, but I don't believe it means that I can never be a loyal, honest and faithful husband."

"Roger," Letty whispered shakily. "I . . . thank you for telling me, but . . ."

"There's something else," Roger said, turning and kneeling before her chair, "I must say *something* about my monstrous treatment of you at Vauxhall—"

Letty held up a restraining hand. "Roger, no—"

"I must. I know how the experience must have disturbed you. I've not been able to forgive myself since the moment I realized that it was you who—"

"Please don't go on. This isn't necessary, I promise you. It was a mistake. I don't blame you at all," she said earnestly.

He grasped her hands and looked at her closely. "But it *was* the barrier that kept you from accepting me, was it not? Tell me the truth, Letty."

She stared at him and then nodded slowly.

He winced. "Oh, my darling," he groaned, "what can I do? I cannot undo what I did that night. But listen to me, Letty, please! I promise you that I will never, never use you so again." He lowered his head until it rested on their clasped hands. "If we were wed," he said in a low voice, "I would treat you with the utmost gentleness. I need not be the kind of man whom you met that night in the gardens. I will be as tender and restrained as a bride could desire."

There was no answer. He looked up at her questioningly. She was staring at him with an enigmatic, wide-eyed expression he could not fathom, as if she were seeing him—or herself—for the first time. "No, Roger, no," she said in a voice that trembled in pain and surprise. "You don't understand. I'm not the girl you think me. I can't be the kind of wife you want. Please let me go. There's no use in talking any more—I don't think I could ever explain it to you. I'm not sure I can explain it to myself. But I can't marry you."

She stood up and made for the door, but he jumped to his feet and caught her arm. "No!" he said, baffled. "You aren't making sense!" He whirled her around so that she fell against him, and he held her fast. "Look at me, Letty," he ordered, lifting her face and forcing her to meet his eyes. "Are you trying to tell me you don't love me? Is that it?"

She looked up with a level gaze. "I'm not trying to tell you anything," she said in a voice that strained to remain steady. "We've already said too much. Perhaps, sometimes, a man and a woman are not suited, no matter what they feel for one another. Let me go, Roger. It's for the best."

He stared at her uncomprehendingly, but the firmness in her eyes seemed unanswerable. There was a frightening finality in her expression. His arms dropped from her, and she stepped back. She took one last look at his face, which was clouded with bewilderment and a kind of numb despair, and she ran from the room.

But even when she had closed the door behind her, climbed the stairs to her room, undressed in the darkness and lain, wide-eyed, in her bed through the weary hours of the night, she could not erase from her mind the look of his face, staring at her with the haunting persistence of a reproachful ghost.

Chapter TWENTY

BRANDON OPENED HIS eyes to bright sunlight streaming into the little window set in a dormer on the other side of his room. His head felt clearer than it had last night, and the sunlight seemed to offer some hope that today might turn out to be less wretched than yesterday. He yawned, stretched, and wondered how long he'd slept. He felt as if he'd slept a week. He raised himself on his elbow to see if he could ascertain the position of the sun to give himself some inkling of the time of day. In front of the window he saw a blur of something that looked like red-gold hair. Puzzled, he put out his hand, felt gingerly on the top of the table for his spectacles and carefully put them on. His vision cleared, and he looked again at the red-gold blur. "Prue!" he gasped.

She was sitting on the window seat, watching him with a half-smile. "Good morning, Brandon," she said with unusual sweetness.

"What on earth—?" He sat up in bed, pulling the blankets up to his neck. "What are you doing here?"

"Do you mean here, in your room, or here in an inn on the road to Gretna Green?"

"I don't know what I mean," he answered, bemused. "Does Letty know you're here?"

"Yes, indeed. We arrived last night and had dinner together."

"We?"

"Roger and I."

"Oh, is Roger with you?" Brandon asked with a feeling

of relief. "Good. Then I'll be able to borrow some blunt." He put his hand to his forehead as his last conversation with Letty came back to him. "I was idiotic enough to go off on an elopement without a farthing in my pocket."

"I'm not at all surprised," Prue remarked cheerfully. "You need someone to remind you of such mundane matters. After all, you have more important things on your mind."

Brandon frowned and regarded her through narrowed eyes. "Even if that remark is meant as a slur on my studies, I shall ignore it. I have no wish to bandy words with you. Why have you come, anyway? Does Roger think he can stop our plans?"

"I believe he already has."

Brandon peered at her. "What? Is Letty going to marry him after all?"

"I don't know. But I believe she'd decided not to marry *you*," Prue explained matter-of-factly, though her eyes were fixed on his face attentively.

"Oh? She has? Why?"

"I think she feels that you don't quite suit."

"I see," Brandon said thoughtfully.

Prue came up to his bedside. "You don't seem very brokenhearted, Brandon," she remarked casually.

"I'm not. To be honest, it was to be a *mariage de convenance*, as the French say."

"And how would the Greeks say it?" Prue teased.

He glared at her for a moment and then returned to his train of thought. "I didn't think it a very good idea, even from the beginning. But since Letty and I had both decided we wanted no more of love, we thought we might brush through. But I think Letty is wise to change her mind. The affair augered ill, and it would not do to 'purchase regret at such a price,' to use the words of Demosthenes."

"Why do you want no more of love, Brandon?" Prue asked brazenly. "And don't answer in the words of

Demosthenes, if you please. I'd like to hear your own words."

"I fell in love once," he said, with a sidelong glance at her face, "but I found the experience too painful."

"Did you? Why?"

"Because the young lady was frivolous, unpredictable and an incorrigible flirt," Brandon said sternly.

"Was she?" Prue said softly, sitting down on the edge of the bed.

"Yes, she was," Brandon declared, throwing caution to the winds. "She called me a stuffy prig, pushed me out of a carriage in the most callous way, and the last time I saw her, she was in the arms of a man-about-town old enough to be her father."

"Really?" Prue said, lowering her lashes in quite fetching remorse. "That was quite dreadful of her, and I'm sure she must be very sorry."

"Do you think so?" Brandon asked, his heart beginning to leap about in his chest in a most disturbing way.

The lowered lashes fluttered. "Oh, yes, I'm sure of it."

"But I thought... It seemed to me... that she had set her heart on becoming Mrs. Eberly."

"Gudgeon! How could she, when her heart has been set on a much more... scholarly type of gentleman?"

"Prue!" He grasped her hands. "You can't mean it!"

"Brandon," Prue said, her lips curled in a mischievous smile and her eyelids fluttering up at him distractingly, "have you ever... kissed anyone?"

He leaned toward her, pulse racing and mind bedazzled in a most unscholarly way. "I'm... afraid not," he admitted, somewhat breathlessly. "I've always been too preoccupied... with the Greeks... to kiss anyone."

"Neither have I," Prue said, her arms stealing around his neck, "but I don't think it can be very difficult..."

Letty had had a most troublesome night. She had reviewed her conversation with Roger over and over. The pain in his eyes had haunted her, but she could think of nothing she could have done to avoid the necessity of causing him pain, short of agreeing to marry him. That she couldn't do. Nothing had changed. It was still clear that he wanted a wife who was—how had he put it?—'delicately reared and sensitive.' After all the talk, all their time together, all the occasions when they had seemed to be attuned to each other, he still expected her to be the girl her Aunt Millicent had described to his mother so many months ago—well-bred, gracious, serene, dutiful and obedient. To play that role, to live with Roger in the polite, indifferent manner of so many other 'arranged' marriages, would be more than she could bear. But as the night had worn on, and she had tried to imagine what that life would be like, and to compare it to the life that now faced her—a life in which she would dwindle into an old maid, to play the fond aunt to her sisters' children, to be the 'extra guest' at dinner parties, to take in cats to have something to love, and to spend her old age dreaming of what might have been—she couldn't help but wonder if the proper and discreet life offered by Roger might not be more bearable than *that*.

She couldn't answer. She was completely ignorant of married life, her father having died before she was old enough to have made sensible observations about her parents' life together, and Aunt Millicent, too, having been widowed early. Perhaps she should discuss the matter with Roger, openly and honestly, as he had suggested. They had been able to talk about Mrs. Brownell quite satisfactorily. Perhaps she could bring herself to explain to him that she was not the delicate, obedient, polite girl that he had supposed her to be. Even if he then decided that she was not a proper wife for him, she would at least have the satisfaction of seeing that haunting look of pain leave his eyes.

By the time the first faint light of dawn had crept into her window, she had decided that she would talk to him first thing in the morning. With a feeling of contentment such as she had not had in weeks, she'd closed her eyes and fallen into a peaceful sleep.

When she awakened, she knew at once that the morning was far advanced. The sun was high in the sky and the voices from the taproom below had the loud, bustling sound that comes when the whole world is wide awake. Guiltily, she washed and dressed and hurriedly went to find the others. Brandon's door was ajar, and she tapped and entered.

Brandon was still in his bed, Prue unnecessarily feeding him soup. When they looked up and saw Letty in the doorway, Brandon looked sheepish. "She insists on treating me like an invalid," he explained quickly. "I've told her repeatedly that my fever has quite gone."

"But a day of rest is very beneficial after a fever, is it not, Letty?" Prue asked. "Roger thinks that we may stay another day, if we wish."

"A day of rest is very beneficial," Letty concurred, and added with a grin, "It's so pleasant to see the two of you getting on so well."

"Wish us happy, Letty," Brandon announced, smiling shyly.

Letty looked from one to the other delightedly, and Prue ran to her and enveloped her in an excited embrace. "Oh, Prue," Letty sighed, "I *am* happy for you both."

Finally, Letty found an opportunity to refer to the subject that had brought her. "Where is Roger?" she asked.

"Oh, he's gone," Prue said, returning to her duties with the soup.

Letty's heart lurched. "G-Gone?" she managed.

"He thought *someone* should return to Bath as soon as possible, to inform the families that all is well. He said that he is impatient to return to London, at any rate, and saw no point in cooling his heels here."

All Letty's old misery descended on her again with a sickening thump. "When did he leave?" she asked in a voice she scarcely recognized.

Prue and Brandon, absorbed in their new happiness, did not notice her perturbation. "Not long ago," Prue answered absently. "Why?"

But Letty didn't answer. She turned and went quickly down the stairs. The innkeeper was clearing tbe remains of a single breakfast from the table in the private parlor. "Has Lord Denham gone?" she asked urgently.

The innkeeper turned and answered deferentially, "Yes, Miss, I b'lieve so. Just 'ad 'is 'orses put to, not two minutes since."

Letty, still hoping desperately that he had not yet gone, ran out the door. There in the courtyard, Roger was helping the boy who served as ostler, porter and errand boy to adjust the reins. She stopped in her tracks and took a quick breath of relief. Roger, not seeing her, was about to swing himself up to the box when she called his name. He turned and saw her running across the courtyard toward him with an expression of joy not unlike the look she had had on her face when she had discovered his presence the day before. Completely bemused, he stood and stared until she came up to him. "Oh," she sighed breathlessly, grasping his arm, "I'm so *glad* you haven't gone!"

He looked at her with a wry smile. "Your greetings could well become the delight of my life," he said drily, "if I hadn't been told that they have no significance and that I mustn't refine too much upon them. Is there something I can do for you before I leave?"

She cast him a sidelong glance. His eyes looked weary and his mouth strained. His hair had been carelessly combed, and a lock fell tantalizingly over his forehead. She itched to brush it away with her hand. But she merely cast her eyes to the ground. "Have you a few minutes to spare? I would like to talk to you."

She could see him stiffen. "I'm really rather pressed," he said coldly. "I'm eager to return to Bath and then to start for London before nightfall."

"I see."

He hesitated. "I thought you had said everything you could last night."

"Not everything."

"Very well, then, what is it?" he asked impatiently. Even to his own ears he sounded childishly sullen.

"May we walk a little way?" she asked shyly, with a glance at the ostler who suddenly began to polish a brass fitting energetically. "I noticed from my window that there's a pretty little garden at the back..."

"Of course," he said contritely and fell into step beside her.

For a while they walked in silence while Letty shored up her failing courage. "It's difficult for me to explain, Roger, but I want you to understand why I couldn't ... why I can't..."

"It's not at all necessary, Letty," he said in a strange, detached way that pierced her heart. "You have finally convinced me that your refusal is final. There is not the slightest need for you to make me any explanations. Although I appreciate your kindness in wishing to do so."

He made a little bow and turned to go. Letty watched him, quite nonplussed. She could not let him go like this. "But, Roger," she said quickly, "I don't want to explain because of kindness. It's only because... I love you so very much..."

He stood stock still for a long, breathless moment. Then, running his fingers through his hair in a gesture of helplessness, he said in a tightly controlled voice, "Letty, all this is very confusing to me—"

"Yes, I know." She put out her hand. "Please come with me. There's a little wooden bench back there, just wide enough for the two of us..."

He took her hand and let her lead him to the bench. They sat down, and he faced her tensely. He couldn't wait to hear what she would say, even though he was convinced it would end with the same pain. Why, he asked himself, am I subjecting myself to further torture? But wild horses could not have dragged him away.

Still clinging to his hand, her eyes lowered, she began. "You've told me many times, my dear, that you think me delicately bred, refined and . . . obedient. That's what everyone thinks. Lady Glendenning's dutiful daughter." She turned her lustrous eyes to him in earnest appeal. "Roger, can't you see that I'm not that girl? Would Lady Glendenning's dutiful daughter refuse to marry the man her family so much desires for her? Would *she* lie, and evade, and make up false betrothals, and elope with the man her sister loves? And . . . and . . . would *she* feel as I do about . . . about what happened at Vauxhall?"

Roger was staring at her in puzzled fascination. "What *is* it you feel about Vauxhall?" he asked, his breath suspended in his throat.

Her eyes flickered down again. "Oh, Roger," she said in a very small voice, "how can I say this? Ever since that day at Vauxhall, I've known . . . I've known . . . that I am *not* the girl you all think me." With a shudder that passed over her whole body, she dropped her hold on him and covered her face with her hands. "I knew then," she said in a mortified voice, "that I didn't want to be your wife. That I couldn't be the dignified, polite, calm, bloodless sort of person that you and my aunt and your mother expect. You see, I would much rather be . . . much rather be . . ."

"Yes?"

"I would much rather be your *mistress*!"

There was no sound, no response. When she could stand the silence no longer, she peeped at him through her fingers. He was staring at her, stunned, trying to understand what she'd said. Then a light seemed to spring on in his eyes, and he threw back his head and gave a shout of laughter. As if a dam had given way inside him, he laughed and laughed until he doubled over in helpless merriment. When at last he could catch his breath, he turned to Letty, who was watching him in some dismay, and gathered her in his arms. "Oh, my sweet little *idiot*!" he said, still gasping with laughter. "My poor, foolish, absurd, adorable idiot!" And he tilted her head back and kissed her with such intensity that it reminded her thrillingly of that terrible kiss in the gardens so long ago. When he let her go, she looked up at him with wide, awed eyes. "Does this mean that I *am* to be your mistress?" she asked shyly.

"Of course you are," he said with a wide grin. "To all the world you will be my well-bred, refined, serene, dignified and dutiful wife. And when we are alone, you'll be the most beautiful, the most exciting, the most delightful mistress a man ever had."

From a window above them, Prue watched the activities on the bench shamelessly. "Oh, look, Brandon," she chortled happily, "they're kissing!"

Brandon knelt on the window seat beside her and peered out to the garden. "Good!" he said contentedly. "I always thought she should have him. 'Sweet is a grief well ended.'"

Prue frowned at him in mock-irritation. "Sophocles?" she asked disdainfully.

"Aeschylus," he retorted promptly.

"Well, I prefer the saying that goes, 'The learned man quotes well the words of others; the wise man quotes his own.'"

Brandon looked at her with a puzzled frown. "Who said *that*? I don't think I recognize the style."

"You'll learn to recognize it soon enough. It's only one of the many Witty Thoughts of Prudence Glendenning." And she stuck out her tongue at him saucily and ran laughing from the room.